CW00515574

# Bonded to the Alpha Trio
## The Last Seraphina: Book One
## Stephanie Swann

# Contents

# Author Note

This book is many things, but one thing it is not is suitable for anyone under 18. If this is you, please put this down. It'll be here when you're of age.

Rating: R

Warnings: rejection, pregnancy, multiple mates, loss, grief, lots of hot, sweaty sex, adventure, twists, turns, darkness, some dubcon, noncon. Generally just an adult book. It does not have infant loss, animal loss, or running back to an abuser.

Copyright © 2023 by Stephanie Swann

All rights reserved.

No part of this publication may be reproduced, distributed, or trans-mitted in any form or by any means, including photocopying, record-ing, or other electronic or mechanical methods, without the prior written permission of the publisher, except as permitted by U.S. copy-right law. For permission requests, contact Stephanie Swann: stepha nieswann.author@gmail.com.

The story, all names, characters, and incidents portrayed in this pro-duction are fictitious. No identification with actual persons (living or deceased), places, buildings, and products is intended or should be inferred.

Book Cover by getcovers.com

Formatting by Stephanie Swann

Editing by Beth A. Freely

First edition 2023

# Dedication

To my husband: for working long days away so that I can play
with the characters in my mind.
To my children: you are the reason I keep trekking on when I
want to quit.

# One: Avery

His touch was alluring and seductive as he traced lines down my back. Braden had a way of making me fall to my knees with just a look. I'd heard what they said about him. *The cruel Alpha heir who took what he wanted.* Well, screw them, I wanted this. I'd been a virgin for too long; all I could think about was him. My 18th birthday was today, and he was my mate. The thought filled me with anticipation and excitement. He hadn't rejected me; he had been sneaking glances and touches all day while he poured me glass after glass of Pinot Grigio.

I could feel the heat rising between us as he leaned closer, his breath hot against my neck. My heart was pounding in my chest as I closed my eyes, savoring the sensation of his fingers dancing over my skin. The noise of our pack milling around was a dull thud compared to the feeling of electricity rising between us.

"Braden," I gasped as he pressed his lips to mine, his tongue slipping into my mouth quickly. I was lost in the moment, drowning in a sea of desire and passion.

As he lifted me onto the kitchen counter, I wrapped my legs around his waist, pulling him closer. Our bodies were pressed together, his hardness pressing against me, driving me wild with need.

"Take me," I whispered, my voice barely audible as he continued to kiss me, his hands roaming over my body. "Please, Braden. I need you."

With a growl, he lifted me and carried me to the bedroom, laying me on the soft sheets. He took his time undressing me, his touch gentle yet firm as he explored every inch of my body. I moaned as he kissed and nipped at my skin, leaving a trail of heat in his wake.

Braden's eyes were dark with desire as he shed his own clothes, revealing a toned and chiseled body that made my mouth water. He crawled over me, positioning himself between my legs, and I could feel his arousal pressing against me. I whimpered at the feeling.

"Shouldn't we...go slower? I haven't done this before." Tears pooled in my eyes as his pushing against my tightness caused my core to ache.

"Just trust me, Avery, I have, and this is how it's done." The confidence in his voice silenced me as I pushed onto him.

With one swift motion, he entered me, filling me in a way I had never experienced before.

I gasped as he started to move, his thrusts deep and insistent. I clung to him, my nails digging into his back as we moved together. There was nothing soft or gentle about the way he used me for his pleasure.

"Say my name," he growled, his voice deep and primal.

"Braden," I panted, my body shaking as the pain subsided and the pleasure came. "Oh, yes, Braden!"

He quickened his pace, his thrusts becoming more urgent as he brought us both close to the edge. I arched my back, meeting him with equal need and desperation.

"I'm coming, I'm coming," I cried out as I shattered around him, my body tightening and releasing in sweet waves of pleasure. I could hear Braden moaning as my core tightened around him in release.

He drove into me once more before his body tensed, his voice rough as he growled, his eyes black with lust. I felt the heat of his release as he filled me, his face a mask of pure pleasure.

I woke up in bed alone, the scent of Braden still lingering on the rumpled sheets. A smile played on my lips as I stretched, feeling the ache of our night. It was a delicious reminder that I had had sex for the first time, and Braden had been my partner. I snickered at the thought that my mom and dad were going to be so pissed that I hadn't waited until the mating ceremony, but why bother waiting? He hadn't rejected me, so obviously, he was perfectly fine accepting a wolfless wolf as his Luna. Yes, unfortunately, I had no wolf. As was expected, nothing happened when the clock struck midnight on my day of birth. My mother was human, so there was always a chance that I, too, would be human. But that's okay because Braden accepted me for how I was.

I decided I was going to run home and grab a shower. I was covered in Braden's scent, and as much as I wanted to bask in it all day, I doubt my dad would react well. Not to mention I felt like a sticky mess after all the extracurriculars I engaged in. Slipping on a sundress I made my way back to my parents' house. It was weird, driving my own car. I kept trying to get used to the feel of the stick shift, but for some reason, I couldn't get it. I never took to driving well, I had to navigate using maps because I had no sense of direction. Obviously, driving from the pack house to mine wasn't an issue, but it always made me feel car sick.

I finally made it back to the house and had to park across the street because our driveway was still being repaved. The house was empty, my parents were at work and the older ones were running pack business. I whistled as I skipped up the stairs, only to stop dead as I saw Braden standing there. His shirt was tight against his muscles as he grinned down at me.

"How are we feeling today?"

"Oh, uh," I blushed, "a little sore, but happy that you accepted me as your mate."

"Accepted you? I did no such thing," he laughed.

"You...you slept with me...I thought..."

"You thought wrong, little girl. I slept with you because my wolf wouldn't shut up about you. We knew you were our mate for the last two years, but obviously couldn't reject you until you knew as well. Amrin wouldn't shut up about accepting you, so I slept with you, dosed him with wolfsbane and now I'm rejecting you."

"What? How could you do this? Fated mates are sacred!" I cried out as he sneered in my face.

"I, Alpha Braden Cooper reject you, wolfless nobody Avery White. Do you accept?"

When I stayed silent, he leaned in closer. Shutting my eyes to drown out sensory overload, I heard him grit his teeth, "Accept Avery, or I will make your life hell. You don't want that do you?"

In a small voice, I relented, "I accept, Alpha."

"Good girl. I don't want to see your pathetic face again."

"You're in my house, Alpha, with all due respect…"

"I own everything and everyone. Don't show your face around me Avery, or I swear to Selene, I will destroy you and everyone you've ever loved."

"Yes, Alpha."

He pushed past me as I sunk to the floor, allowing the pain of the rejection to hit me like a ton of bricks. I held my knees to my chest, rocking back and forth as I cried my heart out for the loss of what could have been.

I didn't know how long I had lay there, sobbing, until I heard a voice.

"Avery? What's going on here? Are you okay?"

I stood up slowly as I wiped my face with the back of my hand. I turned around to see my dad standing in the doorway, looking at me with concern in his eyes.

"I'm fine, Daddy," my voice quivered. "Just got a little emotional over something I saw on TV."

"Avery, honey, I just want you to know that I love you no matter what and you can tell me anything, you know that right?" He gave me a sad smile.

"I know," I sniffed.

"So, again, are you okay? Do I need to crack a bottle over some boy's head?" He chuckled as he wrapped me in his arms.

"No, I'm alright. I will be alright, I promise. Can you make me some tea?"

"Of course, sweetheart."

As my dad went to the kitchen to make me tea, I ran upstairs and shut the door, immediately taking the shower I had come home for.

I stood under the hot water for what felt like an eternity, allowing it to wash away my tears and my pain. I let my mind wander as I watched the water cascade off of me and swirl down the drain. After a while, however, my thoughts were interrupted by a sudden wave of dizziness that came over me. I placed both hands on the wall in front of me, but before I could steady myself the room started spinning faster and faster.

Suddenly, I felt myself slipping and before I knew I was falling forward. My head connected with something hard as everything went black around me. The last thing I heard was a loud thud echoing through the bathroom as I hit the ground, not knowing if or when I would wake up again. The darkness brought me peace.

# Two: Avery

I awoke to the beeping monitors, trying to sit, I found myself strapped to a hospital bed, an IV in my hand.

"Wha-what happened?" I croaked, waking my mom who had been sleeping on the chair beside me.

Mom's face lit up, "Avery! You're awake!" she said, tears streaming down her face. "You had a terrible accident," she said hesitantly.

The memories slowly began to trickle back into my mind. I had been taking a shower when suddenly I slipped and hit my head on the shower floor. The next thing I knew, I woke up here.

As the clouds of confusion settled, reality set in. My mom informed me that due to seizure-like symptoms throughout the coma, they were forced to perform an ultrasound—something they wouldn't have done if they hadn't been so worried and desperate for answers.

To their shock and surprise, it revealed something even more unexpected than a head injury.

"How long was I out, Mom?"

She fiddled with the hem of her shirt. "6 weeks. Avery, uh, there's something I need to tell you."

"What is it? Am I okay?"

"Yes... you both are."

"What... both...?" Realization dawned on me as shock electrified my core. *No, it cannot be, I cannot be pregnant with that bastard Alpha's baby.* "Get it out of me."

"Avery, honey, we can't do that. It's past the time for a safe extraction... you're having a werewolf pregnancy..."

"What does that even mean?"

"It means that despite the fact that it's only been 6 week s...you are progressing much quicker than a normal human pregnancy... double the time and that's how far you are in your wolf pregnancy. 12 weeks. Past the safe point for a choice." Tears welled up in her eyes.

I slammed my fist against my head. "Why didn't you take it out as soon as you found out? This can't be happening to me; this can't be happening to me. God get me out of this nightmare."

"Avery, honey..."

"Stop calling me that!" I snapped. My mom recoiled, startled by my outburst. But I couldn't help it. I felt like my whole world was falling apart. This wasn't how my life was supposed to turn out. I had plans, dreams, aspirations. And now it was all gone, replaced by the looming reality of a pregnancy I never wanted.

I buried my face in my hands, tears streaming down my face. "I can't do this," I murmured. "I can't be a mother. Especially not to a werewolf baby."

My mom put a gentle hand on my shoulder. "Avery, I know this is hard. But you're strong. You'll get through this. And we'll be there with you every step of the way."

I shook my head, feeling hopeless. But a small part of me knew that I couldn't just give up. I had to fight, had to find some way to make this work.

After a moment, I looked up at my mom. "Don't you want to know whose it is?"

She hesitated, "Only if you want me to know. I promise I won't tell dad until you're ready to tell him yourself."

"Oh, mom..." I burst into panic.

"Avery, it's okay," she said softly. "You can tell me. I'm here for you."

The words came tumbling out of my mouth before I could even think them through. "It's Alpha Braden's baby," I whispered, my voice barely audible.

Mom gasped and took a step back as if she'd been burned. "The Alpha?" She shook her head in disbelief. "Oh Avery, what did he do to you?"

Without warning, tears started streaming down my face again as the memories flooded back to me like a tidal wave. "Alpha Braden had used me for sex and then rejected me. Mom, it was like I was a no one to him." I gasped. "He cannot find out about the baby, please. You cannot tell a soul."

A small gasp from the corridor caught my attention as a medical tray clattered. Mom ran out the door to see who it was, but by the time she got there, it was too late. Whoever had heard our conversation was already long gone.

"Avery, I think we need to get you out of here. I don't think it's safe here for you anymore, and I think we need to go now." Her voice was firm, but the slight tremor told me how afraid she was.

"What about you and dad? My brothers?"

"We will be fine, but please, move a bit faster, I know you are woozy still, but there's no time to waste. I've heard the rumors, you know. You need to leave. Right now."

I nodded, slowly getting out of bed, feeling a wave of dizziness wash over me. My mom helped me to my feet, and I swayed for a moment before steadying myself.

"Okay, let's go," I said, my voice barely above a whisper. My heart was pounding in my chest, and I felt like I was in a dream.

We made our way out of the hospital room, trying to be as inconspicuous as possible. My mom had grabbed a bag of my clothes and toiletries before we left, and she tossed it to me before we exited through the back door.

Outside, the air was cool and refreshing, and I took a deep breath, trying to steady my nerves. "Where are we going?" I asked.

"We're going to my sister's cabin. It's in the woods, and it's secluded. You'll be safe there." She looked at me with concern. "Are you feeling okay?" Shoving me in the car, she hustled and got in the driver's seat before high tailing it out of the parking lot.

"Yes, Mom, I'm fine. Shouldn't we talk to Dad, or something?"

"I will fill him in when I get home."

"Wait, you're not staying with me?"

"You know I can't do that Avery. I have responsibilities at home. I promise you'll be safe here."

As we drove, I couldn't help but feel like a fugitive on the run. The reality of my situation was finally starting to sink in. I was pregnant with the Alpha's baby, a werewolf baby no less, and I was on the run from him. If his Beta found out, or the rest of the pack, I'd be done for. The pack that Alpha Braden led with an iron fist were some of the cruelest to outcasts.

I couldn't imagine what he would do if he found out about the baby. *Would he come after me? Would he try to take the baby away from me?* The thought sent shivers down my spine.

When we finally arrived at the cabin, I was surprised to find how secluded it truly was. The cabin itself was small and cozy, nestled in the heart of the woods. It was the perfect place to hide out, at least for a while.

My mom helped me inside and settled me onto the couch, while she went to retrieve some supplies from the car. I sat there and I couldn't help but feel overwhelmed by everything that had happened. As much as I didn't want this baby, I felt a change inside me the longer I thought about it. This was my child. I would protect this little one with my life.

"Yes, okay, yes. Thank you, Sapphire." My mom's quiet voice floated through the air. "It's settled, my dear. My sister is on her way, and she will be here to protect you."

"How can a human protect me from that monster?" I wailed like a small child.

"Sapphire isn't a human honey. Remember having a garden that never died? A river that never dried up? She's a green witch and she will do whatever she can to keep you safe."

"If she's a witch, then why aren't you?"

My mom sighed, "I made a deal with someone a long time ago to trade the source of my powers for something far more worthy. No, my love, do not cry for me. My sacrifice was well worth it."

I couldn't help but feel a wave of admiration for my mom. She had always been an enigma to me, a woman of quiet strength who had sacrificed so much for her family.

As we waited for my aunt to arrive, my mom busied herself with making dinner while I curled up on the couch, lost in thought. I tentatively laid my hand on my belly, shocked when I felt what I thought was movement.

I didn't know how I was going to do this. I didn't know how I was going to be a mother, let alone to a werewolf baby. Being a human meant I was rather inadequate for whatever this baby might need in terms of care, instruction, and education. Sighing, I watched some birds fighting outside the window. As I watched, my tension slowly released, and I found myself enjoying the quiet.

When my aunt arrived, I was surprised to find that she was nothing like I had expected. Instead of a wild-haired, cauldron-stirring witch, she was a calm, collected woman with an air of serenity about her.

"Hello, Avery," she said, smiling, "it's been a long time, hasn't it. I bet you hardly even recognize me."

I shyly held out my hand, but she rushed in for a hug. "No handshakes for family, dear girl."

My mom yelled out, "Dinner's ready! Let's eat and then I'll be on my way back to your father."

We sat down to eat, and my aunt took the lead in the conversation. She told us stories of her travels around the world and her adventures in different parts of the globe. Her stories were fascinating and seemed almost too wild to be true, but somehow, in her calm way, she made it all seem plausible.

As we talked, I felt a sense of comfort settle over me. For the first time since I found out about the baby, I felt like everything was going to be okay.

After dinner, my mom hugged me tightly and whispered in my ear, "I love you, Avery. You'll be okay. I promise."

Then she was gone, and it was just me and my Aunt Sapphire. We sat on the couch, sipping tea, as she looked at me with kind eyes.

"How are you feeling?" she asked, gently.

"Scared," I admitted. "How come I haven't seen you before?"

"You have, dear child, but it was many moons ago. Alpha Ashton forbade witches from being on pack grounds, so I had to stay away. But I always sent a little present on your birthday so your garden would always be green." She smiled kindly.

"Mom was saying that you are a green witch. What does that mean?"

"It means I have a natural ability to connect with the earth and all of its inhabitants. I can help plants grow, heal animals, and even see things that others cannot. It's a unique gift, but also a big responsibility."

I nodded, intrigued by her explanation. "Can you help me with the baby? I don't know anything about being a mother, let alone a werewolf mother."

"Of course, dear. I would be honored to help you in any way I can. But first, we need to make sure you are safe. We don't want the pack finding you here."

"How can we make sure of that?" I asked, feeling a sense of dread.

"We can create a protection spell, but it will require some ingredients that we don't have here. I will need to gather them, but I won't leave you alone. I'll ask some of my contacts to keep an eye on you while I'm gone."

"Thank you, Aunt Sapphire. I... I don't know what to say."

"My dear, you're overwhelmed. You've had so much come at you in such a short period of time. In fact, it's off to bed with you. We will be safe tonight, but tomorrow, we will go find the herbs," she patted my cheek.

"Goodnight, Auntie."

"Goodnight, Avery."

# Three: Braden

"You what?" I gritted out at the young Omega before me.

"I couldn't stop her, sir, as soon as I heard she was pregnant, I ran straight here and I-I..."

A sharp smack caused her to whimper, bringing satisfaction to Amrin. The prick had been hounding me after letting Avery go, and was calling for blood—mine specifically, but any would do— now that he knew she was pregnant with our baby.

The Omega cowered in fear as I stalked around the room, throwing whatever was in my hands across the room. She winced every time something shattered or flew past her head, but she kept her eyes on the floor and never dared to move.

"How could you let her just walk out of here?" I yelled, my voice echoing through the empty chamber. "She is pregnant with MY child! You should have alerted security to watch her! You foolish little imp!"

"I'm sorry sir," she stammered, still not daring to look me in the eye. "But I didn't know what else to do! I froze!"

My rage increased. "And that is why you're nothing but a lowly Omega, and I AM ALPHA!" I screamed. I could see the fear in her eyes grow, but my anger only fueled my desire to punish her. I closed the distance between us, grabbing her chin in my hand and forcing her to look at me.

"You will pay for your incompetence," I growled, pulling her close to me. "But first, you will do something for me."

She trembled in my grasp but didn't dare to resist. I could already smell her fear mixed with arousal; a heady scent that made me grow harder. I leaned in, my lips brushing against her ear.

"You will pleasure me," I whispered, "and you will do it well."

She swallowed hard, but I could feel her nod against me. I let go of her chin and pushed her onto her knees, my cock already straining against my pants. She reached for my belt, fumbling slightly as she struggled to undo it.

I watched her with disgust, but also with a sense of satisfaction. This was all her fault, and no matter how much Amrin tried, I refused to let her go without a suitable punishment. Besides, she was wet, I could smell it, I could see the arousal in her eyes. No one could resist me, least of all a mutt like her.

She tugged at my pants, stroking my length through my pants with her fingers. I was already rock hard, but her skillful touch only served to make me harder. I groaned as she freed my cock from its confines and stroked it tightly with her hand. Pushing Amrin's protests to the back of my mind, I closed my eyes and allowed pleasure to seep into my pores. Since I had rejected Avery, Amrin had sabotaged every sexcapade I had attempted.

But I wouldn't let him ruin this one, and for once, he retreated silently.

She started off slowly, pumping up and down with her hand as she licked the tip, then taking the entire length into her mouth. I threw my head back, the pleasure washing over me. I grabbed her head, pushing myself deeper into her mouth, feeling her gag around me. I pulled her head back and guided her hand up and down my length. She twisted her wrist as she moved, increasing the pleasure I felt with every stroke.

I allowed her to continue for a few minutes, then I grabbed her by the hair and pulled her off me. I tipped her head back and kissed her roughly, before walking behind her. She didn't resist as I pulled her skirt down and bent her over the table.

"Beg for me to fuck you," I ordered.

"Please, sir," she begged, "I need you. I need you to fill me. Please, I'm so wet."

I tipped her head back and bit into her neck, causing her to quiver with pleasure. "I will fill you, mutt, just not in the way you want."

"Spank me," she whispered, "please, I deserve this, I deserve to be punished."

I obliged her, smacking her ass so hard, it left a bright red mark. She moaned, tossing her head back and looking at me with pleading eyes. I smacked her ass again, harder, watching as her round cheeks jiggled with every blow.

"More," she whimpered, and I smacked her again, harder still.

I grabbed her hips and pushed my cock into her, feeling her heat and wetness envelop me. I took a fistful of her hair and smacked her ass one last time, before I began to pound her, the force making her head bang against the table.

She moaned and begged me to go harder, and I complied, ramming my cock into her, listening to the wet squelch with every thrust. She was so wet; she could have been dripping. I held her hips tightly, digging my nails into her flesh, watching as it turned red.

She tilted her head up, her eyes hooded, her pupils dilated. "Harder," she cried, "fuck me harder!"

I thrust as hard as I could, my balls slapping against her, feeling her pussy tighten around me as she came. I didn't give her any time to recover, pulling her up and spinning her around. Her juices were flowing freely down her thighs, and I pushed her on her back on the table, thrusting into her again.

She looked at me, through half-lidded eyes. "I'm yours," she whispered. "You can do whatever you want to me."

I picked up my pace, thrusting into her with abandon, watching as she writhed and clawed at the table as I fucked her. I gripped her hair, leaning down to kiss her hard on the mouth. She moaned into me, biting my lip in the process. I growled, pushing her farther down onto me, forcing the breath out of her lungs.

She struggled to breathe, but I continued to pound her until I felt myself tense up. She bit her lip, and I knew she was close to coming again. I released my seed into her, groaning with every spurt.

"No, don't you dare come again. Your punishment for making a stupid decision. Go clean yourself up and get out of my sight."

She whimpered as she looked up at me.

"I said, GO. Before I find a harsher punishment. I have a mate to find."

*Maddox, Lucas come. I need a meeting. Avery is gone and she's with child. MY child. We need to find her.*

It didn't take long for them to show up, answering my call. Such trusted and faithful companions, these two men.

"What do you mean, she's gone?" Maddox asked.

"Gone. Disappeared. Vanished," I repeated myself, wondering what was so difficult to understand.

"Get Sion and the rest of the guards," Lucas said. "Sion will be able to cast a locate spell, and we will lead the guards to her and bring her home."

Maddox nodded, and the two of them left to gather the guards while I stayed behind and had a moment to myself. Avery was my mate, and I would do anything to get her back. Nothing could stand in my way. After all, this was my chance at redemption.

Dialing Sion's number, he answered immediately, "*Yes?*"

"Is that any way to answer your Alpha, sorcerer?"

"*You're not my Alpha, young buck, what do you want?*" he sneered. I always hated this guy, but my dad said it paid to have a sorcerer in your back pocket, so we kept him on our payroll.

"Look, I need you to cast a locating spell for me. Someone has gone missing."

"*Voluntarily?*"

I scoffed reluctantly, "Yes."

"*And what is it you're looking for?*"

"A woman."

"*A woman? You must be desperate to come to me. Done some naughty things, have we?*"

"Enough. I need you to cast the spell."

"*I don't do spells simple locate spells, let alone for people who have chosen to go missing. Though, perhaps if you doubled my monthly stipend and told me who it is and what you did, then we can talk.*"

"If you think you can threaten—"

"*I'd be quiet if I were you, Braden. You have no allies left, bar me and those who you've kept on such a tight leash, they don't realize that life would be better without you. As far as I'm concerned, this woman is better off without you, and pity her soul that you want to find her,*" he said, impatience lacing his voice.

"She's my mate," I said quietly, rage building up inside me.

"*Oh, I'm sorry, was that supposed to convince me? If I recall, you've been running around town, telling everyone in your pack that she's off limits, laying with half of the female pack members, and all the while, your mate had no idea. Why, pray tell, do you want to find her? Did you hurt her and that's why she ran away? Sorry,* Alpha, *you're SOL. I'm not interested in helping you unless you can agree to my terms.*"

I growled, but he hung up on me, giving me no chance to respond. *How dare Sion talk to me like that!* I was so pissed off; I was literally shaking. Calling Lucas, I told him that we needed to move.

"*Why? What's wrong?*"

"Sion is not cooperating. I doubt he will and I'm not willing to grovel like a bitch. Bring the guards. We will meet in the dining hall, eat some dinner and go find her."

"*Yes sir,*" Lucas replied before hanging up.

# Four: Avery

Aunt Sapphire was so kind. She woke up early to make me breakfast before encouraging me to get outside and lie in the sun. As I stepped outside, the warm rays of the sun bathed my skin, and a soothing breeze blew across my face. I lay down on the grass, closed my eyes, and basked in the peace and quiet of the early morning. She was right, I needed this. I had been so caught up in my work lately that I had forgotten to take care of myself.

As I lay there, I couldn't help but think about how lucky I was to have her in my life. She had always been there for me and had never judged me for my flaws. She was like a mother to me, and I cherished her.

Suddenly, my peaceful reverie was interrupted by the sound of footsteps coming towards me. I opened my eyes to see Aunt Sapphire standing there, looking down at me with a smile on her face.

"I thought you might like a little company," she said, sitting down beside me.

"Thanks auntie," I said, smiling at her. "You know, waking up this morning, I actually feel hopeful? Like it doesn't matter what happens, I will love this baby."

"I know you will, dear. That's a sign that you're becoming a mother. The shift inside you is happening and you will feel more and more attentive to its needs. Speaking of, we need to go search for the herbs for the protective spell."

I nodded in agreement and got up, feeling a newfound sense of energy and purpose. We headed towards the forest, our eyes scanning the ground for the herbs we needed to complete the spell.

As we walked deeper into the forest, we could hear the rustling of leaves and the chirping of birds. The air was cool and fresh, and I could feel my senses heightened. I felt alive.

Suddenly, we stumbled upon a group of fairies, their delicate wings fluttering as they danced around a tree. They didn't seem to have noticed us yet, so Aunt Sapphire motioned for me to stay still and quiet.

As we watched, the fairies began to sing, their voices like tiny bells ringing in the air. It was a lullaby, a sweet melody that was so soothing that I felt my eyes closing. I didn't know how long we stood there, listening to the fairies' song, but when I opened my eyes again, the fairies were gone.

Aunt Sapphire and I continued our walk, picking up the herbs we needed along the way. We talked about the spell and what it would do to protect my baby. She explained that it would create a shield around the baby, keeping it safe from any harm or negativity.

After we gathered all the necessary herbs, we headed back to the house to begin the ritual. We lit candles and incense, and she began to chant in a language I didn't understand. The air felt charged with energy, and I felt a sense of protection and love wrapping around me.

As she finished the chant, she placed her hand on my belly and whispered a prayer for the baby's safety. I felt tears welling up in my eyes. I was overwhelmed with gratitude and love for her, for this protective spell, and for the promise of a new life growing inside of me.

As we sat there in quiet reflection, she turned to me and said, "You know, my dear, this spell is just the beginning. A mother's love and protection is the most powerful magic of all. You will always have the power to keep your baby safe, no matter what comes your way."

I nodded, feeling a sense of responsibility and strength within me. She was right, I was becoming a mother, and with that came a newfound sense of purpose and determination.

We sat in silence for a few more moments, the candlelight flickering around us, before she stood up and said, "It's time for tea. Oh, one more thing, this spell is bound to me. Should anything happen to you, you will be protected, and it will drain from my life force first. So, if you're feeling in danger, please take care to run, as fast and as far as you can. I can withstand much, but I am not impenetrable." She paused, "Should I die, you will be left without my protection."

I felt a shiver run down my spine at her words. I knew that she was powerful, but I never realized just how much she was willing to sacrifice for me and my baby.

"Thank you," I said, my voice choked with emotion.

"It's my pleasure, dear," she replied, smiling kindly at me. "Now let's go have that tea."

We made our way to the kitchen, where she brewed a pot of tea and served us each a cup. As we sipped our tea, we talked about the future and what lay ahead. She assured me that she would always be there for me and my baby, no matter what.

I felt a sense of comfort and calm wash over me as we talked. Her presence was reassuring, and I knew that with her by my side, I could face anything. I loved my mom, with all my heart, but my aunt was one of a kind. She was special in a way I'd never known anyone could be.

The silence was suddenly broken by a loud bang, followed by a cacophony of shouting, and screaming. Through the window, I saw bright flashes of light illuminating the night sky. Panic filled me as Aunt Sapphire sprang into action.

"Dear, that's it for our time together. You must go now. Run, run, and don't look back, no matter what you hear. Keep running until your legs give out and then run some more. I will protect you until my last breath."

"But what about you?"

"Go, now dear." She managed a kind smile while pushing me to the back door just as the front burst open.

I didn't have time to argue. I trusted her with my life, and I knew that she would protect me and my baby at all costs, but a piece of me worried about her own safety.

I raced through the woods, my heart pounding with fear as I heard angry shouts drawing ever closer. More bright flashes of light penetrated the darkness and cut through the air. I could barely breathe, but I kept going, hoping that my aunt's promises would prove true and keep me safe.

Suddenly, I felt a sharp pain in my side, and I stumbled, falling to the ground. I looked up to see a figure standing over me, a dark shadow with glowing eyes. I tried to crawl away, but it was no use. The figure was too strong. *Amrin. They found me.*

As it reached down to grab me, I closed my eyes and whispered a prayer for my aunt. Suddenly, I felt a surge of energy, and the figure was thrown back, its body slamming into a tree.

I opened my eyes to see Aunt Sapphire standing over me, her eyes blazing with power. She had come to my rescue once again.

"Run, dear," she said, grabbing my hand and pulling me to my feet. "I can't hold them off forever."

We ran as fast as we could, dodging trees and jumping over rocks. The sounds of Alpha Braden whooping and hollering as they were pursuing us echoed through the forest, but she was always a few steps ahead, leading us to safety.

Finally, we reached the edge of the forest, and she turned to me. "Go now, dear. Keep running until you reach the next town. There, you will find someone who can help you. I will distract them as long as I can."

"But what about you?" I asked, tears streaming down my face.

"Don't worry about me, dear. I will be alright. Just take care of yourself and the baby. That's all that matters."

"Come with me, please."

"I cannot dear. This is my duty. No, it is my honor. You are everything and more. Protect your son and be well. Goodbye dear Avery." She gently kissed the top of my head before pushing me and summoning a barrier to protect me as I ran.

My feet pounded into the ground while my heart weighed me down, heavy with grief and fear. I could hear battle behind me, the clashing of spells against magic littered with the screams of those who fought. I didn't dare look back, knowing that Aunt Sapphire was sacrificing everything to protect me and my baby.

As I ran, I felt a sudden pain in my abdomen, and I stumbled, falling to my knees. I clutched at my belly, feeling the life inside me stir. Panic rose in my chest, and I felt tears streaming down my face.

I couldn't do this alone. I needed help, someone to guide me and protect me. I closed my eyes and whispered a prayer to Aunt Sapphire, hoping that somehow, she could hear me and help me find a way, but there was no answer. Just as I was about to give up hope, excited howls filled the air.

"This is it little one. We've nothing left... We were so close to making it. I'm so sorry I couldn't protect you."

The world began to spin, but just before I descended into darkness, a pair of strong arms lifted me from the ground.

"Mate."

# Five: Gabriel

S he was the most beautiful thing I'd ever seen. I could feel Silver pacing beneath the surface looking at her bruises, the dirt covering her face and her body before he sniffed out that she was pregnant.

*Mate didn't wait for us!* he screamed.

*Hold up man, you don't know what she's been through before she met us! That's ridiculous. You can see, as I can, that she's been through hell. Clearly, she is not alright. maybe this baby is why she's so abused-looking?*

*Whatever. Call the others, they will want to know about a rogue on the pack-lands. Let me know if you need me.*

I couldn't help but feel a twinge of anger towards Silver's callousness. How could he be so insensitive towards her? But I knew he was just trying to protect our pack. I had to make him understand that we couldn't just abandon her. He knew it, as well as I did, that this woman was our mate, and we couldn't just abandon the gift from Selene.

*Silver, wait. We can't just leave her here. We must help her,* I said to him, trying my best to keep my voice calm.

Silver glared at me. *Help her? She's a rogue, Gabriel. We can't just take her in.*

*But she's pregnant, Silver. She needs our help. We can't just turn our backs on her, plus, if you were in your right mind, you'd sense she's just a human.* I pleaded with him, hoping he would see reason.

Silver hesitated for a moment, his gaze flickering towards the woman, then back to me before he stalked off into the dark recesses of my mind. *Fine. But we have to be careful. We don't know what kind of trouble she might bring.*

I nodded. *I understand. I'll take care of her.*

Holding her close to my body, I felt relief, peace... electricity. She was beautiful. Beautiful ivory skin, smooth to the touch with a twinge of red on her cheeks. Her lips were plump, her hair dark and luscious. *I don't care that she's a human; she's MY human. I'll be damned if that stubborn wolf keeps us apart.*

I carried her back to our pack's infirmary, where our healer, Jasmine, was waiting. She gasped when she saw the woman in my arms, quickly taking her from me and placing her on a bed.

"What happened to her?" Jasmine questioned, taking inventory of the bruises and scars on the woman's body.

"I don't know. Silver smelled that she's pregnant, so we brought her here to get looked at," I explained, my eyes never leaving the woman's unconscious form.

Jasmine nodded, getting to work on examining and treating the woman's injuries. As she worked, I couldn't help but feel a pull towards her. It was like there was a magnetic force between us, drawing me closer to her.

"You know, Gabriel," Jasmine spoke up, breaking me out of my thoughts. "There's something about her scent. It's like...I can't quite put my finger on it."

"What do you mean?" I asked, my curiosity piqued.

"Well, it's like...it's sweet, but with a hint of danger, I've smelled it before, but I can't remember or place it. Like she's been through a lot, but she's still fighting," Jasmine explained, a frown creasing her features.

I nodded, understanding what she meant. This woman was a fighter, and I knew that I would do everything in my power to make sure she never had to fight alone again. As Jasmine finished up, I approached the woman's side, taking her hand in mine.

"She's going to be okay, right?" I asked, trying to keep the worry out of my voice.

Jasmine smiled reassuringly. "She's a tough one. With some rest and care, she should be just fine."

"Thank you, Jasmine," I said, grateful for her help.

As Jasmine left the room, I stayed by the woman's side, just watching her sleep. I couldn't explain the intensity of my feelings for her, but I knew one thing for sure: I would do everything in my power to protect her and her unborn child from any harm that may come their way.

After what felt like hours, the woman stirred, her eyes slowly flickering open. She looked around, confused, before finding me by her side.

"Who are you?" she asked, her voice hoarse from disuse.

"My name is Gabriel. I'm an Alpha in the local pack. You're safe here. We're going to take care of you," I reassured her, giving her hand a gentle squeeze.

Her eyes widened slightly, but then she relaxed, a small smile gracing her lips. "Thank you."

"What's your name?"

She hesitated. "I... I don't know if I can trust you enough to give you that."

"Can you at least tell me where you came from? Or what happened to you?"

'I..." She broke down in tears. Silver stirred inside of me at the sight, and we rushed to embrace her.

"Shhh, it's okay, you're safe now. I'll never let anyone hurt you again, okay? We aren't like that here."

"Why did you call me your mate? I thought you were him?" She looked up at me with haunted eyes.

My throat suddenly dried up. "Um... You're our mate..."

"No... please God no, this can't be happening again." Her words hit me like a ton of bricks.

"Again?" I asked, confused.

She shook her head. "I can't...I can't talk about it," she said, her voice barely above a whisper. "Not yet."

I knew that pushing her would only make things worse, so I decided to change the subject. "It's okay," I said, hoping to offer her some comfort. "You don't have to talk about it right now.

We'll take care of you and your baby, and you can stay here for as long as you need to."

Her tears slowed a bit as she looked into my eyes, and I could see that she was slowly starting to trust me. "Thank you," she whispered. "I don't know what I would do without your help."

I smiled at her, and could feel myself starting to fall for her, not just because of the mate bond, but because this woman was just beautiful. This woman was strong, resilient, and more than anything, she deserved to be loved and protected. And I was going to do just that.

As the night wore on, I stayed by her side, holding her hand and watching over her as she slept. And though I knew that the road ahead would be long and difficult, I also knew that with her by my side, I could face anything that came our way. *I should call the others.*

*Roman, Nikolai, we have a situation, mind stopping by the pack hospital please?*

*On it, boss,* Nikolai responded.

*Don't call him that, we are all equal,* Roman scoffed.

I just chuckled. They were the best brothers to be tied to. Not brothers by biology, but brothers in blood, brothers in arms, brothers in morality. We chose to head this pack, the three of us, instead of dueling for control, as our fathers did before us. We were the Alpha Trio.

When Roman and Nikolai arrived at the hospital while I watched her as she slept, imagine my surprise when they both blurted out, "mate" at the same time.

"The fuck she is," Silver growled.

"She's my mate dude, I can feel it," Roman said, moving towards her.

In a flash, I grabbed his arm and pinned him to the wall, just in time for Nikolai to make his move towards her. Sweeping his leg from under him, I held my foot on his back.

"She is mine," Silver snarled loudly. The room fell silent as we all stared at each other, a tense energy filling the air. I could feel Silver's possessiveness over her, but I also knew that Roman and Nikolai wouldn't back down easily either.

"Let's take a step back," I said firmly, releasing Roman and Nikolai from my grasp. "We don't need to fight over her."

Roman took a step towards me, his eyes still fixed on the woman lying in the hospital bed. "But she's mine," he growled. "I can feel it in my bones."

"I understand that, but we can't just claim her without her consent," I said, trying to reason with him, while simultaneously fighting Silver back from resurfacing. "We need to talk to her, find out what she wants."

We all turned to look at the woman, who was now awake and watching us intently. She sat up in the bed, holding the blanket close to her chest. "What's going on?" she asked, her voice soft but steady.

Silence filled the room as we all tried to figure out who would speak first. Finally, Roman stepped forward. "I'm sorry, we didn't mean to scare you," he said, his voice gentle. "But we all feel a strong connection to you, and we wanted to know..."

"We wanted to know which one of us you want, you know? I don't care that you're pregnant, I'll call that baby mine and no one will know the difference." Nikolai smiled seductively, wiggling his eyebrows at her while I sighed in exasperation.

The woman looked from Roman to Nikolai, then to me. "I... I don't know," she said, her voice barely above a whisper. "I just found out I was pregnant, and I don't know what to do or where to go."

"It's okay," I said, stepping forward. "You don't have to make any decisions right now. We're here to protect you and your baby, no matter what."

The woman looked at me, her eyes filled with confusion and a hint of fear. "But...the mate bond," she said, her voice trailing off.

"We can work through that," I said, trying to reassure her. "We want what's best for you and your baby, and we'll do whatever it takes to make sure you're safe and happy."

Silence fell over the room as we all looked at each other, each of us holding in the intense desire to claim her as our own. I could feel the tension building, the urge to give into our primal instincts almost overwhelming.

But then, the woman spoke up, "I... I don't know what to do," she said, her voice hesitant. "I just need some time to think."

"Take all the time you need," I said, reaching out to take her hand. "We'll be here for you, whatever you decide."

She nodded, looking down at her hand in mine. "Thank you," she said softly.

We stood there for a few more moments, each lost in our own thoughts. I knew that this situation was far from over, and that there was still a lot of talking that needed to be done. But for now, all that mattered was making sure that she was safe and that she knew that we were there for her.

# Six: Roman

*I* *want what I want, is that a damn crime?* The way Gabe cock blocked me from mate was enough to drive me over the edge. I hardly had control over Enzo as it was. Being 27 years old and not having a mate was slowly driving us insane. As the oldest of the trio, I should have found a mate first. Yet here I was, a third of a mate to some woman who hadn't even told anyone her name.

*I had spent a lot of time thinking about my future and my true mate. The one who would complete me and accept me for who I am. The one who could handle me and Enzo and love us equally. I had found her once. Then I lost her just as fast as I'd found her.*

*One night, as I was walking deep in the forest, I caught a whiff of an enticing scent. It was floral, yet musky and it was driving me crazy. It felt like my heart was about to explode with excitement. I followed the scent, and it brought me to a small clearing. That's when I saw her.*

*She was breathtaking. Her long brown hair cascaded down to her waist, and her brown eyes sparkled in the moonlight. Her curves were in all the right places, and she was definitely my type.*

*As soon as she saw me, she took a step back, but I could see the lust in her eyes too.*

*"Hello, beautiful," I said as I walked towards her, not taking my eyes off her.*

*"Who are you?" she asked, taking another step back.*

*"I'm Roman. And you are?"*

*"I'm Cassandra," she replied, still backing away from me.*

*"Well, Cassandra, could I ask what brings you to these woods?" I inquired, attempting to ease her nerves.*

*"I was just out for a walk," she answered shortly.*

*"Well, I'm glad I caught a scent of you. You have an alluring smell," I said, taking another step closer to her.*

*I could feel the tension between us, and my wolf was howling in excitement. I had never felt a connection like this before. My body was begging to touch hers, but I didn't want to scare her away.*

*"Thank you?" Cassandra replied in uncertainty, her eyes flickering over to mine.*

*"I'm not trying to scare you, Cassandra. I just couldn't resist coming closer to you. You smell like my mate," I admitted, not able to hold back anymore.*

*Cassandra's eyes widened in shock, and she took a step back, fear evident in her expression.*

*"Please, don't be afraid. I won't hurt you," I said, suddenly realizing how intimidating I must have appeared.*

*"I have to go," she said, turning to leave.*

*"Wait!" I called out, reaching out to grab her arm. "Please, don't go. I just want to talk to you."*

*Cassandra hesitated for a moment before turning back to me, her eyes still guarded. I released her arm, taking a step back to give her space.*

*"I'm sorry if I scared you. It's just, I've never felt a connection like this before," I said, hoping to reassure her.*

*"Neither have I," she whispered, surprising me with her admission.*

*I could see the hesitation in her eyes, but I couldn't help myself. I leaned in, my lips brushing against hers. Cassandra's lips were soft and plump, and I could feel the electricity coursing through my body. It was like nothing I had ever experienced before.*

*As we broke apart, I could see the same shock and desire reflected in her eyes. I knew then that I would do anything to protect her. She was mine, and no one was going to take her away from me.*

*Little did I know, however, that someone else had been watching us that night. The Beta of the Crescent Scar Pack, Lucas, had been tracking me for some time, and he saw the connection between Cassandra and me as a threat to the growing power of our pack. He waited until I left before jumping out from his hiding spot and attacking Cassandra from behind.*

*I heard her screams in my head, but it was too late by the time I ran back to her. She had already died, her beautiful face marred with scratches and bite marks. Tears streamed down my face as I held her motionless body in my arms, wishing desperately that I could bring her back to life.*

Lucas was long gone by then, leaving behind a shattered heart and an unnamable sorrow in its wake. Cassandra's death will forever haunt me, yet another reason why my second chance mate bond with this mystery girl meant so much to me.

As she stirred in the bed, I glanced at my brothers, my friends, before moving to her side.

"Hello beautiful." I said as her bright eyes landed on mine.

She looked at me with a mix of confusion and fear, not recognizing me from hours before. I immediately knew that my memories of her were not hers of me, the dreams I'd had of her would be mine only. I took a deep breath before introducing myself, hoping to ease her nerves.

"My name is Roman. You don't know me, but I feel a strong connection between us. Can you tell me your name?" I asked, trying to be as gentle as possible. Enzo paced underneath the surface trying to find a crack in my demeanor to take over.

She hesitated for a moment before finally speaking. "Avery. My name is Avery."

I felt a weight lift off my chest at the sound of her name. It was beautiful. A melody after the storm.

"It's nice to meet you." Her face shifted from confusion to shock as she processed my words. I could see the fear in her eyes, but I tried to reassure her.

"I won't force anything on you, Avery. But please, trust me when I say that I will protect you. You are my second chance, and I will do everything in my power to keep you safe," I promised, taking her hand in mine.

My brothers, Nikolai and Gabriel, sound asleep, would do what was needed to protect her. I knew they would do anything to keep her safe too.

Avery looked at me, her eyes flickering with uncertainty. But then, she gave me a small smile, squeezing my hand.

"Okay," she said softly.

Relief flooded through me at her acceptance. I leaned in and placed a soft kiss on her lips, wanting to seal the bond between us. Avery responded, her lips fitting perfectly against mine. I could feel the electricity surge between us, confirming my belief that she was my mate.

As we pulled away, Avery looked at me with trust in her eyes.

"I know this might sound crazy, but I believe we are meant to be together. You smell like my mate, Avery. I've been searching for you my entire life," I admitted, hoping she wouldn't push me away. "My first mate died, and... Selene decided to bless me with a second...you."

Avery's breath hitched at the mention of my first mate's death, but she didn't pull away. Instead, she leaned in closer, her eyes searching mine.

"I don't know how to explain it, but I feel it too. Like we belong together," she said softly, her voice barely above a whisper.

I could see the trust and vulnerability in her eyes, and it only solidified my resolve to keep her safe. I would give anything to protect her from the pain and suffering that I had faced with my first mate.

"We do belong together. And I will do everything in my power to keep you safe," I promised again, feeling the weight of the responsibility of protecting her settling heavily on my shoulders.

Avery smiled at me, a small dimple appearing on her cheek. It was adorable and I felt my heart swell with affection for her.

"I trust you," she said simply, making my wolf howl in delight.

I leaned in, placing a gentle kiss on her forehead before pulling away to give her space. "We should get some rest. We have a lot to discuss tomorrow," I said, looking at my brothers who snored in their slumber.

"You aren't upset that I'm already...pregnant? I know a lot of men struggle with that... I didn't mean to be." She choked back a sob. I could see the fear and guilt in her eyes as she spoke, and my heart ached for her. It was clear that she had experienced pain and trauma in the past, and I wanted nothing more than to protect her from any further harm.

"Avery, please don't worry about that. Your past is your own, and I will be here to support you no matter what," I said softly, cupping her cheek in my hand.

She looked at me with gratitude, and I could see the tears glistening in her eyes.

"Thank you," she whispered, her voice thick with emotion.

I leaned in and kissed her gently, pouring all my love and affection into the touch. Avery responded eagerly, her hands sliding up my chest and tangling in my hair.

The passion between us was electric, and I knew then that I would do anything to protect her.

As we pulled away, I looked into her eyes and saw a glimmer of hope.

"I promise to protect you, Avery. No matter what," I said, my voice firm and resolute.

She nodded, a small smile playing on her lips.

"I believe you," she said softly.

Somehow, this felt like home. After Cassandra was ripped from me, I never thought I'd feel love again, but with Avery, it felt... whole.

# Seven: Nikolai

Hearing Roman's confessions of love and watching her melt in his arms was enough to send my cock into a rage fit. Yes, I wanted her to myself, but damn if I wasn't willing to watch her suck on my brother's dick and get off on it. Perhaps I was the more... lenient, of us all, but quite frankly, I'd have no problems sharing her. She was beautiful and deserved to feel beautiful always.

River lounged around while I watched the interaction. *You going to step in, brother?*

*Na, bro, after what happened with Cassandra, Roman needs a win. I'm not jealous. Besides, we are the obvious pick. If she were to try choosing between us, which would be just straight stupid.*

*He is literally kissing our mate and you're so blasé about it. It's disgusting.*

*He's her mate too. When he backs off, I will go in and swoop her off her feet, alright? Chill the fuck out.*

River scoffed, relaxed, but settled. I knew he was still annoyed, but I could already tell that Avery was different in some ways. She wasn't easily fazed by the presence of all three of us and I was certain she was smart enough to know that she had three mates, three Alphas that would treat her very differently from whoever abused her before. *Prick*.

I respected Roman, so I would let him have his moment with her and offer her all the love she deserves, before I stepped in and pulled her into my arms, vowing to always protect her and love her until our last breath. No man would ever put his hands on her again in a way that made her feel unsafe—not if he wanted to live to see another day. Watching as Roman finally drifted to sleep, I smiled. *My turn*.

"Hey there, princess," I said softly into her ear as I watched Roman snore, his hand wrapped around hers.

She hardly stirred, exhaustion flooding her body. "It's okay, you don't need to be awake for this. Know that my bond to you is more than anything I've ever felt. It transcends the normal love feelings people get for each other; I am literally willing to share you with my brothers because apparently they're your mates too. I am willing to do that for you, but what I'm not willing to do is share you with your demons, so baby girl you better start spilling those soon or I'm afraid I may have to punish you until you do."

I kissed her softly on her forehead, stroking my fingers through her hair until I felt her body stir in her sleep. She was coming to me, to all of us, and I couldn't help but feel like the luckiest man alive. Our love was special, something that no one could ever take away—not even our own demons.

Her eyes opened as she gazed at me. "For the love of Selene, you savages don't understand that I need sleep, eh?" she said weakly with a smirk on her lips, barely able to keep her eyes open.

"I'd apologize, but I'm too damn happy to see you," I whispered as I brought my lips to hers, feeling the electricity between us.

"Hi," she breathed.

I moaned into her mouth, the passion between us almost too much to bear. After a few minutes, I finally pulled away, giving her a gentle smile.

"I love you, Avery," I whispered as she closed her eyes and drifted back to sleep without a word. But I knew she heard me; I knew that she felt my love. And that was enough for me.

As the morning sun came up, I watched her sleep for a few minutes longer, feeling my heart swell with emotion. This was it; I never wanted to let her go, no matter what happened next.

She opened her eyes and found herself surrounded by the three of us. "Um...hi..." she croaked.

We all just stared at her with wide grins and loving eyes.

"Good morning, beautiful," Roman whispered, pressing a kiss to her forehead.

"Sleep well?" I asked as Gabriel leaned in to kiss her other cheek.

"I did," she murmured, her cheeks turning a lovely shade of pink as she looked around. "What is this? The boyfriends' meeting or something?"

We all chuckled, and Gabriel shook his head.

"No, sweetheart. This is all of us loving you and giving you the world."

"It's a bit soon... for saying I love you ... can you guys tone it down... a bit?" She stuttered, her cheeks flushing.

Roman's face hardened, his eyes flashing.

"No, I won't tone it down. I need you like I need air," he said, his tone was harsh, and unforgiving.

"Shut up Roman, you need to give her space. She doesn't know us," Gabriel argued, pulling Roman outside, and giving her some space.

"I'm sorry, princess. Roman means well, but he's suffered a lot in his short life. We will give you all the time you need to process what is happening here." I nodded and turned to go but she grabbed my hand.

"No... stay. I... I don't want to be alone. I need your support."

My heart expanded with pure joy, and I had to fight the urge to pull her into my arms and never let go. Instead, I pulled her into a hug and kissed her forehead. "Always, my love."

Just then the door opened, and Jasmine walked in, carrying a clipboard.

"Ah, good morning, Avery! How are you feeling this morning?" she said as she gave us all a quick glance before making her way to bed.

"I feel... weird." She blushed, looking at the three of us watching her intensely.

Jasmine nodded, and then began to fill Avery in on what was going to happen next. She would have to decide about whether or not she wanted to stay here. Under the protection of the Alpha's, she would have to provide identification, and a few other necessary details.

Avery listened. Her eyes wide as she tried to process what was happening.

After a few minutes, Jasmine smiled and nodded. "It's all settled then. Now we just need you to give you your house and set you up with some documentation showing you are becoming one of us, Avery, and we'll make it official."

"No, she will be staying in the pack house. With us," Gabriel said, stepping forward.

"Oh?" Jasmine said, her eyebrows arching.

"Yes. She is in our care. Set her up with her intake forms Jasmine, and then we will take her home. We will be in the cafeteria. Do not, under any circumstances, allow anyone in here. In fact, call the guards to stand post."

"Understood, Gabriel." Jasmine nodded as we left Avery's room hesitantly.

"Why are we leaving her?" Roman snarled. "She could be in danger?"

"I think it's good, Rom, we need the space, she needs the space. We all need some coffee. A lot has changed in her life in the last 24 hours man," Gabriel said while I just listened.

As we walked to the cafeteria, I couldn't help but feel a mix of emotions—relief, fear, happiness, and love all jumbled up inside me. I knew that Avery was safe now, that we would all protect her with everything we had. But I also knew that she was going through a lot, and I wanted to make it easy for her.

"I think we need to be careful with her, guys," I said, breaking the silence as we walked.

"What do you mean?" Gabriel asked, furrowing his brows.

"I mean her mind has been through a lot. She has been abused, traumatized, and she's pregnant. We need to take it slow and let her process everything before overwhelming her with our feelings," I said, looking at both Roman and Gabriel. "I wish she would tell us who is it, we just need a name, and we can take care of it."

They both nodded, understanding what I meant.

"You're right," Roman said softly, his eyes glancing back towards Avery's room.

We finally made it to the cafeteria, where we were greeted by the smell of coffee and warm pastries. It was comforting and welcoming, and I knew that Avery needed something like that—something that would help her feel at home.

We sat down at a table and ordered some coffee and pastries, trying to keep the mood light and easy. I knew that there would be time for solemn conversations and serious talks later, but for now, it was just the three of us enjoying a moment of peace.

As we sipped our coffee, I couldn't help but wonder what would happen next. Avery's situation was complicated, and I knew that we had a long road ahead of us.

"Guys, I don't know about you, but I think we need to start making plans," Gabriel said, breaking the silence.

"What kind of plans?" Roman asked, his eyes showing concern.

"I mean, we need to figure out what we're going to do with Avery. She can't live her life always looking over her shoulder, and we need to make sure that she's safe," Gabriel said, his voice firm.

Roman looked at me, and then back at Gabriel, nodding in agreement.

"You're right, Gabe. We can't just sit around waiting for something to happen. We need to take action," Roman said, his voice deep and serious.

I knew that they were right. We had to start making some difficult decisions, and fast. Avery's life was on the line, and we couldn't afford to make any mistakes.

"Okay, let's do this. What's the plan?" I said, my heart racing as I tried to keep my emotions in check. Such a short time and this woman has such a hold on my heart.

"We need to find a safe place for her. Somewhere where she can lie low for a while, until we figure things out," Gabriel said.

"The packhouse, right? Like we told Jasmine?" I said.

"Yes, we can keep her there, but she is going to want her own room, and right now we only have three, so someone is going to have to bunk up," Gabe said.

"Or stand watch outside her door in case. We can take turns," Roman offered.

Just then, we heard the cafeteria door open, and all three of us turned to look. There stood Avery, her eyes wide as she took in the sight before her. The sun was peeking through the window, and it illuminated her features, making her look like an angel. Her long brown hair cascaded down her back and her soft curves were evident even under the baggy clothes she wore. I looked at Roman and Gabriel, who had stopped mid-sentence in admiration. Even from across the cafeteria, she had taken their breath away with just a glimpse of her beauty. But Avery's expression quickly turned to one of worry as she took note of our serious faces.

"What's going on?" she asked, approaching us cautiously.

"We need to talk to you," I said, leading her over to a nearby table.

As we all took our seats, Gabriel started to explain the situation. "Avery, we've been doing some thinking, and we don't feel safe with you out in the open like this. We think it's best that you lay low for a while until you feel up to telling us who you were running from and what happened," he said.

Avery looked at us with concern in her eyes, tears beginning to well. "Okay, I trust you guys, but I don't want to talk about it yet...What do we need to do?" she said, her voice barely above a whisper.

"We were thinking that the packhouse would be the safest place for you right now. We'll put you up in a room and take turns watching over you," Roman explained.

She nodded slowly, her lips compressed into a thin line. "I understand. Thank you, guys, for looking out for me," she said. "I...um..." She bit her lip. "I still don't know where I stand on this whole mate thing. I clearly am not made for one mate, let alone three. The last one... clearly didn't work out so well."

Roman reached across the table and grabbed Avery's hand. "We understand. It's not easy to accept something like this, but we're here to support you. We'll figure it out together."

She smiled weakly at him; her eyes filled with emotion. "Thank you, Roman."

Gabriel leaned forward; his intense gaze fixed on her. "But for now, we need to focus on keeping you safe. Whoever you're running from is still out there and he's dangerous. We won't take any chances with your safety."

Avery nodded in agreement, a determined look on her face. "I'm ready. Let's do this."

With that, we all stood up from the table and made our way out of the cafeteria. As we walked down the hallway, I couldn't help but feel a sense of unease. The situation was far from perfect, and I knew that danger lurked around every corner. But I also knew that we were stronger together than apart.

As we walked through the packhouse, we attracted a lot of attention. People glanced at us curiously, whispering among themselves. But we didn't stop to acknowledge them. Our priority was Avery's safety, and nothing else mattered.

# Eight: Avery

These men were intense. Constantly staring at me like I was a prime cut of steak they couldn't wait to sink their teeth into. To be honest though, it was refreshing. My last memory of a man who I thought was my mate, looked at me with utter disgust. But these three were different. They made me feel safe, protected, and loved. And yet, the idea of having three mates still didn't sit well with me. How could I possibly love three men? It seemed like an impossible task.

As we walked down the hallway, I couldn't help but feel a strange pull towards Gabriel. There was something about him that made my heart race and my palms sweat. Maybe it was his intense gaze or the way he carried himself with confidence. Either way, I knew that I needed to keep my distance.

*The sound of footsteps echoed behind us, and I turned around to see who it was. It was Braden. My heart started beating faster as I felt the grip of fear clenching my chest.*

"Braden!" Roman growled, his eyes narrowing at the sight of him.

Braden smirked, his eyes trailing over me. "Hello, Avery. I've missed you."

I stepped back, my heart racing. "Stay away from me," I warned him.

Braden took a step closer, his eyes darkening with anger. "You're mine, Avery. You belong to me."

I backed away, trying to put as much distance between us as possible. "I don't belong to anyone. Not you, not anyone."

The sound of a snarl interrupted us. I turned to see Gabriel, his eyes flashing with anger as he stepped in front of me protectively.

"Avery is ours," he growled, his fists clenched at his sides.

Braden smirked, his eyes flickering over Gabriel. "And who are you to claim her? Just another mutt in the pack?"

Gabriel's eyes blazed with fury as he lunged forward, his fists connecting with Braden's jaw. The sound echoed through the hallway as Braden stumbled back, his eyes wide with shock.

Roman stepped forward, grabbing Braden by the collar of his shirt. "You're not welcome here, Braden. Leave now before we make you."

Braden sneered, his eyes flickering over me one last time before turning and walking away.

I breathed a sigh of relief as the tension in the hallway dissipated. But as I looked up at Gabriel, his eyes still dark with anger, I couldn't help but feel drawn to him. As if he was the only one who could truly protect me from the dangers of the pack.

*It was then that I realized, maybe loving three men wasn't so impossible after all. Maybe, just maybe, we were better together than apart.*

The dreams I'd had in the hospital of these three protecting me and subsequently destroying Braden were powerful. Now as I looked around my new room, I could smell him everywhere. My mind was closing in on me, and I could feel the bile rising in my chest.

Just as I felt like I was about to have a full-on panic attack, Roman stepped in and wrapped his arms around me. His touch was comforting, and for the first time in my life, I felt safe. His embrace filled me with a warmth that settled over my entire body and eased away my fears.

"It's alright," he whispered gently, running the back of his hand down my face soothingly. "You don't have to be afraid anymore. We'll take care of you."

I nodded, tears streaming down my face, but no longer feeling scared.. Warmth and love came from him, like the scent of the sun's rays on the beach. Roman's scent was musky, strong and most of all, protective. It smelled of pine and salt. Giving me a sense of security that was beyond measure.

"Should we go fix some dinner?" His deep voice rumbled through his chest. "You don't have to worry about meeting anyone, the packhouse is just for us 3. Well 4 now that you're here."

I smiled weakly, still feeling a little overwhelmed by everything that had happened in such a short period of time. "Yeah, that sounds good," I replied, my voice barely above a whisper.

As Gabriel and Roman led me to the kitchen, I couldn't help but notice the way they moved together. It was as if they were in sync, every action perfectly coordinated. Even the way they looked at each other was different. There was a deep understanding and respect that I had never seen before.

While we began to prepare dinner, I found myself lost in thought. *What would it be like to be with both at the same time? Could we really make it work?* My thoughts turned back to my dream.

Sighing, I called for their attention as I put my heart on the line and explained the entirety of my situation. I was careful to explain that Braden and I had hardly been mates, so I wouldn't trigger any feelings of jealousy. It was only when I mentioned that he found out I was pregnant and needing to hide with my aunt, that the men's gazes turned feral. The table went deathly silent as they processed this information, allowing me to swallow my feelings of insecurity and angst.

"We will never let him hurt you, Avery," Nikolai spoke first. "You are safe, here, with us."

"We promise. You and the baby," Gabriel added, while watching Roman slide his arms around me for comfort before Gabriel turned to stir something on the stove.

Looking up at these three, I almost believed it.

It was then that Gabriel turned back to me, his eyes intense. "I know you're thinking about it," he said, his voice low. "And the answer is yes. We can make this work. The four of us together."

I felt my heart skip a beat as he spoke. Could it really be that simple?

"What about jealousy?" I asked, my voice hesitant.

Roman chuckled, placing a hand on my shoulder as he poured me a glass of wine.

"Jealousy only happens when there's competition," he said, his eyes meeting mine. "But with the three of us, there's no need for competition. We each bring something different to the table. We each bring something unique to you. I am kind, listen first, react second type. Roman is a big goof ball once he gets past his insecurities and Nikolai is... he's... domineering. You will get to know each of us and find that we complement each other, and subsequently, you, in different ways. Ways that make you feel whole and complete."

Nikolai stepped out of the shadows. "We will all die for you, Avery, no hesitation. None of us would dream of treating you the way Braden did." I felt a lump form in my throat at Nikolai's words. It was hard to fathom that these three men, who barely knew me, were willing to put their lives on the line for me. But then again, they had already proven that by saving me from Braden.

I looked at each of them in turn, studying their faces. Gabriel's eyes were full of warmth and understanding, Roman's were shining with excitement and humor, and Nikolai's were intense and almost predatory. They were all so different, yet they fit together like pieces of a puzzle.

"Okay," I said finally, a smile spreading across my face. "Let's do it. I'll try to be open and accepting of our... unconventional mateship. I wonder why I don't feel the mate bond though... like I did with... him...?"

The men tensed. "We can find out. Not tonight though, tonight we relax, enjoy ourselves and get to know you a little better," Gabriel said with a slight smirk.

The rest of the evening was a blur of laughter, good food, and getting to know each other better. We talked about everything under the sun, from our favorite movies to our deepest fears. We found that we had a lot in common, but we also had our differences. And that was okay.

As the night wore on, I found myself growing more and more comfortable around them. It could have been the copious amounts of drinking they did. I never saw them without a glass of wine in their hands. Their relaxation bled into me, allowing me grace to relax too, despite my drink of choice being flavored water. I felt light, happy, and comforted, like I was on top of the world. We ended up on the couch, with me nestled between Gabriel and Roman, while Nikolai sat in a nearby armchair. It was as if we had been doing this for years, not just a few hours.

"I have an idea," Roman said suddenly, a mischievous grin on his face. "Let's play Truth or Dare."

I groaned inwardly, knowing that this game never ended well for me. But before I could protest, Gabriel chimed in with an enthusiastic, "Yes!"

Nikolai raised an eyebrow but gave a nod of approval.

"Okay, who wants to go first?" Roman asked, bouncing in his seat.

"I will," Nikolai said, his voice low and commanding. "Avery, truth or dare?"

I swallowed nervously but knew that I couldn't back down now. "Truth," I said firmly.

Nikolai leaned forward, his gaze piercing. "What is your deepest, darkest desire?"

I felt a flush rise to my cheeks as I considered my answer. I had always been taught to keep my desires and fantasies to myself, but something about Nikolai's question made me want to open up.

"My deepest, darkest desire is to be completely dominated and taken care of by someone who knows exactly what I need," I whispered.

There was a moment of stunned silence, then Nikolai leaned back in his chair with a satisfied smirk on his face. "Thank you for sharing, Avery," he said, his voice almost a purr.

The game continued, each round becoming more and more intense. We laughed and pushed each other's boundaries, but it was clear that Nikolai was the most dominant of the group. His questions were always the most provocative and he seemed to be enjoying himself immensely.

It was my turn again, and Gabriel leaned in with a mischievous glint in his eyes.

"Avery, truth or dare?" he asked.

"Dare," I said, feeling quite brave.

Gabriel's grin widened. "I dare you to kiss whoever you want."

My heart skipped a beat as I looked at the three men next to me. But then I realized that I didn't have to choose. I could have them all.

Without hesitation, I turned to Gabriel and kissed him deeply, his lips soft and warm. Then I turned to Roman and did the same, his kisses playful and teasing. Finally, I turned to Nikolai and felt his strong arms wrap around me as he claimed my lips aggressively.

In that moment, I realized that they were all right. We didn't need to compete for each other's affections. We could all love each other equally and be fulfilled in different ways.

As we pulled away from each other, panting and flushed, I felt a sense of belonging that I had never felt before.

"I think we'll all be very happy together," Nikolai said with a devilish grin.

# Nine: Avery

I awoke in the morning with a wicked emotional hangover and bare bones recollection of the night before. All I remembered was having the courage to kiss the three of them and then the world faded to black. Reality and exhaustion were hitting me like a truck this morning. Groaning as I sat, I looked around my new room.

The room was airy and spacious, the walls and floor accented with cream colors, giving off a peaceful, serene atmosphere. The full-sized bed I woke up in sat right in the middle of the room and was large enough to fit four people. A deep mahogany dresser was stationed against one wall while a full-length mirror leaned against another. On either side of the bed were two white nightstands topped with soft pink lamps while billowy white curtains hung from two high windows that overlooked the gardens outside. In one corner there was an armchair draped with a fuzzy blanket and plush pillows.

Taking in my surroundings, I felt my tight body relax as I had nothing but comfort around me for miles. Not wanting to waste any moment in this blissful space, I quickly gathered my things and headed into the ensuite bathroom connected to my bedroom door.

As soon as I opened it, my senses were overwhelmed: The brightness of the white marble tile covering every surface bounced light all around me making everything look so pristinely clean. Above me was a skylight that illuminated everything even more—like natural sunlight streaming down from Heaven itself—casting its blessing onto whoever chose to enter such a heavenly oasis. An extra-long bathtub filled one side of the room complete with a tray for reading or holding a glass of wine. The shower opposite it featured a rainfall showerhead and a steam function, promising to wash away all my troubles. I let out a contented sigh before grabbing a fresh towel and starting to peel off my clothes.

As I stepped into the shower, the warm water cascaded over my aching body, and I relished the feeling of it restoring me back to life. The steam fogged up the glass doors, and I danced around, letting the water and steam wake me up.

After finishing my shower, I wrapped myself in a plush robe and walked back into my room, feeling like Dione, the goddess of love. I walked around the room, luxuriating in the clean, fresh sensations and feeling utterly spoiled. It was then that I decided I wanted to stay here in this gorgeous packhouse, but a feeling of dread pitted in my stomach.

I was just about to get dressed when a knock sounded at my door. Raising an eyebrow, I wrapped the robe more tightly around myself and opened the door to find Nikolai standing in front of me, no shirt on, his rippling abs dotted with water. My heart skipped a beat at the sight of him. The man was a walking, talking definition of sexy, and his chiseled features and bulging muscles made my knees weak.

"Good morning," he said, his voice deep and husky. "I hope you slept well."

I nodded, unable to find my voice as I took in his sculptured chest and toned biceps. "Yeah, I did," I managed to say, my eyes tracing the tattoos on his arms. "Thanks for the room, by the way. It's amazing."

He smiled, revealing a row of perfect teeth. "I'm glad you like it. And I hope you don't mind me coming in like this. I wanted to check on you and make sure you're okay."

The concern in his voice made my heart swell, and I felt a sudden urge to hug him. But instead, I stood there, still wrapped in my robe, trying to compose myself.

"I'm fine," I said, finally finding my voice. "Just a little emotionally stretched, that's all. Everything that's happened seems to be pushing and pulling at my mind and it's shutting down."

He chuckled. "Yeah, I know the feeling. But don't worry, we'll take care of you."

"We," I repeated.

"Yeah." He nodded, his eyes twinkling. "We went over this last night... even ended the evening with a kiss. You must be drained if you're blanking on that amazing experience." He winked. "Gabe and Rom are in the kitchen making us breakfast, care to join? Or you know, I could have you for breakfast."

I gulped as his eyes darkened. Heat crept up my cheeks as I nervously tugged at my robe. The way Nikolai looked at me made me feel like I was the main course on a platter.

"I'll join you for breakfast," I said, my voice barely above a whisper.

He grinned, and I couldn't help but feel a flutter in my chest. "Great, let's go then."

"I need to get dressed first...," I said, my voice trembling.

Nikolai chuckled. "Only if you must... I'll wait outside." I closed the door and stood against it, my heart pounding. I needed to pull myself together if I wanted any semblance of normalcy. From the sounds of it, I had agreed to a 4-some. What kind of harlot does that?

My head struggled to wrap itself around the news that I was now in a relationship with not one, not two, but three men. HOT men. As my fingers trembled pulling up my shorts and pulling on a tank, I took deep breaths and started counting backwards from 10.

Once I was done, I opened the door and found Nikolai—who suddenly had a shirt on—standing outside waiting for me.

Leading me by the hand, Nikolai walked me towards the kitchen where Gabe and Rom were already cooking up a storm. The delicious aroma of bacon and eggs filled the air, and my mouth watered at the sight of the piled-up plates on the counter.

"Morning, Avery!" Gabe called out, his eyes alight with joy. "You look great after all that sleep!"

Rom grinned and gave me a nod of greeting.

"Good morning, guys," I said, smiling at them both. "Thanks for the breakfast. It smells amazing."

Nikolai pulled out a chair for me, and I lowered myself down, still feeling a bit overwhelmed by everything. The packhouse was so much more than I expected, and I couldn't help but feel like I was out of my league being here.

"So...," I said, looking around the trio. "You guys mentioned something about your pack last night?"

Gabe and Rom shared a knowing glance before Gabe turned back to me and nodded.

"Yes, we are part of a pack called The Raven Moon," he explained. "We all share Alpha status in this pack— me, Rom and Nikolai."

Roman took over from there. "Our pack has quite a long and storied history," he began. "It started out with my family as our founding members over two centuries ago." He motioned for us to join him at the large dining table near the kitchen, where he proceeded to tell me all about the Raven Moon Pack.

Rom talked animatedly about his ancestors and how they made sure that each generation would carry on their legacy of strength and courage while keeping their wolf heritage alive. He explained that his ancestors had been some of the first werewolves to have gone through the transformation publicly without fear or hiding what they were.

As time went on, their descendants kept these values alive by protecting not just themselves but all supernatural creatures who lived in harmony with nature, leading up until today when they became well known throughout supernatural communities as guardians of peace and justice among wolf packs and other clans alike.

He also went on to talk about how Gabriel's ancestors had joined the pack a few decades later and eventually married into the family, Gabriel being a product of that original blessed union, centuries ago. Nikolai then shared his story — of course still with the same pride in their heritage that all of the men shared — of how his family had been granted sanctuary in the Raven Moon when they were being hunted by their previous pack.

His ancestors were warmly welcomed into their new home, but even more so, they were truly embraced by Rom's family who took Nikolai's under their wing and taught them the ways of their pack and how to be true guardians of the supernatural world. Because of this special relationship, the two families remained close throughout the years, leading up until now — and the expansion of the pack and pack duties is why there needs to be three Alphas from 3 different ancestries to serve and protect the will of Selene.

"That's beautiful," I said in awe.

Roman smiled at me warmly. "It is," he agreed. "And now, we continue that legacy by protecting not just our pack but all supernatural creatures who need our help. It's an honor to serve as an Alpha, and we take that responsibility very seriously."

I nodded, feeling humbled to be invited onto such an incredible and vivid ancestral land. As we continued talking, I couldn't help but feel drawn to Nikolai, once again. There was something about him that just pulled me in, his fierce loyalty and unwavering determination sparking something deep within me. Roman and Gabriel were gorgeous, no doubt, but Nikolai hid a storm under that ultra masculine temperament.

As if sensing my thoughts, Nikolai turned to me and met my gaze. "Is something on your mind, princess?" he asked, his deep voice sending shivers down my spine.

I swallowed hard, caught off guard by the sudden intensity of his stare. "Uh...no, I was just...I mean, well, I was just thinking about how amazing it is to be a part of such a rich and powerful history," I stammered.

Nikolai smiled, his eyes twinkling with amusement. "Yes, it is quite something, isn't it?" he said, his hand reaching out to brush against mine. "But there's more to it than just history. There's the present, and the future. And I want you to be part of our future. You can help us take Raven Moon to new heights. To be the most powerful and safest of all the pack lands."

My heart skipped a beat at Nikolai's words. Was he asking me to join the pack as an Alpha? Or did he want me to be their Luna? It was something I had never even considered before. But the way he looked at me, with such intensity and desire, made me feel like it was my destiny. This was moving all too fast, and panic once again rose in my chest.

"I... I don't know what to say," I stuttered, my cheeks flushing with heat.

Nikolai leaned in closer, his breath hot against my ear. "Say yes," he whispered, his lips grazing my skin.

I shivered at his touch, feeling a rush of desire flood through me. Hesitating a moment, but acting on impulse before I lost my nerve, I turned to him and kissed him deeply, my hands tangling in his hair as we lost ourselves in the passion of the moment.

As we pulled apart, Nikolai grinned at me hungrily, his eyes dark with desire. "Is that a yes," he said, before claiming my lips once more in a heated kiss.

"It's a 'let's see how this relationship goes before I commit any further.' Take it as you will."

Roman smiled from across the table and Gabriel laughed as everyone got up to start clearing breakfast dishes.

# Ten: Braden

"**W**here the fuck is she?" I screamed at Lucas.

"I don't know! We've been at it trying to track her, but that bitch of an aunt cast a protection spell on her and unless we kill her, we can't track her. Something you refuse to do!" he yelled back.

"Watch your damn tone with me, Luke. I know we are friends, but I am your Alpha first." I spit at him.

I was angry. Angry that I didn't know where Avery was, and that we couldn't use our usual methods to track her. We had been at it for days and without any luck. I just kept asking myself why she couldn't be found. She should be locked in my dungeon by now. My heart blackened at the thought of not ever seeing her again or having access to my heir. My son.

My hands balled into fists as my anger boiled inside me like a volcano waiting to erupt. My breaths turned into deep growls as my wolf started to take control over me, begging to be released so he could go out searching for his mate himself. But I knew that would be futile; if even we couldn't find her with our best wolves searching, then Lucas must be right. We needed to deal with her aunt.

Lucas looked at me warily; he knew better than anyone what my anger could do when pushed too far. He put his hands up in a placating gesture and tried calming me down, but his voice was drowned out by the rage that consumed my body with every passing second.

Avery had been gone for too long now and it seemed like there was no sign of her anywhere, making Amrin increasingly angry and volatile. I had been experiencing black outs and waking up covered in blood.

"Is... Amrin okay?" Maddox dared to ask.

"He's fine, why?" I answered curtly.

"Just... we have noticed some Omega's going missing..."

"Since when do you care what I do to MY Omega's?"

He stuttered, "I don't... it's just starting to get the attention of... you know who."

I raised a brow, intrigued. "Enlighten me," I demanded.

Maddox hesitated for a moment, but then took a deep breath and spoke in a hushed voice, "The Council has been receiving complaints from some of the neighboring packs. They are concerned about the disappearances of the Omegas that are under your care."

I scoffed, rolling my eyes as I let Amrin to the surface. "Of course, they are. They always find something to complain about."

"But, Amrin, this is different. They fear that you might be... harming them."

I sighed heavily, knowing that this was going to be a pain in the ass. "I'm not harming them, Maddox. They're mine. I can do whatever I want with them."

"But, Amrin, the Council—"

"I don't give a damn about the Council, Maddox," I interrupted him. "I am the Alpha of this pack, and I make the rules. If they have a problem with that, then they can come and talk to me themselves."

Maddox nodded, looking relieved. "Understood, Alpha. I just wanted to make sure that you were aware of the situation."

"I am," I replied shortly. "Now, if you don't have any more stupid issues to bother me about, how about we go see that aunt of hers?"

I took off without waiting for an answer, my wolf howling in my head as we made our way to the dungeon. I still couldn't understand why we had to go through this hassle; surely, she would show up somewhere. I hated witches, they were a stain on society. I hated them more when they were mated to wolves. Diluting our bloodlines and making us weak. Like Avery. She was weak, but the fact that she could get pregnant and hold an Alpha's baby means she was special. I just didn't know what she was... yet. I could feel Lucas and Maddox trailing behind me, but I was determined to get there as fast as possible.

When we reached Avery's aunt's cell, I snarled loudly and demanded access. The guard immediately complied with my request and opened her door to let us in. She cowered in the corner of her cell, her eyes slit with anger when she saw me enter.

Once I reached the end of the room and stood directly in front of her cell door, I spoke in a gruff voice that reverberated against the dungeon walls: "Tell me where Avery is."

Her aunt just snorted obnoxiously before replying, "I'll never tell. You can do whatever you want to me, but I will never betray my family."

I sneered at her response. "You mean my property. Avery is mine, and I'll do whatever it takes to find her."

Her aunt just chuckled at my words, clearly unimpressed. "You think you're special because you're an Alpha? You're just another pawn in the game. There are higher powers at work here, and you're just a means to an end."

I was about to retort when a low growl interrupted me. Lucas, who had been silent all this time, now released his inner wolf and it was clear that he was not happy. "You fucking witch. You have no idea what you're getting into."

The aunt just smirked at the sight of Lucas, revealing her true intentions. "Ah, the loyal friend. How sweet. You do realize, though, that he's just using you, don't you?" she taunted.

I could see Lucas shaking with fury. He had always been protective of our family and pack, and he didn't take kindly to anyone who threatened them. "We'll see about that," he growled before lunging at the cell bars with his teeth bared.

I watched as he tried to break through the barrier, but to no avail. She just laughed at his attempt. "You're wasting your time, little wolf. You'll never find her."

I was starting to feel a sense of dread creeping up inside me. What if she was right? What if we never found Avery? The thought of never seeing her again caused a pang in my chest and my wolf howled in agony. We needed to find her, no matter the cost.

I took a deep breath to calm myself and then spoke in a low voice that brooked no argument. "You will tell us where she is, or you will suffer the consequences."

Her aunt just scoffed again, clearly unimpressed. "And what consequences would those be? Torture? Death? Believe me, I've been through worse."

I glowered at her, my anger simmering just below the surface. "You have no idea what we are capable of," I warned her before turning to Maddox. "Get me the whip. I've had enough of her defiance."

Maddox hesitated, his eyes flickering between me and her. "Amrin, I don't think—"

"I said get me the whip!" I roared, my patience wearing thin.

Maddox scurried off, knowing better than to argue with me when I was like this. When he returned with the whip, I snatched it from his hands and marched over to the cell door. I cracked the whip against the bars, the sound echoing through the dungeon. The aunt flinched, but she didn't look scared.

"Last chance," I warned her.

"You're just like your father," she spat at me. "Cruel and heartless. You'll never find her. She's too smart for you."

That was it. I couldn't take it anymore. Without another word, I opened her cell and stepped inside, Amrin had pushed me out and I was powerless to stop him. The whip was forgotten as my hands closed around her throat, squeezing the life out of her. She struggled beneath me, but my grip only tightened until finally, she went limp.

Lucas and Maddox stood frozen in shock at my actions. I released the woman's lifeless body and turned to face them, my chest heaving with anger and adrenaline.

"Clean this up," I growled at them before leaving the dungeon.

My wolf was still roaring inside me as I made my way back to my chambers. I couldn't believe what I had just done, but at the same time, a part of me felt satisfied. That witch had no right to taunt me like that, to challenge my authority. And she certainly had no right to keep Avery from me.

As I entered my room, I saw a note on my desk. It was from a member of my pack, informing me that they had spotted a witch's caravan heading towards the southern border. *Could Avery be with them?*

I felt a glimmer of hope inside me as I read the note. Maybe there was a chance to find her after all. I picked up my phone and video called Lucas and Maddox.

"We're going on a hunt," I told them, my voice cold and determined. "We're going to find Avery, no matter what it takes. Fuck the aunt, she can rot for all I care." Lucas and Maddox nodded, their faces solemn as they understood the gravity of the situation. We quickly prepared and set out towards the southern border. Our wolves were on high alert, sniffing out any trace of Avery's scent.

As we travelled further south, we came across several villages that were notorious for harboring witches. We questioned the locals, but they were tight-lipped and refused to divulge any information. I could feel my frustration building with each dead end we encountered.

Just as we were about to give up hope, we spotted a group of caravans in the distance. My heart leapt in my chest as I recognized the markings on one of them. It was the same caravan that had been spotted by my pack member.

Without hesitating, we made our way towards the caravans, our wolves snarling and growling dangerously. As we got closer, we could see figures moving around inside the caravans. But there was one caravan that caught my attention. It was the one with the same markings as the one we had been tracking.

I approached cautiously, my wolf prowling alongside me. Suddenly, the door was thrown open and a figure stumbled out. It was just a human.

"Worthless! THE LOT OF YOU!" I screamed loudly, shifting into Amrin before tearing towards the caravan.

# Eleven: Braden

My anger and strength were unquenchable as I tore through the caravan of witches like a tornado. Witches screamed and scurried away in horror as I ripped apart their tents, shattering magical artifacts and destroying any sign of them being here. With each powerful blow, my energy only seemed to increase. I felt invincible at that moment, and nothing could stop me from doing what I felt was right.

Soon enough, the caravan had been reduced to rubble. There was no trace left of the witches' presence but a few scattered items around the area. I felt powerful again, whole. I needed this.

The sound of flesh tearing and bones crunching against my raw power was exhilarating. I loved feeling the rush of force as I decimated people who deserved it. Sure, some witches managed to get in some good strikes, but they were low level. Nobodies. No one could compete with me. NO ONE.

Finally relenting control back to Braden, I retreated and left him to deal with the mess. He deserved it after what he did to our mate.

"What the hell man?" Lucas screamed. "This is insane!!!"

"I... they deserved it," I snarled at him.

"No... man they really didn't. They were going to some fair and you just... women... children..." Lucas looked around as Maddox slowly backed away.

"Don't take another step unless you want to be next, Dox. I don't have the time or patience for cowardice. Are you two with me, or not?" I growled.

Maddox and Lucas stared at me with fear in their eyes. I watched as their fear slowly changed to determination.

"We're with you," they said in unison.

"We need to find the person who gave me bad intel. I want him hung and dried for this," I said, anger overcoming me once again.

We headed back to the packhouse, determined to find the traitor. We had just reached the entrance when a hooded figure suddenly appeared in front of us. It was Avery's aunt, looking disheveled and fuming with rage.

"You will never catch me, and you'll never find her," she hissed at us before painfully vanishing into thin air. I looked at Maddox and Lucas in shock. Lucas looked stunned, but Maddox met my gaze with a silent warning— someone had helped her escape from the dungeon.

We searched through every room of the packhouse for any clues or traces of our traitor without success until finally we gave up and returned outside. We knew that whoever had freed Avery's aunt was powerful, and probably still out there somewhere plotting against us. But we also knew that if we were ever going to catch them, we would have to work together as a team— no matter how hard it might be.

We had another enemy now, and it was time to take them down.

The next few weeks were tense. Every day, we would search for clues about who was responsible for freeing Avery's aunt. We also kept a close eye on the happenings of the pack, making sure nobody was plotting anything behind our backs. We knew from experience that it was only a matter of time before the traitor might strike again, so we stayed prepared and vigilant.

Finally, we got a break. Someone had snuck into the pack-house late at night, and in the morning, we knew who it was. It was the former Beta of the pack, Lucas's father. He had been helping Avery's aunt escape and was planning to overthrow our pack. But we had finally caught him.

"Alpha, please... let him explain..." Lucas pled on behalf of his father.

"He betrayed us... what explanation could you possibly want?" I hissed.

"He's—"

"He's what? Your father? So, I killed mine and I'm fine. You don't need him, and I don't want him. Think twice about whether you want to stand by his side, or mine."

Lucas resigned himself to his bedroom and I didn't hear from him for the rest of the night.

That night, we held a trial. Every pack member was there to support us and witness. We presented our evidence and gave

Lucas's father a chance to defend himself, but it was clear he had no defense. He refused to answer why he did it, and what motive he had for trying to keep Avery from me, but it didn't matter. I wanted justice and there would be nothing but justice for my lost prisoner. In the end, he was sentenced to death. We all watched silently as he was dragged away and hung by his feet.

The next morning, all that remained of the former Beta was his lifeless, rotting corpse and the lesson he had taught all of us— the pack was only ever as strong as its packmates. We had an order of authority, and no one would ever challenge me for my title. This pack was mine and mine alone.

"It is done, Alpha," Lucas said, his eyes blank.

"Thank you, Luke. Now. Shall we get back to discussing the small issue of where the FUCK is Avery?"

We all gathered around, Maddox and Lucas included, and tried to come up with a plan of action. We knew that wherever she was, whoever had taken her would not have wanted to be detected by anyone. We decided to start by sending scouts in all directions to find the most powerful sorcerer they could and bring him to me. They had instructions to keep their eyes open for anything suspicious and report back as soon as possible.

We also sent out letters to everyone in our pack and beyond; wherever Avery may have gone, someone must know something about it. Perhaps somebody had seen her on one of the roads or heard something from one of her relatives living nearby. Maddox suggested spreading a reward for information which could lead us to finding her; this way we could be sure that anyone who held a possible clue or hint would share it. It was beautiful, really—a heartfelt letter, penned by her mate.

"It's been a week. There's no trace of her." Lucas and Maddox were becoming more and more withdrawn from me as my rage increased. "I'm going to let Amrin go search. Join me for a hunt tonight and we will become like brothers again. It feels like this nonsense with Lucas' dad has soured our friendship."

Lucas inhaled sharply.

"I mean, you did kill his dad man... you didn't even apologize..." Maddox started before catching my sharp look and trailing off.

"You want an apology, Luke?"

He looked at me, hope filling his eyes.

"You don't get one. Your dad was scum. He aided and abetted a witch that was our only ticket to finding Avery and now we have to resort to less savory means to find her, this is literally, ALL your dad's fault," I yelled.

Lucas nodded and looked away, defeated. We all silently agreed to go on a hunt that night in search of Avery, or at the very least clues as to her whereabouts.

I followed Lucas as we set out along the lake, our werewolves looking for any signs of life that could lead to Avery's location. As I took in the gleam of the moonlight on the water, I noticed a young woman bathing in the lake. I immediately stopped and watched as Lucas turned towards her, his tail stiff in the air.

*Mate.*

I could feel the call of something powerful between them, like a current of electricity had touched their hearts. Lucas moved towards her and began speaking, his voice low and gentle. Even though I couldn't hear what he said, it was obvious he had found something special in this beautiful young woman. Moving closer to hear what they were speaking of, I sat on the embankment to eavesdrop.

"You are so beautiful," he murmured as he went into the lake, closer to her.

"Who are you?" She turned, a frightened expression on her face.

"I... my name is Lucas. I'm the second in command of the local werewolf pack. Have you seen any sign of a woman? She might be a captive of a witch," he asked her, his voice calm yet firm.

She looked at him with a mixture of fear and confusion, but shook her head, nonetheless. "No, I haven't seen anyone like that. Are you okay? You're bleeding." She pointed to his side where a gash had been torn in his shirt, revealing a deep cut on his ribs.

Lucas groaned but tried to brush it off. "It's nothing, just a scratch. Please, if you hear or see anything, let me know." He was about to lose courage when he turned back to her. "You're my mate. My chosen one."

She gasped. "No... that can't be right; I am pledged to Sion."

Lucas snarled.

"Sion is nothing. He's just a human. You're my mate, and you will be by my side."

The woman's eyes widened in fear at his sudden aggression. "Please, I don't know what you're talking about. I have to go."

Lucas grabbed her arm, his grip tight and possessive. "You're not going anywhere until you acknowledge me as your mate."

Maddox stood up, ready to intervene, but I held him back. "Let him handle this." I was half hoping he would rip her heart out. We needed laser focus on finding Avery, not all this fluff about mates.

I watched as Lucas continued to intimidate the woman; his eyes wild with the frenzy of the hunt. But then, something in her expression shifted. It was like she found the courage to stand up to him.

"You're hurting me." She pulled her arm away from his grip. "I don't know you, and I don't owe you anything. Leave me alone."

Lucas recoiled as if he had been slapped. "You don't unders tand... you're my—"

"No, I don't understand. And I don't want to. Now leave me alone, or I will call Sion."

That was my cue. We did not want Sion here.

"Lucas, time to go bud. Leave the maiden," I shouted as his eyes blazed a trail towards me.

"But she's mine!"

"We will come back for her, man, but we can't afford Sion to show up here. Not now."

"Sion? That traitor?" His eyes turned dangerous, and I saw his fangs elongate. "He'll pay for taking her from me."

"Lucas, calm down." I stepped forward, ready to intervene.

"He took my mate, Alpha. He's going to pay," Lucas growled.

I paused, taking a deep breath. "Alright. We'll deal with him, but first we have to find Avery. We can't lose focus."

# Twelve: Avery

The guys were sweet and attentive, always trying to follow me around as I explored the pack lands. "Worried about my safety" was always the claim, though I had a feeling they just needed to be close to me. I needed space and the only way I would get it was by sneaking out in the middle of the night after I'd gotten them tipsy enough that they didn't hear me sneak out my window.

Tonight was no different. I had found a beautiful pool of water with a small waterfall that flowed down a small hillside. I'd sneak out and go straight there, just in time to watch the beautiful Omega's shift and play in the water. The way they bounded, so carefree and happy, sent a jealous chill down my spine. Why didn't I have a wolf, and more importantly, was I ever going to get one? I sat on a fallen log, just out of view, though I was sure they could smell my presence. It was almost impossible to hide from a wolf's nose, let alone hide an Alpha pregnancy, but I wanted to feel like I was a part of something.

"Hi." The noise startled me, and I jumped.

"Oh...hi," I said nervously, looking up at a plain-looking girl with mouse brown hair and flat brown eyes.

"What are you doing here? You shouldn't really be here without someone..." She was worried for me, and it felt nice.

"I know, I just needed some time alone," I replied, feeling the weight of my secret weighing heavily on my chest. The girl nodded, but her eyes seemed to bore into me as if she knew there was something more.

"Is everything okay?" she asked, and I could feel the concern in her voice.

I hesitated for a moment before taking a deep breath and admitting the truth. "I'm pregnant." The words came out in a whisper, but they echoed loudly in the silent forest.

Her eyes widened at my blatant confession. "I know...I can hear the heartbeat. Who's the father?" she asked softly.

"That's the thing," I said, tears welling in my eyes. "It's an Alpha from another pack who never wanted me and now I have three amazingly sexy men who all want me, and I can't bring myself to be vulnerable around them. I can't let go of the pain I felt when I was rejected the first time. What if they reject me the minute the baby is born? I don't think my heart could handle it."

The girl listened intently, her eyes never leaving mine. She seemed to be considering something before she spoke. "I know what it's like to feel rejected and scared," she said softly. "But you can't keep living in fear of what might happen. You have three men who love you and want to be there for you. You need to trust them and let them in. They won't reject you, not when they see the beautiful baby you're carrying."

I sniffled, wiping away my tears. "How do I do that? How do I open up and trust them?"

"It won't be easy, but it starts with being honest with yourself and with them," she replied, giving my hand a gentle squeeze. "Tell them how you feel, what you're afraid of. Let them be there for you and support you."

I nodded, feeling a glimmer of hope shining through the darkness. She was right. I couldn't keep pushing them away and living in fear. I had to be honest with them, no matter how scary it seemed.

"Thank you," I said, smiling gratefully at the girl. "You're one of the wisest people I've ever met."

She returned the smile. "Just remember, you're not alone. You have people who care about you and are ready to stand in the way of fire for you. I know, because I've watched how they interact with you, even in the short time you've been here."

I sniffed and studied her face as she spoke. She had the quiet resilience of someone who had also experienced the pain of rejection. "I realized I didn't ask what your name was…"

She chuckled softly. "I'm Hannah," she said, extending her hand.

I shook her hand, taking in the warm energy it transmitted. "Hi Hannah, I'm Avery, though I suppose you already know that," I replied.

We sat in silence for a little while longer, just enjoying each other's company. Eventually, Hannah stood up, smoothing out her skirt. "Well, it was lovely talking to you, Avery. But I should be going now."

"Wait," I said, reaching out to grab her arm. "Can we do this again sometime? You're the first person I've met here that I feel like I can really talk to."

Hannah's eyes lit up with delight. "Of course, Avery. I'd love to. How about we meet up again next week? Same time, same place?"

I grinned, feeling lighter than I had in weeks. "Sounds perfect."

As Hannah walked away, my heart was filled with joy. I'd never had any friends back home, and out of respect, the trio weren't announcing who I was until I felt safe again. They weren't keeping me a secret, but they knew I wasn't ready for a big celebration. It was nice that someone had seen me and finally reached out.

"There you are!" Gabriel yelled as strong arms crushed me in their grip.

"We were so worried!" Roman said as he lifted me and cradled me into his chest.

Nikolai watched, his eyes dark and his face twisted in simmering anger. I felt my heart race as Gabriel and Roman held me tightly, their concern for my well-being evident in their embrace. But as I looked up at Nikolai, I couldn't help but feel a twinge of regret.

"What's wrong?" I asked, trying to keep my voice steady.

Nikolai's jaw clenched as he glared at me. "I told you not to wander off," he growled.

"I was just talking to someone," I protested, struggling to free myself from Gabriel and Roman's grip.

"You were supposed to stay with us," Nikolai snapped, his eyes flashing dangerously.

"I'm sorry," I said quickly. "I know I shouldn't have wandered off." Walking up to him and placing my hand over his heart, I leaned into him, allowing myself to sink as he wrapped his arms around me and breathed in my scent.

"Sorry, little princess, I didn't mean to snap. It's just... I finally found you and you're flighty and feisty and I don't know how to show you that you mean the world to me. I... lose myself in my emotions sometimes."

I felt a shiver run down my spine as Nikolai's words washed over me. I could feel the intensity of his emotions, the passion and possessiveness he had over me. In that moment, I knew there was no one else in the world that I wanted to be with more than him.

"It's okay," I whispered, pressing my body against his. "I know you didn't mean it."

Nikolai's lips found mine before I could say another word, and the kiss was bruising and rough as if he was trying to stake his claim on me. But I returned his passion with equal fervor, letting myself get lost in the intensity of our emotions.

As our kiss deepened, I could feel Nikolai's hands roaming over my body, possessively claiming every inch of me. I moaned into his mouth, my body responding to his touch, craving more.

Suddenly, Gabriel and Roman's presence faded away, leaving me alone with Nikolai. He pulled away from our kiss to look at me, his dark eyes burning with desire.

"I need you," he growled, his voice low and husky. "Right here, right now."

I didn't hesitate for a moment, knowing that I wanted him just as badly. I gave him a nod, my body trembling with anticipation.

"There's a cave, just beyond the edge of the pond."

I smiled and looked around for Gabriel and Roman.

"They went home. They respect that I need my time with you. They said to tell you dinner will be ready when we're done."

Nikolai didn't waste another moment. He scooped me up in his arms and carried me to the cave, his lips never leaving mine. The cool air of the cave sent shivers through my body, but Nikolai's warmth kept me from freezing.

He set me down on a large rock, his hands immediately unbuttoning my shirt and exposing my bare chest to the cool air of the cave. He leaned down and took a nipple into his mouth, swirling his tongue around it. I threw my head back in pleasure, moaning loudly.

Nikolai's hands found their way to my pants, undoing them and sliding them down my legs, his lips trailing down my skin, leaving goosebumps where they touched. I lifted my hips to help him, eager for him to be inside me.

He stood up, towering over me, and unbuttoned his own pants. His hardness sprang free, and I couldn't resist the urge to wrap my lips around him. I took him deep into my mouth, stroking his length with my tongue. Nikolai groaned, tangling his fingers in my hair.

I felt his fingers graze my entrance, teasing me before pushing inside. I gasped, my back arching off the rock, as he began to thrust his fingers in and out of me. I was already so wet, and I couldn't help but let out moans of pleasure.

His other hand found its way between my legs, caressing my clit in circles. The pressure began to build up inside me, the intensity threatening to overwhelm me until I could no longer contain it. Releasing a cry, I climaxed around his fingers, my body trembling with pleasure.

Nikolai quickly entered me, pushing himself deep inside. My eyes rolled back into my head as he began to thrust in and out of me, each movement harder and faster than the last. Our bodies were slick with sweat, our breathing ragged and labored. He pulled my hair back as his hand went to my throat. His black eyes stared deep into my soul as he watched pleasure write itself on my face.

"What do you want?" he rasped.

"You."

"No, what do you want?"

"I want you to spank me, pull my hair and..."

"And?"

"Lose yourself in me."

His grunts filled the cave, sending me on a high. My walls convulsed around him as I moaned his name louder and louder. He quickened his pace, slapping against my pussy as he pushed deeper within me.

His thrusts grew more frenzied and desperate as the orgasm rocked through our bodies. His grip tightened on my hair, a deep guttural moan erupting from his throat as he released himself within me, biting my neck as he did so.

We collapsed onto the rock, both spent and exhausted. We lay in each other's embrace, our sweaty limbs tangled together. Coming down from the sensations, my hand flew to my neck.

"Did you just..."

His eyes returned to normal as they filled with sorrow. "I'm so sorry, Avery... I... lost myself..."

My heart filled with turmoil. I wanted so badly to be a part of this mate bond, but the feeling that my choice was stripped from me was fighting the bond slowly clicking into place.

"I... Avery, I don't know what to say." He reached for me as I slipped out of his grasp, rushing to dress myself.

"You know, I was finally thinking that being a part of this was a good idea. I let my guard down... and... and..." I started sobbing.

He stepped towards me, and I stepped back. "Please take me home."

His face fell as he nodded, pulling me onto his back as he walked out of the cave in silence.

# Thirteen: Nikolai

"**F**uck you, so hard River," I screamed at the very satisfied wolf inside me.

*Yeah, like I just fucked her, eh?* He laughed.

"This is not funny man. She wasn't ready and now you've gotten us labeled as psychotic!"

I slammed my hand on the wall, feeling the rush of anger and fear wash over me. The wolf within me had taken control once again, luring me into a moment of passion that I now regretted bitterly. How could I let this happen? It was as if I had no control over myself anymore, no sense of right or wrong. I wanted our marking to be sacred, special. But nope. Once again, River proved he could not be trusted.

And River, he didn't care. He relished in the wildness that consumed me, delighted in the chaos that he created within my soul. He was always there, whispering in my ear, urging me to take what I wanted without regard for anyone else's feelings or well-being. And I had fallen for it. Again.

I sank to the ground, feeling the weight of my shame and guilt crushing me from all sides. What had I become? How could I keep living like this, with the constant battle between my human self and the beast within me?

River chuckled, a low sound that grated on my nerves. *Come on, man. Don't be so hard on yourself. It's not like we hurt her or anything. And besides, you know she wanted it too. The more you deny me, deny us and the savages we are, the worse the battle for "who is who" will be.*

I wanted to scream at him, to tell him that he was wrong, that I didn't want this. But the words caught in my throat, choked by the overwhelming sense of shame and self-doubt. Deep down, I knew he was right. The wolf within me was a part of who I was, and try as I might, I could not deny it forever.

But I couldn't let go of my humanity either. I couldn't let the beast take control, no matter how much it called out to me. I had to find a balance, a way to live with the duality of my nature without losing sight of who I was.

I closed my eyes, taking deep breaths to calm myself. It was time for me to decide, to take control of my life and my destiny. I had to find *her* and ask her what the hell I was. None of my brothers struggled with their wolves the way I struggled with River. The first time we shifted, I blacked out for days. I wound up somewhere south, hundreds of miles away from home. No one was with me, no one saw me, no one helped me.

Her face drifted towards me the longer I held my eyes closed. I thought she loved me, but she abandoned me the day before I turned 18 and I never saw her again. My own mother. The one who was supposed to love me and care about me. While

Gabe and Rom's moms stepped up and stepped in, I longed for my own, often withdrawing into myself and losing days at a time. I'd ask the guys about their shifts, and they always told me how they remembered everything. Every bone breaking, every prance, every hunt. But not me.

My wolf was defective. Essentially shutting me out to a point where he saw through my eyes, but I could never see through his. As I heard Avery laugh downstairs, I let go into the darkness.

*I opened my eyes to find myself in the same dark, eerie forest where I had woken up after that fateful night of shifting. The trees swayed gently in the wind as if whispering secrets to each other. I took a step forward, feeling the crunch of dried leaves underfoot.*

*Suddenly, I heard a low growl, and my instincts kicked in. I froze, looking for the source of the sound. A shadowy figure emerged from behind a tree, its eyes glinting in the darkness. It was a wolf, but not just any wolf. Its fur was jet black, and its eyes were an icy blue that bore into mine with an intensity that made me shudder.*

*I took a step back, but the wolf advanced towards me, its growling becoming more menacing. I knew what it wanted— a fight to establish dominance.*

*I closed my eyes and focused on my breathing, trying to calm myself as the wolf circled me. It bared its teeth, ready to attack, but I refused to let fear take over. Suddenly, I felt something snap inside of me, and before I even knew what was happening, I felt my own wolf taking control.*

*As if seeing myself for the first time, I watched my shift. It was magnificent. My bones crackled and popped as they elongated, my face shifted, and I stood upright. Strength coursed through my veins as River cracked his neck.*

*We are Lycan.*

*The black wolf stopped her advance and looked at me with a sense of recognition. I stared back, feeling my heart swell in my chest as I finally realized who she was— my mother.*

*Tears filled my eyes as River approached the wolf cautiously, sniffing the air around her. He then bowed his head in respect and placed his muzzle on her shoulder. A deep understanding passed between us before she gracefully padded away into the night.*

"My son," she spoke. "You are everything. I am so sorry I abandoned you, I waited as long as I could. Your father... he... he's not a very good man. If he knew that you carried the gene of the last Lycan, he would end your life. My son, all the abuse you carried on your little shoulders at his hands, I weep for, but know, that you come from a long line of very strong Lycans."

"What do you mean? I can't be a Lycan, they've been extinct for many years..."

"It is true son. Hide your identity, keep the others in the dark. Your father lurks where he cannot be seen."

"But..."

"The girl. She is good for you. She too, has immeasurable powers, many of which I do not know. You must see Selene. She will be waiting for you when you are ready. And son...?"

*I fell silent, watching her as she shifted into the mother I always knew her to be. "I am so proud of you. And I love you."*

I awoke to dainty hands trailing small circles through the hair on my chest. It was Avery, her eyes staring up at me with concern. "Are you okay?" she asked softly.

I took a deep breath, still reeling from the revelation of my true identity. "Yeah," I lied. "I just had a weird dream."

She leaned up to give me a soft kiss, her lips warm and comforting against mine. "Well, you're awake now. And that's all that matters."

I wrapped my arms around her, pulling her close as I tried to make sense of what I had just experienced. My mother was alive, and I was a Lycan— a member of a race that had supposedly gone extinct.

"Wait, aren't you angry with me? For marking you without your consent?" I looked at her, struggling to contain my urge to look at my mark.

"Honestly? A little yeah. I am a tiny bit angry that we didn't talk about it... but the guys chatted to me and told me that you've always had trouble containing your dark side and... I get it. I want to help you. I want to help calm down and be at peace."

I sighed, feeling grateful for Avery's understanding. "Thank you," I said, holding her close. "I don't know what I'd do without you."

Avery leaned back, looking up at me with a mischievous glint in her eye. "Well, lucky for you, you don't have to find out," she said as she straddled me on the bed. "Because I'm not going anywhere."

I grinned, feeling my heart lift as Avery's lips found mine once again. For a moment, I forgot all about my Lycan identity and my mother's warning. All I could feel was the heat of Avery's body against mine and the overwhelming sense of love and desire that we shared.

As we moved together in unison, I couldn't help but wonder what other secrets lay hidden within me. What other powers and abilities did I possess? And what would become of me and Avery if my father ever found out about my true nature?

But for now, I pushed those thoughts aside, choosing to focus on the present moment. With Avery by my side, I knew that anything was possible. And as we surrendered to our passion, I felt a deep sense of peace wash over me, knowing that I was exactly where I was meant to be— right here, with the woman I loved.

"I don't know what it is about you, Nik, but I can't seem to keep my hands off of you." She blushed, a sheen of sweat covering her brow.

"Well, maybe I'm just that sexy?" I chuckled into her hair.

"No, I just feel… drawn to you. Your darkness… it calls me. I feel at home with it."

I froze, unsure of how to respond to Avery's words. I had never met anyone who was so welcoming of my darkness, so accepting of the parts of me that I had always tried to hide.

"Avery... I don't know what to say," I admitted, my voice hesitant.

She reached up to trace a gentle finger along my jawline. "You don't have to say anything," she whispered. "Just let me love you, even during moments when you don't love yourself."

"Guys, can you stop banging for one goddamn second? Breakfast is ready and it's getting cold," Roman yelled from the bottom of the stairs.

I couldn't help but laugh, feeling slightly embarrassed at the thought of Roman catching us in the act. Though, technically I had nothing to feel weird about. We were all supposed to share her, though as far as I knew, I was the only one that had her since she came into our lives.

"Come on, let's go," I said, pulling Avery up from the bed and heading towards the door. "We can continue this later."

As we made our way down to the kitchen, I couldn't shake the feeling of unease that settled in my gut. Avery's words had left me feeling exposed, vulnerable in a way that I wasn't used to.

"Hey man, everything okay?" Roman asked, sensing my mood.

I shrugged, not wanting to burden him with my problems. "Just tired, I guess."

"You sure? Cuz I'm here for you, you know?"

"I know man. Just a lot on my mind."

"A lot on your dick too, I guess."

"I heard that," Avery laughed as she poured herself a cup of coffee.

Home. This is what home felt like.

# Fourteen: Gabriel

When I saw the mark on her neck the next morning, I almost shifted and went after Nik right there. But then I saw it.

It wasn't just a mark. It was *the mark*. The one from the Prophesy of the Lycan.

I had heard the legends of the Prophesy from an elder werewolf in a distant pack many years ago. He told me that one day, the world would be thrown into chaos, and only one Lycan would remain. An unstoppable killing machine with a heart of bravery. A being so powerful they could easily level cities in a single night if they wished it.

But this being would not be destructive, instead he would bring peace to the world and lead his kind with compassion and understanding. The elder told me that this prophecy was foretold on the neck of every true Lycan mate—the mark of a crescent moon surrounded by nine stars. One for each of the supernatural races, either in existence or extinct.

And here she was, part of the Alpha Trio. How had this not been part of the Prophesy? Her being the one for all three of us. I needed to do some digging.

As Roman remained oblivious to her new mark, I sat and watched them interact. She was the most at ease with him, as I suspected she would be. He was the funny one. She had yet to see the darkness of his insecurities come to the surface, because when they did, they swallowed all that was light in him. But I knew that he would do anything to protect her. And he wasn't the only one.

I had never felt so protective of a woman before, but something about her drew me in. Maybe it was the mate bond, or maybe it was just the way she held herself. Whatever it was, I knew that I needed to protect her too.

I watched as she laughed with Roman, her eyes lighting up as he made a joke. He put a hand on her shoulder, and she leaned into him, her head resting on his chest. It was a tender moment, and a pang of jealousy ran through me.

But I quickly pushed aside my green goblin and focused on the bigger picture. We needed to figure out what her mark meant for all of us, and how it fit into the prophecy. As the oldest and most experienced member of the Alpha Trio, it was up to me to take charge and lead us forward.

I stood up from where I had been sitting and approached the two of them. They looked up at me, startled by my sudden movement.

"Something on your mind, Gabe?" Roman asked, his hand still lingering on her shoulder.

"Yes," I replied, my eyes fixed on hers. "I think we need to go into town and visit our resident witch."

Roman's eyebrows shot up. "What for?"

Avery started twitching. "Um, excuse me, I think I need some air."

"I'll come with you," Nik's voice came out of nowhere.

"Where were you all morning, sleepy head?" Roman joked.

"Getting a new tattoo, doofus."

Avery blushed. "Can I see it?"

"Sure, next time you rip my clothes off." He smirked.

"Okay, you two..." I started, bursting into laughter when Nik rolled his eyes at me, grabbing an apple before taking off after Avery outside.

"Rom, we need to talk."

"Yes, I saw the mark, Gabe. I know you think I'm the idiot of the group, but I smelled it on her the second she waltzed in here yesterday."

I couldn't help but smile at my brother's uncharacteristically perceptive comment. "You're not an idiot, Roman. You're just...you."

He laughed, running his fingers through his hair. "Thanks, I think."

"But seriously," I continued, all humor dropping from my voice. "We need to make sure she's safe. That mark is more than just a decoration. It has to do with the Prophesy."

Roman nodded, his face set in a determined expression. "Between the three of us, there's no way she's going anywhere. And we'll go see the witch in town, like you said."

"Good. Now we do have pack business to attend to, there's only so much work we can push off and it's been weeks since we checked in with the progress of the rescue center." I sighed. We had been building a rescue for abused women and children and it was slow going. With so many packs who were cruel and defiant to the oath to take care of each other, it was almost constantly overrun. We needed more manpower and finding it was difficult. As we made our way to the pack house, I could feel the gravity of the situation weighing down on me. The rescue center was important work, but with the recent Prophesy and Avery's arrival, it felt like just a drop in the bucket.

As we entered the pack house, the smell of fresh coffee greeted us. "Good morning, Alpha," our pack secretary, Maria, said as she handed me a steaming cup.

"Morning, Maria. How's the progress on the rescue center?"

"It's slow-going, as usual. But we have some new volunteers coming in today to help with the construction."

"Great. Thank you for keeping things running while we've been otherwise busy."

She smiled knowingly. "No worries Alpha Gabriel. We have it under control."

Walking into the office was like walking into a warzone. Paperwork was scattered haphazardly on every available surface, but we did our best to navigate it as we sat down at our desks.

"Okay, let's start with the funding. We need more money if we're going to expand the center. I think we should reach out to the human community and see if they'd be willing to donate. Maybe we could even do a fundraiser," I suggested, brainstorming ways to increase our resources.

Roman shrugged. "We could ask Nik to design some t-shirts or something. People love that kind of stuff."

"Nik? You want Nik to design t-shirts? He'd sooner rip the throats of anyone who looks at Avery wrong than do some frilly girl nonsense."

Roman gasped, "Are you being sexist, Gabe? My heart!"

I chuckled, "You know me better than that, Roman. I just meant that Nik is a bit... aggressive, to say the least. Maybe we should find someone else for the t-shirt designs."

Roman nodded in agreement. "Fair point. How about we reach out to some local businesses for donations? Or even start a GoFundMe page?"

"That's a great idea, Roman. We'll need to make sure we have a solid plan for how the donated funds will be used though," I replied, feeling optimistic about our fundraising possibilities.

As we continued to discuss different ideas for fundraising, my mind drifted to Avery. She had been on my mind constantly and I longed for the closeness Nik had already felt with her. Even Roman. Why was I last? Ugh, I needed to refocus.

I caught the tailspin of Roman asking what else we could do to raise money.

I leaned forward, resting my elbows on my desk. "Well, we can reach out to local celebrities as well. Maybe we can convince them to make a public statement in support of our cause, and that should help us attract more donations."

Roman nodded, impressed. "That's a fantastic idea, Gabe. Which celebrities do you have in mind?"

"I was thinking about reaching out to Emily Rolozinsky. She's known for her activism, and I think she might be interested in what we're doing," I said, feeling hopeful.

Roman grinned. "I like it. Let's see if we can get in touch with her. Maybe we could even arrange for her to visit the center, and that would give us some great publicity."

"We could even try to get a hold of some of the wealthy donors we have had in the past. Maybe they'd be willing to increase their contributions or even sponsor an event for us."

Roman nodded and grabbed a notepad, ready to jot down any potential leads. As we continued to brainstorm, my mind kept drifting to a certain beautiful young lady.

Suddenly, a knock on the door interrupted our conversation. I looked up to see Nikolai standing in the doorway, a scowl on his face.

"What's up, Nik?" Roman asked.

Nik sighed heavily, his fists in tight balls as his look became a glare. "Avery's missing."

# Fifteen: Roman

"What the fuck do you mean, she's missing?" Gabriel roared as I got up and crossed the room in less than a second.

Nikolai looked at us, his face pale. "I don't know what happened man. We were going into town, crossed over the border and she just... disappeared."

Gabriel's eyes narrowed, his jaw clenching tightly. "Are you telling me that she vanished into thin air?" he asked in a low voice.

Nikolai nodded, beads of sweat forming on his forehead. "Yes, I swear it. We were just walking down the street when she stepped into an alleyway and then... she was gone."

Gabriel slammed his fist onto the table, splintering its surface. "That doesn't make any sense. She couldn't have just disappeared," he growled.

But even as he spoke, a sick feeling started to pool in the pit of my stomach.

Gabriel slammed his fist onto the table again, causing the glasses and bottles to rattle and papers to fly off the table. "You better start talking, Nikolai. What the hell did you do to her?"

Nikolai's eyes widened. "I swear, Gabriel, I didn't do anything to her. She was right behind me and then she was gone. It's like she vanished into thin air."

Gabriel paced back and forth, his mind racing with various scenarios. "That simply isn't possible...unless..."

I glanced sharply at him. "Unless what?"

"Unless a witch had something to do with it."

"You don't think there is a witch on Braden's payroll, do you?" My eyes felt like they were on fire from how long I'd held the glare towards Nik.

"I mean, yes. He rules through fear and brutality. Why wouldn't he have a witch on his payroll?" Gabe said, running his hands through his hair and sighing deeply.

Suddenly, the room fell silent. We all heard the creaking of the floorboards as a figure stepped into the room. The room twisted and spun until we were no longer in the safety of our home. It was a woman, dressed in rags with a hood covering her face. She was holding a small wooden box in one hand.

Without making any sound, she walked towards us and placed the box on the table. Gabriel reached for it, but the woman pulled it back. My hackles rose at the sight of someone so freely entering our domain without an invitation.

"I have something that belongs to you," she said in a raspy voice.

"What is it?" I asked, trying to see her face under the hood.

"It's a charm that will help you find your mate," she replied.

"How do you know about her?" I demanded, anger lacing my voice. *We should end her life just for daring to show her face here.* She stunk of magic.

The woman chuckled, her hood falling back to reveal a small smile on her face. She didn't look particularly cruel, but one could not be too careful when witches are involved. "I know all about her. And I can help you find her."

I exchanged a look with Gabriel and Nikolai. We all knew the risks of dealing with the unknown, but finding my mate was worth it.

"What do you want in return?" I asked, trying to keep my tone level.

The woman's smile grew wider. "Just a small favor. Nothing much."

I narrowed my eyes. "What kind of favor?"

"Nothing to concern yourself with at the moment," she said cryptically. "Are you interested in the charm or not?"

I hesitated for a split second before grabbing it. "How does it work?"

"A locate ceremony. Though, I don't hold out much hope you'll be able to find her. Not with the Prophesy hanging over your heads and no knowledge of the power that it holds." She laughed, looking at Nikolai.

"How do you know about that," he said sharply, making a move towards her.

"Not so fast, young Lycan. I can be friend or foe, you must decide." She looked at him intensely.

Nikolai stood his ground, eyeing the woman warily. "What do you mean by that? Are you trying to bait me?"

The woman chuckled again, her eyes scanning our faces. "I don't mean to bait you, dear. But I have information that could help you in your quest to find your mate and fulfill the Prophesy."

"And what is that information?" Gabriel spoke up, his voice calm but firm.

The woman's smile disappeared, replaced with a serious expression. "There is a way to break the curse of the Prophesy. But it requires a sacrifice. One of you must give up something precious in order to break the curse."

My heart sank at the thought of what that could mean. I knew what was most precious to me, and I couldn't imagine giving it up.

"What kind of sacrifice?" I asked, my voice barely above a whisper.

The woman looked at me with a mixture of pity and amusement. "Oh, dear. I cannot say. It varies from species to species. But if you are truly committed to breaking the curse, then you will know what must be given up."

I felt a lump form in my throat.

"We don't even know the details of what the Prophesy is," Gabriel said, his voice hesitant.

"They didn't teach you much, did they?" She scoffed before reciting an ancient Prophesy.

*In days of old where winds anew,*

*Two beings of different kind shall choose,*
*To unite their power and bind their hearts,*
*And bring an end to worlds apart.*

"But what does that even mean?" Nikolai asked, frustration seeping into his voice.

"It means one of you is destined to unite with someone from another kind to bring about the end of the divide between species," she explained. "Only one of you. As I have heard through the grapevine, all three of you lay claim. The only way to circumvent the Prophesy and erase the curse while fulfilling your duties is through sacrifice."

We all exchanged looks, unsure of what to say or do next. The weight of the Prophesy and the sacrifices that may be required of us now hung heavily in the air.

But one thing was clear, we couldn't let the divide between our species continue any longer. Our ancestors had come together to protect all kinds. It would be our undoing if we ended the purpose of our pack.

"I will do whatever it takes to break the curse and unite our species," I said, finally breaking the silence. "But we need more information."

The woman nodded, seemingly pleased with my answer. "Of course. I suggest you start by finding your mate. The charm will lead you to her, and then the rest will follow."

I slipped the charm into my pocket, feeling its weight on my chest. "And what of the sacrifice?"

"When the time comes, you will know what you must do," she said cryptically before turning to leave.

"Wait!" I called after her. "What is your name?"

She turned back to us, a small smile creeping over her face. "My name is Sapphire." With that, Sapphire disappeared into the night, leaving us to ponder her words and the fate that lay before us. The weight of the prophecy hung heavy on my mind, along with the realization that saving my mate might be the key to saving our species. The haze disappeared and we found ourselves in the middle of the forest.

Nikolai broke the silence. "We should leave. We can discuss our next steps on the way back to the pack."

Gabriel and I nodded, and we headed back towards the denser parts of the forest, our thoughts swirling with the knowledge of what must be done.

As we walked, I felt the charm burning hot in my pocket, and I couldn't help but think of the mysterious woman and how she knew about us. Was she on the side of the natural order, or was she poised to strike and end the delicate balance that we have begun to create?

"Guys, I am dying with worry. We need to go find Avery," Nik spoke, breaking the tense silence again.

"You're the one that lost her," I snarled.

"Thats not fair man, and you know it," Gabe said, surprising me by sticking up for him.

"Yes, it is totally fair, all he had to do was watch her and keep her safe. My God, we are ALL supposed to protect her but no, you believed only one of us was sufficient. And now? Now I'm going to lose her. Like I lost Cassandra." I lashed out. I couldn't help it. My old fears and insecurities were sitting right there under the surface.

Gabriel put a hand on my shoulder, his touch calming me down. "We'll find her, Roman. We'll get her back. I promise, we won't fail. Not this time."

Nikolai nodded in agreement. "We have to. She's our mate. We can't lose her."

We quickened our pace, following the path back to the packhouse. As we moved forward, I couldn't help but think of the sacrifices that might be required of me. What was I willing to give up to save our species? Would it be my life, my love, or something else entirely? The idea gnawed at me like a constant hunger, a deep desire to protect and preserve the pack at any cost.

When we arrived at the packhouse, chaos had erupted. Fires were burning as our people screamed.

"What the hell happened? We couldn't have been gone that long!" I screamed over the noise.

"I don't know! Maybe this was all a big distraction." Gabriel panicked. "Get to the rescue, save the women and children, go now!" Without hesitation, we all shifted into our wolves and bounded towards the chaos. The smell of smoke filled our nostrils as we raced through the trees.

As we approached the packhouse, we could hear the screams growing louder, a mixture of fear and pain. We howled to each other, letting out a warning and sending a signal to the others that we were on our way.

When we reached the clearing, the sight before us made me stop in my tracks. The packhouse was engulfed in flames, the roof caving in, and the walls crumbling down. The screams grew louder, but they were not coming from the packhouse.

In the center of the clearing, a group of wolves had our pack members surrounded. They had our pack pinned down, barely clinging to life. I growled, the anger and protective instincts inside me kicking into overdrive.

*We have to act fast,* I sent a mind link to Gabriel and Nikolai, my voice laced with fury. *We can't let them hurt our pack.*

Together, we charged towards the intruders, our fur bristling with anger. They didn't stand a chance against us, our strength and speed too much for them to handle. We tore through their ranks, taking them down one by one until they ran off in defeat. It was then that I heard a long howl and watched as a massive black Alpha called his attackers to him, watching him as he turned and ran.

*Get to the rescue, now!*

# Sixteen: Roman

I tore off towards the rescue, dread filling the pit of my stomach. To my utter surprise, it had been left largely unscathed. Whether that was because we interrupted the destruction or because of another reason, my heart filled with gratitude. We had over a thousand women and children here.

*They're safe guys,* I mind linked my friends.

*We need to ramp up security around here,* Gabriel said back. *We've been lax.*

*Yeah, probably because we found our mate and let things slide,* Nikolai snarled.

*Get this fire under control,* Gabriel said, before shutting us out.

I took a deep breath and surveyed the area. The damage was minimal, but the fear and trauma would last for a long time. I walked towards the main hall, where the women and children were ushered to safety.

As I entered the hall, I saw the women huddled together, some crying, others holding onto their children tightly. I knew I had to bring some reassurance to these women, and my heart was heavy with the responsibility.

"Everyone, listen up!" I projected my voice, trying to sound confident. "We are safe, the danger is over. You are all brave and strong, and I promise that our pack will keep you safe. We will not let anything happen to you or your children."

I saw some of the women relax and wipe away their tears. It was a small victory, but it gave me hope.

"We will be increasing security checks, and we will have patrols around the clock to make sure that nothing like this ever happens again. We are all in this together, and we will overcome any obstacle that comes our way."

I could see some of the women nodding in agreement, and I knew that they were beginning to trust us.

"If anyone needs anything, please do not hesitate to ask. We will try our best to accommodate your needs."

I saw one woman in particular, step forward from the crowd. She held a young baby in her arms, and her face was etched with worry.

"Please, can you tell us what happened? Who did this?" Her voice was trembling.

I knew I had to be honest with them, even if it meant revealing the truth, one we weren't ready to reveal yet.

"We suspect that a rival pack may have been behind this. They have been seeking my mate, our mate. But rest assured, we will not let them harm you or us."

The woman nodded, her eyes still filled with fear, but also with a glimmer of hope.

As I was speaking, I noticed a young male standing off to the side. Approaching him, he looked anywhere but at my face.

"Who might you be?" I asked curiously.

"My name is Stephen, sir."

"Are you with these rescues or are you part of us already?"

"I ran here as soon as the fires started. My dad is in the pack guard and my mom died when I was born. He told me to come here, and it'll be safer."

I observed Stephen closely, noticing a hint of fear in his eyes that he tried to mask. It was clear that he had been through a lot.

"Your dad is in the guard?" I repeated, slowly.

"Yes sir."

I put a reassuring hand on his shoulder, hoping to ease some of his worries. "You're safe here, Stephen. We will take care of you."

He looked up at me, his eyes filling with a glimmer of hope. "Thank you, sir."

I smiled at him, hoping to make him feel a little bit better. "Don't worry, we'll find your dad and make sure he's safe too. Do you think you could try to mind linking him and tell him to meet you here? Alpha Gabriel and Alpha Nikolai are tending the matters in the pack village."

Stephen nodded as his eyes glazed over. "He said he is on his way."

I hardly had to wait 5 minutes and a distinguished but exhausted man came into the center.

"Alpha Roman," he said with a nod, grabbed Stephen and gave him the once over.

"Your son here tells me you're part of the guard?"

"That's correct."

"Do you have intel on what happened here today?" I asked.

He shook his head. "No, I am just an officer, you'd have to talk to Chief Mal about that. But sir..." he trailed off. "Shouldn't you know more than I do? Don't you run the forces?"

I smiled tentatively. "Actually, my leadership expertise lies elsewhere. While I have a hand in pack matters, we have another Alpha assigned to our security and training. He hasn't been derelict in his duties, but we now have more enemies than we did a few weeks ago."

The guard officer's eyebrow raised in surprise. "More enemies? Who could possibly want to attack us?"

"Our rival pack," I said grimly. "They have been looking for our mate, and they won't stop until they find her. But we won't let them harm anyone in our pack."

The guard officer's expression tightened in anger. "We must find a way to take them down before they can hurt anyone else. We should launch a counterattack."

I shook my head. "We need to be careful. We don't know their numbers or their strengths. If we launch an attack without enough information, it could lead to disaster. We need to gather more intel on our rivals first." I conveniently leave out the part where Avery is missing. That is not supposed to be shared yet.

The guard officer nodded in agreement. "I understand, Alpha. But what do we do in the meantime?"

"We'll increase security measures around the pack, set up additional patrols, and monitor all pack borders carefully. We need to prevent another attack from happening. I will have Alpha Nikolai look into more extensive and strategic planning."

The guard officer looked satisfied with my answer. "Understood, Alpha. I'll make sure the other guards are informed."

"Good. And make sure Stephen is taken care of. We need to protect our young ones."

The guard officer nodded and turned to leave, taking Stephen with him.

Sighing, I watched as the women began to settle their kids in for the night. Making sure that there was an increased presence of protection, I set off back to the packhouse to debrief with Gabe and Nik.

As I walked, my mind couldn't help but think about Avery. Was she safe? Was she with the rival pack? Or was she on her own, lost in the wilderness? The thought of her being hurt or worse made my chest constrict with worry.

I needed to find her, but without any leads or information, it seemed like a near-impossible task.

Once I arrived at the makeshift packhouse, I made my way to where Gabe and Nik were waiting for me.

"Any news on Avery?" Gabe asked as soon as I entered the room.

I shook my head. "No, not yet. Unfortunately, she didn't magically appear at the rescue. But we need to step up our efforts to find her. We can't just sit around waiting for something to happen. If tonight is any indication, we are in for war over her."

Nikolai leaned forward. "Agreed, but we need to be careful. We can't risk any more of our own getting hurt."

"I know," I said, rubbing my temples. "But we need to do something. Avery is out there somewhere, alone and vulnerable. We can't just abandon her."

Gabriel put a hand on my shoulder. "We won't abandon her. Sapphire gave us the charm and we can use it."

"Then let's do that," I said urgently.

"Roman, we also have our pack to think about. Thousands of lives are on the line."

"Right, so how about I use the charm and go after Avery and you two can deal with the pack safety. Afterall, this could have been avoided if Nikolai just did his job."

Nikolai's fists clenched as his jaw tensed. Gabriel interjected before the tension could escalate any further. "Let's not assign blame here. We need to work together to find Avery and protect our pack. Roman, using the charm is a risky move. We don't know the consequences or if it will even work."

"I know that but we're running out of options here. We can't just sit around and let our enemies come after us. Avery is the key to all of this. If we find her, we can end this once and for all. Laying claim on her will likely cause Braden to back off. He can't claim her if she already bares our marks."

Nikolai sighed heavily. "She bares mine already..."

"Yes, but 3 mates mean 3 marks... Hey Nik, can't you link to her now that you're bonded?" I asked.

"No. I've tried, something is blocking the connection..."

I frowned. "That's unusual. What could be blocking it?"

"Maybe the rival pack put a spell on her?" Nikolai suggested.

"That's possible," Gabriel agreed. "We need to find out for sure and see if we can break the spell."

Nikolai leaned back in his chair. "I'll talk to our pack witches and see if they know anything about this. We'll also need to talk about fixing the security issues. Nik, that's on you."

He nodded. "Let's get to work."

# Seventeen: Braden

"Lucas, Maddox, report!" I screamed as they joined me in retreat.

"Packhouse is incinerated, the village grounds are burning, but are quickly getting under control. The rescue was spared because those three dicks managed to get in the way," Lucas barked while running beside me.

"Maddox, status of my mate."

"Unknown," he simply replied.

We continued sprinting through the forest, trying to outrun the flames that were quickly approaching us. It seems some of my soldiers are pathetic at arson. My heart was filled with hatred and bitterness. Avery was all I wanted. Amrin had gone silent, it felt strange that my mind was quiet instead of filled with the usual berating I would be getting.

As we neared the edge of the forest, I caught a glimpse of movement in the nearby bushes. Without thinking, I leaped forward, using my enhanced senses to track the figure. It was Avery stumbling through the underbrush, her clothes singed, and her skin covered in soot.

I rushed towards her, scooping her up in my arms and cradling her against my chest. Her body was limp, and her breaths were shallow, but she was alive. I let out a relieved breath, my heart warming at the sight of her.

"Avery, my love, are you alright?" I whispered, running my fingers through her hair.

She stirred in my arms, her eyes fluttering open to reveal pools of confusion and panic. She looked up at me, a small mewl crossing her lips before she passed out.

"Lucas, Maddox, call ahead to the nearest safe house. I need to make sure she's guarded. Make sure she receives proper medical attention," I ordered, passing her to my trusted soldiers. "Make sure that baby is okay."

As they did that, I raced ahead to the nearest house.

When we arrived, I had them carry her directly to the bedroom and instructed them to chain her to the bed until the doctor arrived.

"Sir, are you sure you want to do that?" Maddox said hesitantly.

"Yes," I snarled. "I don't need her running away again."

Once that was done, I sat next to Avery on the bed and took a moment to catch my breath. Taking in her appearance, it was clear she had suffered greatly from whatever she had gone through, but she would make it through. She had to—she was carrying my baby.

"Alpha Braden. Is this your mate?" Orville said as he took in her poor form.

"Yes. She is carrying my child, please attend to her as gently as possible."

Orville nodded and began his examination, checking her vitals and tending to the wounds on her skin. I watched him work, Amrin growling at every whimper that escaped Avery's lips. She was in so much pain, and all he wanted to do was murder the doctor for helping her.

"Alpha Braden, she's in stable condition now. She's been through a lot, but she'll pull through," Orville said finally, stepping back from the bed and giving me a reassuring pat on the shoulder.

"Thank you. And the baby?"

"Gone, sir. It did not survive whatever she has been through."

Amrin forced me to shift, ripping the doctor to shreds before I could utter a word. Then he looked at Avery, rage flowing through his veins.

*You did this,* he hissed at me.

*No, I didn't, this isn't my fault.*

*You rejected her. You made her leave. This is your fault. You will pay for your sins; I'll make sure of it.*

Terror clutched at my heart as I tried to shift back, but Amrin held the reigns, refusing to let me.

He shut me out, leaving me in the dark.

**Amrin**

Stupid fucking human. I tried guiding him, I tried coaching him. But no, his idiot of a father raised him to be an utter imbecile that abused his own mate, so what did I expect? How Selene could have given me to such a moron, I'd never know, but I did know that I would never give him the control back. If that meant we stayed in my form, then that's what we would do. My rage wasn't directed towards Avery. It was directed towards him. My own flesh, my counterpart.

I could feel his fear and desperation to regain control, but it was too late for that now. He had caused too much damage, and I wasn't going to let him hurt anyone again. Avery was safe now, and I would make sure she never suffered at his hands again.

As the night wore on, I paced around the room, Avery's whimpers the only sounds to break the silence. She was restless, her body writhing in pain as she clutched at her stomach. The thought of the baby, my child, not surviving ripped through me like a knife. But it was nothing compared to the anger I felt towards my counterpart. I had wanted her, wanted our child more than anything.

He had rejected Avery, driven her to leave. And now, she was paying the price for his idiocy. If it was up to me, I would tear him apart limb by limb. But I knew that wasn't possible, at least not yet. I needed him to pay penance and repent. If he refused, I would move to plan B. Finding a way to separate us so I could end his miserable life. Pathetic waste of skin.

I nosed at her belly, pausing a moment as I smelled her. She still smelled different. Before I had time to ponder what that meant, her beautiful eyes opened, meeting him.

She gasped, a terrified sound as she tried to pull at the chains that held her prisoner on the bed.

*Shit. I didn't think of those when I forced my asshole into his corner. I'll have to try mind link Maddox to release her.*

"Are you here to kill me?" she finally said, tears welling in her eyes as she moved her hands over her stomach.

Curious reaction.

I couldn't very well speak to her since we never marked each other, but I could move up into her space and lay down. So that's exactly what I did.

"Oh...um...hi," she said through her fear.

I gently nuzzled her side, my way of assuring her that I meant no harm. I never wanted her to be afraid of me.

"Please don't hurt me, I'm not strong enough." Her voice was barely audible, but I could make out every word.

I nipped at her side again in response and moved my body up against hers. It seemed to help reassure her and draw her out of her fearful state.

"Thank you," she whispered, and I licked her face reassuringly before settling down next to her. "Who are you?"

I growled in response, nosing her mark as I realized someone had claimed her already.

"Are you...his wolf?"

My growl deepened as I recognized the scent of the one who had marked her. One of those Alphas from the burning. I turned my head to look at her, meeting her gaze with eyes that burned with fury. She flinched slightly, but I did not move away. Instead, I leaned in close and sniffed at her neck, inhaling the scent of him on her skin.

She whimpered but didn't try to pull away, and I knew in that moment that I would not let him keep her. She was mine. Yesterday. Today. Forever.

I let out a low rumbling sound and moved closer, pressing my body against hers so tightly, I was almost in her lap, before licking her mark one more time. Her hands trembled as she reached up to stroke my fur.

"You're beautiful."

My heart raced as I shivered under her touch, and I vowed that I would never leave her side. Fuck everyone who would come in our way. She would always be mine.

Maddox stepped into the room, shocked at the image before him.

Jumping off the bed, I mind linked him to undo her cuffs and bring her some food.

"You sure that's a good idea? Wouldn't um... Braden be kind of angry that you're releasing her?" His eyes shone with terror.

*He's not the one you should be afraid of, pup,* I growled back. *I may be showing her kindness, but do not think that extends to you, Lucas, or anyone in my way. I am more than I appear, and I won't let any of you get in my way.*

Maddox stared at me for a moment, then nodded and hurried to do as I asked.

Once he left, I curled up next to her again, pressing my body against hers protectively. She flinched slightly and rubbed at her wrists rubbed raw from the chains. Fury rose in me, and I desperately tried to reign it in. When rage flowed through me, I had no control over myself.

Maddox returned with a plate of food for her, simple food. Eggs, some stale bread, and a bit of deli meat that thankfully wasn't off yet.

"You good, Amrin?" he asked, watching my lip curl upwards.

*Get the fuck out of here pipsqueak. Don't bother me until I call for you again.*

He scurried off and I was finally left alone with the woman who would fulfill the prophesy.

# Eighteen: Avery

The last few days were a whirlwind of *what the absolute hell?*

First, I was somehow separated from Nik. One second, he was there, the next... I couldn't see him, and I was transported to some random area with a voice telling me to run. So, I did. I ran. I tried to run back to the guys, but I had no idea which way to go, and I ended up in the back of some cave, where I then had to fight off a pack of bats who tried to attack me. Presumably to eat me. Or make me into a vampire. Only half kidding.

As I caught my breath, I looked around the cave and realized that it was not a natural formation. It was too symmetrical, too ornate. Intricate patterns of vines were etched into the walls, and tiny glowing crystals glimmered in the darkness. The air hummed with energy, and I felt a tingling sensation all over my skin.

Suddenly, a figure emerged from the shadows. It was a woman, or at least she appeared to be a woman. She was tall and slender, with long, flowing hair the color of moonlight. Her eyes were large and luminous, and her skin was as pale as alabaster.

"Who are you?" I demanded of the ethereal figure.

"You know who I am, child," she spoke softly, her voice illuminating the cave with a softness that caressed my fear and drove my darkness into the light. I tried to recall where I had seen her before, but to no avail. The woman sensed my confusion and smiled.

"Do not fret, child. You will soon remember everything. We have been waiting for you."

"We?" I asked, intrigued, and slightly unnerved.

The woman nodded and gestured towards the glowing crystals that lined the walls of the cave. As if on cue, they began to pulsate and emit a blinding light. I closed my eyes, shielding them from the intensity of the light.

When I opened them again, everything had changed. The cave had transformed into a grand hall, with a high ceiling and golden pillars stretching towards the sky. In the center of the hall stood a throne with intricate carvings of mythical creatures, and on it sat an imposing figure cloaked in black.

The woman led me towards the throne, and as we got closer, I could feel the power emanating from the figure seated upon it. My heart raced as he spoke.

"Welcome, child," the figure said in a deep, commanding voice. "We have been waiting for you."

I couldn't help but feel a sense of familiarity, like I had met this figure before. But I couldn't place where or when. The figure stood up, towering over me, and placed a hand on my shoulder. I could feel the weight of his touch, the power that flowed from him.

"As the chosen one, you have a great destiny ahead of you," the figure continued. "The fate of our world rests in your hands."

I looked up at him, trying to process everything that had just happened. The woman had disappeared, leaving me alone with this mysterious figure.

"What do you mean by, "chosen one?" What fate?"

The figure looked down at me with piercing eyes that seemed to see right through me.

"You possess a gift, a power that has been dormant within you. With it, you can change the course of our world and bring peace to those who deserve it."

"We have a proposition for you," the figure continued, his voice echoing through the grand hall. "Our world is in peril, and we require your assistance to restore the balance."

"What do you mean?" I asked, my curiosity piqued.

The figure looked at me with intensity, as if he was gauging my worthiness. "You possess a unique ability, child. One that could shift the tides in our favor. Will you help us?"

I hesitated for a moment, unsure of what my ability could possibly be. But the woman reappeared beside me and placed a reassuring hand on my shoulder, and I felt a surge of courage.

"I don't understand. Where am I? Who are all of you? I don't have any powers... I'm a wolfless wolf. Pregnant, no less, because I am a failure to my kind. To Selene," I said bitterly.

"My dear, you did not fail me." The woman beside me spoke and suddenly a rush of memories flooded into my mind.

Selene talking with my mother.

My mother was being given the gift of pregnancy by way of a small crystal being absorbed into her skin.

My father doting on her as she grew round with child.

My birth in this very hall, with these very mystical beings watching on.

This imposing figure putting a hand on me and blessing my future.

I shattered, fell to the floor as tears ran down my face. "What am I? What are you?" My voice was meek, small, as it echoed in the hall. The woman beside me, Selene, bent down and wrapped her arms around me, holding me close as I trembled with emotion. I felt the surge of strength flow through her arms, into me before breathing a sigh of peace.

"We are the guardians of this world," she said softly, her voice soothing me. "And you are our last hope."

I looked up at her, confused. "What do you mean, last hope?"

She hesitated for a moment before continuing. "There is a great evil in our world. It seeks to destroy everything we hold dear, and it grows stronger every day. We have fought it for centuries, but we are losing. We need someone with your abilities to help us stop it."

"What abilities?" I asked. "I don't have a wolf. I am nothing."

Selene smiled at me, a small glint of mischief in her eyes. "Oh, but you do have an ability my dear. You just haven't found it yet." She stood up and helped me to my feet before leading me towards a set of doors that I had not noticed before.

"Come with me. I will show you," she said as the doors opened to reveal a large training room.

The room was filled with weapons of all kinds: swords, spears, bows, and arrows, but what caught my eye was a small, glowing crystal sitting on a pedestal at the far end of the room. It pulsed with energy, and I could feel its power even from where I stood. Selene noticed my fascination with the crystal and smiled.

"That is the source of your ability," she said, walking towards it. "It is called the Spirit Stone, and it has been passed down through generations of our guardians. It gives the wielder the power to control the elements."

She held out her hand, and the crystal flew into her palm, glowing brighter than before. She closed her eyes and took a deep breath, and suddenly a gust of wind erupted from her hand, blowing my hair back.

"Wow," I breathed, my eyes wide in wonder.

Selene turned to me, holding it out for me to take. "Take it," she said, "and embrace your destiny. You are the only one who can save us."

I hesitated for a moment, unsure if I was ready to accept such a responsibility. But then I thought of everything I held dear and remembered how much it would hurt me to lose them. I reached out my hand and took the Spirit Stone from Selene.

As soon as the crystal touched my palm, a jolt of energy shot through my body. I felt my senses awaken, and suddenly, I could feel the elements around me—the air, the water, and the earth.

I panicked and packed it into my pocket before turning back to her. "Right, so this magical crystal grants me magical powers, but what am I?"

"My dear child. You are the last of a very special species."

"Right, you keep saying that. What is the species?" I was getting anxious now. Why wouldn't they just tell me what I am?

Selene took me back into the great hall, where the hooded figure stood with outstretched arms.

"Come. Let me show you what you are." He touched a finger to my forehead, plunging me into a swirling mass of darkness before being sucked into the light.

Suddenly, I was surrounded by these beautiful creatures. They shimmered in the light, their wings glimmering as they hovered around me. These were not angels like I have seen before, but something more... ethereal.

"These are Seraphim," Selene said softly, her voice filled with awe. "You are one of them. The last Ethereal Seraphina."

I looked up at her in shock, unable to process what she was saying. "What?" I started laughing, unable to hold in the anxiety attack that was pulsing through me. "No. Nope. I am not a... what? A Seraphina? What even is that? No. I reject this. Just take me back to the bat cave, I am perfectly fine being a bat snack."

Selene placed a comforting hand on my shoulder. "I understand this is a lot to take in. But you have been chosen for a great purpose. Your powers as an Ethereal Seraphina are unlike any other. You have the ability to control the elements and heal the sick with just a touch."

I looked at her incredulously. "Heal the sick? Control the elements? What am I, some kind of superhero?"

"In a sense, yes. You have been chosen to protect the world from evil forces that threaten to destroy it."

I scoffed. "And what if I don't want to be a superhero? What if I just want to be free from fear and live my life peacefully with my child and... three mates?"

Selene approached me calmly and took my hands into hers. "It's okay, child. This is a lot to take in, but you are special. You have a gift, a power that can protect this world from the darkness that threatens it."

I shook my head, not wanting to hear any of it. "I'm sorry, but I can't accept this. I'm just a regular person. I don't want any of this responsibility."

The hooded figure spoke up, his voice grave. "The darkness grows stronger with each passing day. It won't wait for you to come to terms with your destiny. You either accept it or watch as the world falls into chaos."

I looked at him, his eyes piercing through mine. A shiver ran down my spine, making me realize the gravity of the situation. I had to make a choice.

Taking a deep breath, I made up my mind. "Okay," I said, nodding my head. "I'll do it. I don't know how, but I'll try."

Selene smiled gently, her hand still holding mine. "That's all we ask. We'll train you and guide you every step of the way. You won't be alone in this."

The hooded figure stepped forward, holding out his hand. "Do you want to talk to your ancestors before we send you back?"

"I... I can do that?"

"Yes," he said, his voice softening. "Close your eyes and take a deep breath. Focus on the ones who came before you, those who share your bloodline. They will guide you and offer their wisdom."

I took a deep breath and closed my eyes, feeling the weight of the situation settle on my shoulders. I focused on my ancestors, feeling their presence around me, guiding me. Memories flashed in my mind, ones from centuries ago, of powerful men and women who had fought to protect their land and their people.

"Hello, dear Avery." A woman's voice came from behind me. The field was filled with light, the wings of a hundred Seraphim outstretched against the sky. "Welcome home."

# Nineteen: Avery

I whirled around and was face to face with the most beautiful woman I'd ever seen.

"Hi," I said shyly.

"Oh child, we have been waiting for you. You are infinitely powerful, desperately needed, and wanted beyond knowledge. You know that don't you?" she said, caressing my face in her hands.

I had no idea what to say to that, and my mind blanked as I blurted out, "so when do I get wings?"

The woman chuckled softly, and her eyes sparkled with amusement. "Wings? My dear, you are already capable of far greater things than just wings," she replied with a mysterious glint in her eyes.

As soon as she finished her sentence, the room around us started to change. The walls and floors shifted and morphed into an otherworldly landscape. Trees with sprawling branches filled with vibrant leaves towered above me, and a river flowed gently nearby, its water shimmering in the sun.

I looked around, my mouth agape in awe. "What's happening?" I asked breathlessly.

The woman smiled at me, her eyes now reflecting the blue of the sky.

"You are in a realm where magic reigns supreme. This is your true home, my child," she said, her voice soft and melodious.

I tried to take it all in as I stumbled forward, nearly losing my footing on the new terrain. The air smelled of lilacs and honey, and I felt a strange energy pulsing through me, making my skin tingle.

Suddenly, a low growling sound interrupted the peaceful scene. I turned towards the direction of the noise to see a massive, fiery dragon heading towards us. I tried to run, but I was frozen in place by both fear and fascination.

"Oh, dear child. Don't worry, that is Oblisk. He is my pet." Her laugh tinkled gently. "Did you want to ask any questions? Our time is rather limited."

"Why am I the only one left? What even is an Ethereal Seraphim? Why haven't I had powers my entire life?"

She chuckled, "perhaps we shall start at the beginning... Ethereal Seraphines are intermediaries between the realms of magic and divinity, often we deal with blessings, enchantment and healing. We bring peace and harmony to the world. You possess magical abilities, capable of granting wishes, bringing forth healing energy, and inspiring spiritual enlightenment."

As she spoke, I felt a warm energy surge through me, like a dormant power awakening within my very being. "But why am I the only one left? Where are the others?" I pressed, desperate for answers.

The woman's expression turned solemn. "There was a great war between the Ethereal Seraphim and the darkness that threatened to consume us all. Many were lost, but your crystal essence was hidden away in the mortal world to protect you from harm. Now, as the last of your kind, it is up to you to harness your powers and fight against the darkness that still threatens this realm."

I swallowed hard, feeling the weight of responsibility settle heavily in my chest. I listened intently, my mind racing with possibilities. "But why haven't I had these powers before?" I asked again.

The woman tilted her head, her eyes studying me carefully. "It is not uncommon for Seraphim to have a delayed awakening," she said. "However, there is something different about you, child. Something that has prevented your powers from manifesting until now."

I frowned, feeling like there was more to the story. "What do you mean?" I asked, my voice shaking slightly.

The woman sighed, her gaze flickering towards Oblisk as he landed gracefully beside us. "There are dark forces at work in this world, child," she said gravely. "Powers that seek to keep the Seraphim from fulfilling their divine duties. It is quite possible that someone has been blocking your powers, preventing you from reaching your full potential."

I felt a cold shiver run down my spine at the thought of some unknown force working against me. "Who would do such a thing?" I asked in a hushed tone.

"That, my dear," the woman said with a sad smile, "is a mystery we have yet to unravel. But fear not, for we will aid you in uncovering the truth and help you strengthen your powers. Together, we will fight back against the darkness and restore balance to this realm."

I nodded slowly, feeling a sense of determination rise within me. I was no longer alone in this battle, and the knowledge that others believed in me gave me strength. I looked up at Oblisk, who looked at me curiously.

"We should leave this place," he said in his deep, gravelly voice, shocking me. "There is danger lurking in the shadows, and we cannot stay here for long."

The woman nodded in agreement, her wings unfurling behind her. "I will guide you to safety," she said, gesturing for us to follow her.

"Wait, this is our home? Why are we leaving? I like it here!" I protested like a petulant child.

"Sweet dear, this land doesn't exist as you're seeing it. Not anymore. It's been taken as part of our destruction. We must go. Our time is over."

As quickly as I'd arrived, I was thrown back through the swirls of darkness and thrown on the floor in the great hall. "Well...that was interesting."

"Did Alara help you understand more about who you are?"

"I mean, yes and no. To be honest, I'm just kind of shocked at all of this. I won't lie." I sighed, my mind still reeling from the experience. "But at least now I know that I'm not alone in this.

Alara and Oblisk, they believe in me. And if they can help me unlock my true potential, then maybe I can make a difference."

Selene nodded, her expression softening. "You are stronger than you realize, my child. And together, we will help you become even more powerful. But first, we must prepare you for what lies ahead."

I looked at her in confusion. "What do you mean? How are you going to prepare me," I asked.

"There are those who seek to use your powers for their own gain," she explained, as if to a 5-year-old. "We've been over this, there are..."

"Yes, dark forces. But how can they take what is mine to hold?"

"The same way they destroyed those before you."

Cryptic. Unhelpful. Frustrating. "Right, and that was how?"

"They will try to break you, use your fears and emotions against you. They will try to manipulate you, control you, and force you to do their bidding," Selene answered gravely.

"And what can I do to stop them?" I asked, feeling a mix of fear and determination.

"We will train you to be strong, both physically and mentally. We will teach you how to harness your powers and use them to protect yourself and those around you. And most importantly, we will teach you how to trust your instincts and make the right decisions in the face of danger," Selene said firmly.

"I don't have any weaknesses," I said proudly.

"Oh, but you do." She nodded at my stomach, where my child slept, nestled peacefully in the safety of her cocoon. "That," Selene said, "is your greatest weakness."

"What?" I was confused. "My child?"

"Yes," Selene said. "The Dark Forces will use your child against you. They will threaten to harm her, take her away from you, and you will do anything to protect her. Do not underestimate the power of a mother's love."

I felt my heart drop. Selene was right. I would do anything to protect my child, even if it meant putting myself in danger.

"But that doesn't mean I won't fight back," I said, determination in my voice. "I'll do whatever it takes to keep her safe. My child is my weakness, but she's also my strength."

"That's good to hear." Selene smiled. "Your child will be your motivation to keep fighting, no matter what challenges come your way."

"So... what do we do now?"

"Now, I dump you back in the bat cave, place a spell of protection on your child. It won't hold forever, but it will still her heart for those listening. She will be beautiful, strong, and proud."

"...her father is none of those," I said, sadness creeping into my heart as I thought about the contrast between Braden and the Alpha Trio.

"Avery, a father is more than a bloodline. You have those in your life that I placed there to love, protect and nurture both of you."

"But why did you give me Braden first?" Tears welled in my eyes. "I wish this baby could be one of theirs."

She held me tightly. "There is no good, without darkness. No pleasure without pain, no growth without struggle. Braden and Amrin were given the greatest love of their lives, and Braden destroyed that. He couldn't break free from the shackles that bound him to mediocrity."

I nodded, understanding Selene's words. "But what about the Alpha Trio? They seem to be everything Braden wasn't."

Selene's eyes twinkled mischievously. "Ah, the Alpha Trio. They are quite... intriguing, aren't they?"

I raised my eyebrows. "What do you mean?"

"They have darkness within them, just like Braden. But unlike him, they have found a way to balance it with their light. They have each other, and together, they are unstoppable."

I couldn't help but feel a shiver run down my spine at Selene's words. The Alpha Trio was powerful, dangerous even, but they were the balance. My heart swelled at the thought of going home to them. Images flashed before my eyes. Labor, birth, nurturing and caring for this little being alongside three strong men to guide and love her.

Selene must have seen the excitement in my eyes, for she chuckled lightly. "I take it that you're eager to return to your men?" she asked.

I couldn't help but grin sheepishly. "Yes, I miss them so much. I'm still scared, but..."

"Then go, Avery. I gave them to you for a reason." Selene stepped back and gave me a gentle push towards the large black hole that suddenly appeared in the floor. "Be with those who love you and will protect you."

I nodded, tears streaming down my face. "Thank you, Selene. For everything."

She smiled warmly. "Remember, Avery. You have the power within you to protect and love your child fiercely. And with your men by your side, nothing can stop you."

The hooded figure stepped forward. "Selene. He's here, she must go," he said urgently.

"It's time."

"Wait, when will I see you again?" I said, desperation clawing at my chest.

"When the time is right."

A single tear trickled down her face as she pushed me through the floor as darkness engulfed me.

# Twenty: Avery

After that whirlwind of a strange, yet enlightening dream, I was unceremoniously dumped on my ass, back in the cave, just as I was promised. Walking out into the densely treed forest, I palmed the Spirit Stone in my hand. A loud roar nearby indicated a waterfall was close, and it called to me. Heeding its summon, I dove right into the shimmering pool beneath the falls.

The Stone started whispering, glowing brightly as the wind picked up around me. Holding up to the sun, it swirled with life before flying straight into my chest. Shock ran through my body as it absorbed into my skin, setting fire to my nerves, not in a painful way, but in a pleasing, warm sensation that filled me with peace and a sense of knowledge. As I emerged from the pool, my body felt lighter, as though I could almost float on air. And then it happened— the world around me seemed to shift and change in an instant. The trees around me took on a soft pink hue as their leaves slowly turned into feathers of the palest pink. Their branches stretched out towards me, beckoning me forward.

I felt myself being pulled forward, as if by some invisible force. Following the tree's lead, I walked forward, not quite sure where I was going, but trusting that the Spirit Stone would guide me.

Soon enough, I found myself standing in the middle of a brightly lit field, butterflies dancing around me. My arms were weightless as they lifted above my head, dancing in time with nature.

Whispers started around me, beginning as lilting melodies before turning ominous. My heart twisted painfully in my chest as darkness descended in this mystical field. I turned around to run, but the butterflies had turned into black crows, their wings beating against the sky like a heavy drum. I could feel my feet sinking into the earth, as if it was trying to swallow me whole.

In the distance, I could hear faint whispers and murmurs, but I couldn't understand what they were saying. They were getting louder and closer, and I felt a sudden urge to run away. But my feet wouldn't budge. It felt like roots had grown from the ground, wrapping themselves around my ankles. Panic set in, and I started sprinting towards a path that seemed to appear out of nowhere.

It was a narrow, winding trail that cut through the darkness. The whispers grew louder, and I could hear strange, guttural noises coming from deep within the forest. Every step felt like I was wading through thick, heavy mud. I pushed on, my breaths coming in ragged gasps as I ran.

Before I had a moment to try collect myself, strong arms captured me as I was on the verge of collapse. My eyes fluttered open and took in the face of my savior.

Braden. My heart set off in an anxious roar as my body shut down. *No, no, no, no, this can't be happening. I'm a Seraphina, I can fight him.* But try as I might, my limbs grew numb, and my body stilled.

When I awoke, I was chained to a bed with a large wolf watching me. My head spun with fear as I lay there on the bed, waiting for his next move. All I wanted was to get out of here alive—but would he let me go? Maybe if I placated him and did as he asked, he would let me go? Sighing, I let go of silly fantasies and returned my gaze to the giant wolf in front of me.

Much to my surprise, it seemed to want to be close to me, responding to each of my pleas with comfort, which brought me a sense of peace. It was only when Maddox came in that I realized this was Braden's wolf, Amrin. It sent shocks through my core when I realized Amrin had never agreed with the way Braden had callously pushed me aside.

When he had Maddox undo my chains, I decided that I would try to make a run for it when he was asleep, but through the day and night, he lay beside me, refusing to let me move.

Bile rose in my throat as I understood... he wasn't about to let me go. Even as he licked the mark from Nikolai, he would never let me go back to them. Desperately, I tried to open a mind link to my mate.

*Nik... Nik, please say you're there. Please, I need you.* Looking at the big black wolf beside me, watching as his even breaths rose and fell, I did everything in my power to maintain a calm composure. Any change in my heart rate and he would hear it, alerting him.

As minutes turned into hours and hours turned into days, I felt myself falling deeper into a state of despair. The only sliver of hope to escape was the rare moments I was allowed to sit outside or use the bathroom. He had Maddox continue to bring me mediocre food, which ruled out using any kitchen utensils to fight my way out.

Was this really it? Would I be trapped here forever with a giant wolf watching my every move? I couldn't bear the thought of never seeing Nikolai again, never feeling his touch or hearing his voice. My mind drifted to Roman and Gabriel, wanting nothing more than to give myself fully to my three Alpha men and accept what they wanted to give me.

But then, something remarkable happened. Amrin started to shift. At first, it was slow and painful, but eventually, he stood before me in his human form. His eyes flickering black.

"Avery," he said, his voice deep and gravelly. "I've been waiting for you."

I started screaming, kicking back against him as he lunged forward. But he easily overpowered me, pinning me to the ground with a strength I couldn't believe. "Stop struggling, Avery," he growled. "You're mine now."

Tears streamed down my face as I realized the truth of his words. I was trapped, completely at Amrin's mercy. And judging by the way he was staring at me with darkened eyes, he had no intention of showing me any mercy.

"What do you want from me?" I asked, my voice trembling. "Why are you doing this? You let me go."

Braden leaned in closer, his hot breath washing over my face. "I need you, Avery," he whispered. "I was a fool before, but that child was supposed to be mine. You let it die and now you owe me an heir."

I whimpered, fear gripping my heart. I had known that Braden was obsessed with the idea of having an heir, I was warned as much, but I never thought he would go this far.

"I can't," I said, my voice barely above a whisper. "I can't have a child with you. Please, Braden, this is wrong."

"Oh, but you will," he said, his grip tightening on my arms. "You will do whatever it takes to make it happen."

I struggled against him, but it was no use. He was too strong, too determined. Just as I opened my mouth to scream again, the door opened, slamming against the wall.

Braden looked up, his face calm and collected. "Lucas. What can we help you with?"

I looked at the person who entered the room and my heart leaped with hope. Maybe Lucas could help me escape from Braden's grasp.

But as Lucas approached us, I saw the look in his eyes— it was one of fear and submission. He bowed down to Braden, avoiding my gaze completely.

"Alpha," Lucas said in a low voice. "The council has called for your presence. They require your immediate attention."

Braden sighed, releasing me from his hold. "Very well. Avery, you'll stay here until I return." He locked and bolted the door as he left, taking my hope of escape with him.

He walked out of the room without another word, followed closely by Lucas. As soon as the door closed, I exhaled. I was safe... for now, but unless something drastically changed, no one was coming for me. No one knew where I was... I didn't even know where I was.

I looked around the room, trying to find anything that could help me escape. The room was empty except for a small window high up near the ceiling. My feet ran towards it, hoping to find something outside that could indicate my whereabouts.

I pulled myself up and peered through the window. My heart sank when I saw nothing but dense forest surrounding the building. There were no signs of civilization, no roads, no people, nothing. I was completely isolated.

Tears streamed down my face as I slumped back onto the floor. I knew that I had to come up with a plan to escape, but my mind was blank. I was trapped, left desolate and afraid with a man who clearly had no regard for me or my feelings. Just what lay between my legs.

The sound of footsteps outside the door brought me back to reality. I quickly wiped away my tears and tried to compose myself. The door creaked open, and Lucas entered the room holding a tray with food and water.

"Alpha has instructed me to bring you your dinner," he said, placing the tray on the small table in the corner of the room.

I looked at him, hoping to find some compassion in his eyes, but all I saw was fear... and hatred. He quickly left the room without another word.

I approached the tray, realizing how hungry I was. I couldn't believe that I was eating food from these people. But then again, I had no other choice if I wanted to keep my strength. I swallowed my pride.

As I ate, I thought about what I could do to escape. I needed a plan, and fast. But how could I possibly escape from an isolated building in the middle of nowhere? I held the power of a Seraphina, with no idea how to access it. Sobs wracked my body, sending me into a panic induced spiral until eventually, my mind went blank, and I fell into a restless slumber.

# Twenty-One: Braden

Amrin was a tough son of a bitch, but without sleep and food, he was easy enough to subdue. Locking him away in the back of my mind was the first step once I was in control. The second was stuffing back a shot of wolfsbane. If I could keep him quiet and pliable, he wouldn't interfere with my plans for Avery. Idiot. He wanted to dote on her, *love* her. *Love is weakness. No woman deserves to be loved on. They need to stay in their place.*

Bleeders. Cleaners. Breeders. I was about to get what was mine after she stupidly lost my child, when low-and-behold, the Council had to show up at juuuuust the right time. *Assholes. Who needed a group of stuffy old wolves making rules and shoving them down our throats? Out of touch, the lot of them.* Sitting in this room with them was nothing short of torture. All I wanted was to rake my claws across the delicate skin of a certain female a couple of rooms over.

But as I watched them from the shadows, I realized something was off. The way they moved, the way they spoke, it was as if they were a hive mind, a single entity. Their eyes fixed on me, and I knew I had to get out of there. But before I could make a break for it, they cornered me, their expressions stoic and emotionless.

"We have been watching you," one of them said in a voice that reverberated through my skull. "We know what you have done."

"I've done nothing that isn't well within my right to do, back off," I snarled. The Council members didn't budge. "Your actions have consequences," another member said, his voice just as unsettling as the first.

"You can't give me consequences. Who are you? Some stupid figureheads who run around and swing their dicks as if you're better than the rest of us. I am the Alpha of Crescent Scar, the most powerful pack in the North. You are nothing but skin and bones. A relic of times of old." I pushed one of them before walking out of their circle of saggy skin and old breath.

"You will be made an example of," the first member said. "We have watched you abuse those beneath you, reject your given mate. We have watched suffering at your hands. You still stand judgement."

I rolled my eyes at their sanctimonious speeches. They had always been a thorn in my side, ever since I gained power over the Crescent Scar pack. With a snarl, I lunged towards them, ready to stand my ground.

But as I bared my teeth and prepared to strike, a sudden pain shot through my body. I howled, dropping to the ground as my vision blurred. Something was wrong, something was...

changing. It felt like my insides were being twisted and turned inside out.

They began to cackle as none other than Sion stepped out from behind them. "Hello Braden. Nice to see you again."

"Traitor," I spat as the pain rolled over me in waves. "You took Lucas' mate for yourself, you refused to help me find Avery—" A scream erupted from my throat before I could finish the list of wrongdoings.

Sion just chuckled; his eyes glowing with amusement. "Oh Braden," he said, "you always had a one-track mind. This has nothing to do with any of that."

The pain intensified, and I felt something shift within me. It was like a fire burning inside me, changing me in some fundamental way that I couldn't even begin to understand.

"What the hell did you do to me?" I snarled, struggling to stand up on my hands and knees.

Sion just smiled serenely. "You'll see," he said. "But for now, I think it's time we left."

The council members began to melt before disappearing entirely, leaving me on the floor writhing in pain.

"Lucas...Maddox...," I gasped. "Help me."

Two figures appeared out of the shadows, walking towards me with concern etched into their faces. As they knelt beside me, the pain ebbed and flowed with the beat of my heart.

"Braden, what's happening?" Lucas asked, his voice filled with worry.

I tried to speak, but my throat felt parched like I hadn't had a drink in days. Maddox stood up and grabbed a bottle of water from the table, handing it to Lucas who brought it to my lips.

I took a few sips before I was able to speak again. "Something...changed. Sion did something to me."

"What did he do?"

"I don't know, but it hurts. Take me to the bedroom," I rasped. "Where's Avery?"

"She's locked up good and tight. Don't worry, she will be there when you... gain control of whatever this is."

Lucas and Maddox helped me up, their hands supporting me as we made our way to the master bedroom. The pain had lessened somewhat, but I still felt like something was crawling under my skin, itching to be released.

As I lay down on the bed, I exhaled sharply, trying to steady my breathing. I closed my eyes and tried to focus on my surroundings, but the pain was making it almost impossible.

Suddenly, a strange sensation swept over me, and I felt like I was being consumed by something otherworldly. It was as if I was being overtaken by a force that was not my own.

"Braden?" Maddox said as he watched me writhing. "Uh, something is... happening to you."

"What? What's happening?" My sight started blurring as I pulled my hand up to my face to try figure out what Maddox was so slack jawed about. That's when I saw it. My hand was changing, transforming into something that resembled a claw— black, sharp, and deadly.

I tried to scream, but the pain became unbearable. The claw extended from my hand and pierced through the mattress like it was made of butter. The room filled with the sound of tearing fabric and metal as my body began to transform.

"I've never seen a transformation like this, ever," Lucas muttered under his breath.

As the transformation continued, the feeling of ripping and tearing continued to build. The muscles in my body were pulling apart and healing, over and over again. The pain was excruciating, but as I opened my eyes, I saw the world in a new light. Everything was sharper, clearer, and more vibrant than before, even with the senses I had when Amrin was in control, then suddenly, I plunged into darkness.

I let out a deep growl as I stood up on all fours, my body now covered in jet-black fur. My senses were heightened, and the room was filled with a scent that I had never noticed before.

"Braden, what's going on?" Maddox asked, his voice trembling.

"I don't know," I snarled, not recognizing my own voice as a deep, guttural sound erupted from within me. I'd shifted thousands of times, but this was like none of them.

The sound of ripping flesh filled the room as my screams pierced the air.

"Oh, my goddess... Lucas... he's..."

"Amrin is crawling right out of him..."

I felt something emerging from within my body, and then a sudden burst of energy coursed through me. A second voice filled the room as my vision began to return until everything was just a light blur. I touched my skin, feeling it slick with something wet, long strips hung off my body as I let out another loud scream before collapsing.

**Amrin**

"Ah, hello Lucas, Maddox." I felt good. Great. Finally, Sion had found the spell to rip me from that sack of skins body and set me free from the confines of his pathetic intentions.

"How... how is this possible?" Lucas said, his eyes darting towards the door. "How are you talking?"

"Oh, dear boy. Sion is an old bat, as old as time, and he knew just the right spell to split me from your pathetic Alpha and remake me in my own image." I watched in amusement as Lucas tried to back away slowly, fear etched on his face. Maddox just stood there, staring at me with wide eyes.

"Amrin, what do you want?" Maddox asked cautiously.

"What do I want? Oh, my dear, Maddox. I want everything that was taken from me. The power, the control, the respect that I deserve." My eyes tracked his as he avoided looking at me. "Mostly, I want Avery."

I could feel the energy coursing through my body, and it was unlike anything I had ever felt before. The world around me seemed to vibrate with my presence.

"I see the confusion on your faces," I said with a chuckle. "You see, you insipid fools, Sion killed the wolf inside Braden, and put my soul into a demon that was just begging to have a chance to roam earth. Now that I am rid of that... lump, I can finally fulfill my duties." I watched as Maddox took a step back, fear and confusion etched across his face.

"Your... duties?" he asked, his voice trembling slightly.

"Yes. My duties are to wreak havoc, destruction, and chaos upon the world. And that's exactly what I'll do." I took a step forward, relishing the power that flowed through me. "You two still don't get it. Braden was given a gift. I was that gift. The first wolf our dear little Moon Goddess ever made. I am the only one who is reincarnated through the centuries. Always to the same lineage from which I was first born into. I have watched these idiots turn my pack into a thriving, flourishing place of love and contentment, into a rigid wasteland of abuse. The last 4 generations of Alpha's have lost sight of what it means to have a blessed Luna. So, I made a deal to right their wrongs. Unfortunately, it came at the price of sharing a mind with Belial, which somewhat taints the wrongs I can right, but nevertheless, I digress."

Lucas had backed himself into a corner, his breathing labored as he stared at me with wide eyes.

"What about Avery?" Maddox asked, his jaw set in determination.

"What about her? She will be mine. And with her by my side, nothing will stop me."

# Twenty-Two: Nikolai

"There, the voice," I said urgently as Roman and Gabriel gathered around me. "It's her, I'm telling you. It's her."

Gabriel looked at me. "Roman, go get Isabella. We need her help."

Isabella was a trusted witch, in our inner circle. Our inside group had various supernaturals, but Isabella used to be my favorite. Until I fucked her. It got a bit messy. "Do you have to get her? Can you get Isla instead?"

"Just because you stuck your dick in her, doesn't mean the rest of us can't use her. She's the most powerful witch we have here. Suck it up."

Roman snickered under his breath as he slammed the door shut.

"The only reason I'm agreeing is because this is Avery and I want her to be safe. Let's be clear, I'd rather stick hot toothpicks in my eyes than meet with Isabella again. But since I can't locate her voice... ugh." I cringed. Isabella wasn't a bad lay, it was what she did after that really sent me in a tailspin.

Gabriel just shook his head, amusement in his eyes as he turned away from me. Roman came back in, dragging a bedazzled Isabella with him. "Of course, I'll help you, Roman," her voice dripped with seduction as she eyeballed me from her peripherals.

"Isabella, really, we just need your help to do a locate spell inside Nik's mind," Roman said.

Isabella ignored Roman and instead just looked at me. "My, my, who do we have here? Nik's latest play for a one-night stand?"

"Shut it Isabella, we need your help," Gabriel said sternly.

Isabella just smirked. "You know, I am a witch, not a tracker." She sniffed. "But I'll see what I can do. Sit, Nik."

I walked stiffly to the chair and sat, grimacing as her hands wrapped around my head.

"Now think about the voice you've been hearing." Then she muttered, "I'm sure you hear many of the slut voices reverberating around in that empty head of yours."

Just as I was about to shift and take her head clean off her body, Roman silenced her with a glare. "Isabella. This is our mate. All of ours. Please, do what you need to do and don't antagonize Nikolai any further. He's volatile enough."

Isabella muttered something under her breath, and I gritted my teeth. Roman was right. I had to control my anger and let her do her magic. I closed my eyes and focused on the voice I'd heard.

Isabella's grip tightened around my head, and I felt the heat radiating off her hands. She kept up her spell, chanting and mumbling and I felt my body begin to relax. That was the thing about witches, no matter how annoying they were, they could make you calm in seconds.

I felt a warmth settling in behind my eyes, and I was instantly pulled into my own mind. I floated in between space and time, looking for that voice. Then, there it was, loud and clear. I clung to it, the warmth and safety wrapping around me like a blanket. Isabella pulled away and I opened my eyes, her face inches away from mine. Her eyes slid down to my lips as she licked her own before trailing her fingertip down my cheek.

She smiled and said, "in the woods, there's a clearing, so small you'd miss it. There's an old cabin, falling apart at the seams. She is there." As our chairs scraped against the floor, she cautioned, "be quick. Something dark is ascending at a rapid pace. I don't think your precious mate will survive whatever it is."

"Thank you," Roman said curtly.

"Of course, you owe me. Be sure to bring me something nice when you return." She winked and I ducked around her.

"Come on, let's move," I said gruffly, already on edge. I walked to the door and stopped as I felt a hand on my shoulder.

"Be careful," Isabella said softly, her eyes filled with worry. I nodded and stepped out with Roman and Gabriel hot on my heels. My heart was racing, I had to get to Avery before it was too late. Whatever it was had Isabella worried and that's never a good sign when dealing with the supernatural.

Flying through the trees, we ran, not stopping for a moment, even when our lungs felt like they were on fire.

*Here!* Gabriel linked.

The clearing was small and barely visible, hidden beneath a thick layer of shrubs and trees. We pushed through the undergrowth and there it was, a small, crumbling cabin at the edge of the glade.

"Slow and steady. We don't need to alert anyone to our presence," Roman warned as he stalked towards the window. "She's here!"

My heart squeezed as I saw her pale face staring back at us through the small window. "It's pounding time."

Before I had a chance to rip the door down, Gabe stopped me. "Nik, River. Whichever one of you is in control right now, please... don't. We need to do this quietly. Whatever lurks inside can and will kill her. We need to get her out without destruction and mayhem." The plea in his voice stopped me short. He was right. Without ever having seen what we were up against, we couldn't just barge in and face it head on.

I closed my eyes and focused on reaching Avery, my hands quivering with need and want to simply take her away from this place. Suddenly, I heard a click and the window opened slowly. Roman, Gabe and I slowly entered, ready to fight whatever it was that had our mate trapped.

What was inside the cabin was not a creature, it was stillness and silence, thick with tension and grief. Avery was huddled in a corner of the room, her body trembling, and her eyes glassy and vacant.

"I thought I was just seeing things," she whispered, her eyes locking onto mine before she scanned Gabriel and Roman.

Roman stepped towards her and gently touched her shoulder. "It's ok, Avery. We're here to take you home." He spoke softly and I could tell he was trying to calm her, but there was a sickening feeling in my gut. Something was terribly wrong here, I could feel it.

Gabe bent down to pick her up, but she resisted. "No!" she shouted, her body twisting away from him. "I can't leave. I can't. Please, don't make me leave." She dropped her head into her hands, her shoulders shaking with sobs.

Gabriel looked up at Roman before looking at me.

"He will kill you. He will kill all of you, he's not himself. He's... something else, something more. A darkness that has descended. Please. Just let me go. I will be fine. Please, go," she begged, tears streaming down her face, cleaning small paths in the dirt and grime.

"We can't do that. We're here to protect you," I said, my voice firm but soft. I moved closer to her and held her tightly as she sobbed into my chest.

"Listen to me Avery. You are safe. We are here to protect you. Whatever it is that is here, we will face it together, ok? You don't have to be scared anymore," I said, my voice low and soothing, whilst simultaneously gripping the hilt of my sword tighter.

She loosened her grip on me and looked up into my eyes. She nodded slowly and wiped her face with her sleeve before standing. "You can't fight him. No one can," she said simply, before she grabbed a broken piece of glass and sliced it across her wrist.

"No!" I screamed, grabbing her hand, I squeezed until she let the glass go. Turning her wrist over, I saw that she had healed in a matter of seconds. Puzzled, I looked to my brothers before hearing thundering footsteps racing down the hallway.

"We need to go. Now." I looked at Roman. "Take her and run. You are the fastest. Go. Now." Shoving Avery towards him, he took her and leapt out the window.

Gabriel and I shared a look before jumping out after him, just as the door behind us shattered. A gutted scream rung out, echoing in the still air.

We ran through the thick of the trees, our feet pounding over the fallen leaves and broken twigs. The night sky above us started to turn a dusky purple, soon giving way to streaks of pink and orange in the horizon.

As we approached our makeshift packhouse I could feel some of the tension easing from my body. We were all safe for now, there was nothing following us. Perhaps it grew tired, or maybe it was saving its strength for what lay ahead, either way, I was grateful.

"Avery," I whispered to the broken girl in front of me. She had been quiet the whole way back, her eyes now fixed on the ground as she shuffled her feet. I could tell that something was still weighing heavily on her mind.

"Hey," I whispered again, this time placing a soft hand on her shoulder. "What happened in there?"

Avery took a deep breath before speaking, her words slow and hesitant. "It... It wasn't him. My ex-boyfriend, the one who had been stalking me, wasn't the one in there. It was something else, something dark and terrifying."

I frowned, gathering her in my arms. "What do you mean?"

"Braden. He was there, with Lucas and Maddox... but there is that thing... it's... it's big, it's dark... It sends chills down your spine even looking at it. I don't know what it is, but I caught a glimpse of it through the door when Lucas took me to the bathroom. I'm scared. I'm so, so scared."

I held her tightly, my mind racing with possibilities and questions. Whatever was happening, it was clear that we were dealing with something beyond our understanding. I didn't want to let her go, but my brothers were anxiously waiting for their own slice of peace.

I handed her off to Gabriel before motioning for Roman to follow me into the kitchen. As we entered the kitchen, I pulled out a chair for Roman and myself. We both sat down, and I ran my hands through my hair, trying to make sense of what Avery had said.

"What do you think it could be?" Roman asked, his voice low and cautious. "I mean, we've dealt with supernatural beings before, but this feels different."

"I don't know," I responded, my mind racing with possibilities. "But whatever it is, we need to be prepared. We need to figure out what we're dealing with, and how to stop it."

Roman nodded. "Agreed. We'll need Avery to tell us what she saw... we don't have much, if anything, to go off of—"

As if on cue, Avery walked into the kitchen and took a seat across from us. Her eyes were puffy, and her face was still streaked with tears, but she looked determined. She took a deep breath and began to speak.

"I didn't see much, but it was enough. It was big, really big, and dark. I could see its eyes glowing, like they were on fire. It was like nothing I've ever seen before," she said, her voice shaking slightly. "And Braden was... he was..." Her face crumpled.

"He was what, Avery?" Gabriel said gently, wrapping his arms around her waist from behind.

"Shredded. His skin hung off him in clumps... the blood..." Avery broke off, unable to finish the sentence.

I reached out and grasped her hand, pushing back the tears that threatened to spill. We all sat in silence for a long moment, trying to digest this new horror.

Finally, Roman spoke, "We need to be prepared. We need to gather our resources and make a plan. A plan to stop this thing, whatever it is. We failed our pack, and Avery, once already, we need to make sure that we don't make the same mistake twice."

I nodded, my grip on Avery's hand tightening. We all knew it was time to stop letting the chips fall where they may. We had it so good the last decade. Peace among all supernatural's to cross into our pack lands, but it appears that with the arrival of our mate, that peace was shattered to bits.

Avery gasped, "he said something about Belial. I just remembered."

Roman and I shared a look. "Belial?" Roman echoed, an eyebrow raised in surprise. "That's a demon."

My mind raced, trying to piece together what this could mean. Why would a demon be involved in our mate? And how did it relate to Avery's ex-boyfriend, or the dark creature that had attacked him?

"We need to know more," I said firmly. "We need to find out everything we can about Belial, and how it might be connected to what we're dealing with."

Roman nodded. "Agreed. And we need to do it fast. We can't afford to waste any more time."

"Guys...can you..." she trailed off.

"What, Avery? What do you need?" Roman said tenderly, his hand caressing her cheek.

"Can you all sleep with me tonight?"

# Twenty-Three: Avery

I felt safe here, squished in the middle of three giant Alpha men. They were warm and inviting, I could easily reach them and derive pleasure from their bodies. Instead, I lay still in the comfort of their steady breathing, knowing that no one would tear me from their grasp. As relaxed as they were, I knew none of them were sleeping just yet.

So much had happened in the last few days, and they deserved to know everything, but where did I even start? I took a deep breath and moved closer to Gabriel, who was snuggling me from the right, his arm wrapped around my waist. It was comforting, and I felt my muscles relax.

"Guys," I began quietly. "I need to tell you something."

They all turned to look at me, concern etched on their handsome faces. I took another deep breath.

"I... I'm not what you think I am."

Their expressions shifted to confusion. I continued, "I'm not a human, wolf or witch. I'm not even a vampire or anything like that."

Their jaws tensed, but they stayed silent, waiting for me to continue.

"I'm a Seraphina."

Roman sat up. "A what? The Seraphim have been gone for a century. How?"

"My mother was the vessel. It's a really long story. But basically, while I was missing, Selene came to me and took me to the high council, and I met Gods and Goddesses who warned me about a darkness that's coming." I rubbed my hands on his arms, trying to soothe both of us.

"Wait, you went to their meeting place? How?" Gabriel breathed in awe. "I've heard about it, but I've never seen it. How amazing that must have been."

"It was quite terrifying, actually. No one told me their names, except Selene. Anyway..." I paused. "She told me that I am the last of the Seraphim. Basically, my ancestors saved a Spirit Stone from one of the fallen Seraphim. They allowed me to choose what I wanted, and I picked the stone that called to me. Ugh, I'm not explaining this right." Frustrated, I crawled over limbs and got out of bed. "I need a coffee." As I walked towards the door, Roman caught my wrist, pulling me back towards him.

"Wait," he said. "You don't have to go. We will grab your coffee and bring it to you."

Nikolai all but ran down the stairs and came back in a flash, holding a can of cold brew coffee. "Here, now come sit in between us. We will listen to everything, even if it takes all night."

I hesitated for a moment but nodded, returning to the warm embrace of my lovers. "The Spirit Stone gives me immense power," I began. "It basically was absorbed into me, so I now possess the power of the Seraphim. Except... I don't know how to use it or what to even do with it. All I know is that they will reach out when the time is right to teach me and that I need to be prepared for something to happen, and step in and defend this world."

The three of them looked at me incredulously, shock etched in their expressions.

"That's... a lot to digest. But we did hear from a witch that you were part of a Prophesy so it's not entirely new information. Though, she got some things wrong. Funny how that works, isn't it?" Roman chuckled, wrapping me in his arms.

I smiled softly, grateful for their understanding and support. "Yeah, it is. But there's more. Selene also warned me about someone trying to harm me, someone who knows about my power and wants to use it for their own gain. She didn't give me any specifics, but she made it clear that I need to be cautious."

Gabriel pressed a kiss to my temple as Nikolai rubbed soothing circles on my back. "We'll protect you, love. No matter what, we'll keep you safe," Gabriel said.

"I know you will," I said, sinking back into their embrace. "That's why I trust you with this. I wish you could have been there to see it. It was amazing."

"I do too, no offense, but your recounting skills need a bit of work," Roman chuckled.

I laughed too, feeling a bit relieved that they weren't completely rejecting me after spilling such a huge secret. "Yeah, it's almost like a game of telephone, huh?"

Nikolai moved behind me, slowly rubbing my thighs as his engulfed me. "We'll figure this out together. You don't have to do this alone. You're amazing, you know that?"

A flush creeped over my cheeks as he massaged circles into my skin, his fingers working out the tension and creating a whole new one as he travelled closer and closer towards the heat that lay between my legs.

"You want us to make you feel good, Avery?" Gabriel said, his eyes roaming the length of my body before stopping on the mark that lay against my neck. "Do you want us to complete the mark?"

I shuddered at the thought of them completing the mark, knowing that it would bind us even closer together. But in that moment, with their hands on my body and their lips on my skin, all I could think about was the overwhelming desire coursing through me.

"Yes, please," I moaned, feeling my body respond to their touch.

Gabriel leaned in and placed a soft kiss on my lips before moving down to kiss my neck, his teeth grazing the mark. Nikolai's hands moved up to cup my breasts, his thumbs rubbing against my nipples, making them harden under his touch. Gabe and Roman shed their boxers, standing proudly with their impossibly hard dicks jutting out proudly. They were monsters. Thick and veiny, one straight, one slightly curved. My stomach lurched at the sight. Handling Nikolai was a lot, but all three?

I hardly had time to think before they were around me again, encompassing me in their scent, their limbs, their love.

Roman's hands glided down to my hips, spreading my legs. He looked at Nik who whispered for me to relax as he opened me wider, giving Roman a clear view of my glistening pussy. I fixed my gaze on Gabriel who cupped my breast and licked my neck. Just as I was about to tense, Roman grabbed my hips and impaled me on his cock as Gabriel sunk his teeth into my neck.

The sensation was overwhelming, but in the best way possible. I felt my body clench as Gabriel's teeth sunk deeper into my skin followed by a surge of intense emotions that consumed me. I lost control, my hips moving faster and faster, my muscles tightening around Roman's cock. All at once the sensations were too much, and I felt the first powerful wave crash over me, sending ripples through my entire body.

The feeling of my release was so powerful it left me breathless. The three of them working together to bring pleasure that I had never felt before. They moved in harmony, crashing against me and over me, hitting spots I had never known existed within me. I felt alive, like I was being reborn as an entirely new version of myself. I was free and liberated from all my insecurities and fears.

Roman didn't pause for a moment. He slid out of me, his cock shining with my arousal as Gabriel took over. Once more nodding at each other, Gabriel pulled me from Nikolai's arms before pushing me down on the bed. He pulled my hair, exposing my neck to Roman as Nikolai watched with burning passion. In a split-second Roman bit me, soft at first, increasing pressure as Gabriel pushed his way inside of me.

I screamed out as my body shuddered, sending sparks of bliss through me. The fervor was too much, but I clung to it as Roman released my neck and Gabriel pounded inside me. The pain and rapture mixed in a way I had never felt before, pushing me closer and closer towards unravelling entirely.

Finally, I let go, the orgasm rippling through my body, waves crashing over me with such intensity that it caused me to see stars. I collapsed back onto the bed, completely spent and completely in awe. I looked up at the three of them, all staring down at me with satisfied grins. That's when I felt it. The click. Suddenly, every emotion they were feeling pushed and pulled at me. I could feel the love and connection radiating from them, like a physical touch that swirled around me, supporting me in the most profound and beautiful way. All of them stared at me, my vulnerability on display as they pressed words of love and affirmation through the link.

We stayed like that for some time, the connection binding us together until Nikolai broke the spell. He grinned and spoke the words that solidified our bond.

"So, I guess this means you accept all of us now, doesn't it?"

# Twenty-Four: Avery

They were all passed out, naked, exhausted, and fulfilled. I sat quietly at the window sipping on my coffee, sore from our extracurriculars, but finally finding myself experiencing peace for the first time since I turned 18. It felt like it had been years, but the reality was that it had only been a few months. My bump was already showing, and I was overdue for a check-up. I could feel the baby, but like every first-time mother, my anxieties needed to be quelled by someone who knew more. Running my hand over my stomach, my mind drifted towards Braden. Amrin, more explicitly. What was he? What had he turned into?

He was terrifying and I didn't understand it. So different from the wolf that had laid beside me and brought me a small sense of comfort in my captivity. Yet he transformed into something... monstrous. While they were gone, I had been working on jiggling the old knob on the door and when he roared, the lock just... snapped. Somehow, I felt safer with that tiny piece of metal when I saw him. He was... different. His eyes were glowing red, his skin stretched and twitched, charred black as tendrils of smoke puffed behind him as he walked, and his nails had turned into sharp claws. It was like watching a horror movie come to life. The image of Braden laying there, a skinned sack of flesh was ingrained in my mind. But how? What had happened?

As I gazed out of the window, I couldn't shake the feeling that something was coming. Something ominous and foreboding. The room was silent except for the sound of my sipping and sighing, but it felt like there was a storm brewing outside. A storm that would unleash something dark and terrible.

My thoughts were interrupted by a hand on my shoulder. Looking up, I saw Gabriel searching my face. "You alright?"

"No. Not really, but I feel better now." I grabbed his hand. "Sit with me?"

He nodded and sat next to me, his eyes scanning the darkness outside. "What were you thinking about?"

I hesitated; I'd burdened them so much already. But I could feel his patience, his encouragement as he absently stroked my hand with his thumb. "I was thinking about Amrin. And what he did—what he turned into."

Gabriel's face grew serious. "I can't even fathom it. It's unnatural. Even for us."

I leaned into him, feeling comforted as he wrapped an arm around my shoulders. "What is he?" I whispered.

"I don't know," Gabriel admitted. "I do know that he's dangerous. That's all we need to know for now. We'll figure out what to do about him later."

I nodded, accepting his words as truth. Deep down, I couldn't stop my mind from wondering and fearing what Amrin could be capable of. The weight of my pregnancy only added to my anxiety. Would he come for me? Selene had masked the baby, but... what if he knew? I didn't want this baby to be born into a world where monsters roamed freely, where I couldn't guarantee their safety.

As if sensing my worries, Gabriel gave me a reassuring squeeze. "We'll keep you and the baby safe. That's a promise."

Tears welled up in my eyes as I looked up at him. "Do you think he is the darkness that Selene was talking about?"

He looked away, but I caught the fear that flashed in his eyes. "I don't know, Avery. I really don't."

Suddenly it hit me like a sack of bricks. "I am the Seraphina. This is my duty to fulfill. I'm the one who is supposed to end the darkness before it can consume our world."

Gabriel turned his gaze back to me, studying my face. "You don't have to take on that burden alone. We are here to help you. We are in your corner."

I shook my head. "I don't know." It was all too much to handle, the weight of the world on my shoulders. All I knew was that I couldn't sit back and let the darkness win. "I have to try."

Gabriel gave me a small smile. "Then we'll try with you. Together."

I let out a small laugh, feeling some of the tension in my shoulders ease. "Together. I like the sound of that."

"Speaking of, we need to get you in to see the doc, tomorrow."

"I was just thinking about that, how did you—" I said. "The mate bond. Duh." Lightly smacking my forehead, we laughed.

"Jasmine will make sure that there is an opening for you."

"Are... are you sure about this? About us?" I laid my hand back on my stomach, gently caressing the bump, imagining it was my baby.

"Avery, are you seriously asking if we accept you and the baby?" His face twisted in shock with a hint of anger.

"I'm sorry, Gabriel," I said quickly, feeling a wave of guilt wash over me. "I know you do, it's just... Sometimes I can't believe it myself. Why would you? It's not even yours." A tear fell and just as quickly as it trailed down my face, his finger was there to wipe it.

Gabriel softened, his dark eyes meeting mine. "We love you, Avery. And that means we love your baby too, no matter what. All three of us. Please, you must believe that, if nothing else. That baby is ours, even if he—or she—didn't come from us."

I let out a shaky breath, feeling overwhelmed with emotion. "Thank you. I'm sorry, I'm just an emotional wreck."

He leaned in and placed a gentle kiss on my forehead. "You've been through a lot. You have every right to be emotional, but Avery, I won't let you keep doubting our love for you. Roman, Nik and I love each other, but we've never shared a woman. But for you? We do. We accept that each of us will have our own slice of time with you and we are willing to put you in the front and center of all of us. Think of our relationship like a diamond. You are the point, and we fill the shape."

I giggled at his analogy, feeling warmth spread through my chest. "I don't know what I did to deserve you guys."

Gabriel grinned, his hand now back on my stomach. "You existed. That's all it took for us to fall in love with you."

I leaned into him, resting my head on his shoulder. "I love you, Gabriel."

"I love you too, Avery. We all do." He kissed the top of my head and ruffled my hair, and we sat in comfortable silence for a few moments.

"Did you feel that?" I said quickly, awe spreading through my body as I tried to grab his hand and put it on my belly in time.

"Was that a...?"

"Yes... yes it was. Her first kick."

Gabriel's face lit up with a smile. "That's amazing, Avery. I wish I could have felt it too."

I gestured for him to keep talking as I pushed down on his hand. As he did, we both waited in anticipation. And then it happened again. This time, Gabriel felt it too.

He looked at me with amazement. "That was incredible. She's strong... just like her mom."

"I know. It's like she knows we're talking about her," I said, giggling at the thought.

Eventually, he pulled away. "We should get some rest. We have a big day tomorrow with the doctor's appointment and whatever else comes up. It seems like with you, every day is a mystery." He stood, pulling me into his arms before lifting me bridal style and carrying us to his room.

"Don't want to share me with the guys?" I giggled.

"No, not right now."

I felt the heat of his body as he lay me in his plush bed. I could feel the warmth radiating off him, enjoying how the muscles in his forearm strained as he held my hand. I felt the smoothness of his hair as I ran my fingers through it every few minutes.

Relishing the warmth of his skin, I settled my body around his, my thigh on top of his stomach, my head in the crook of his arm. As we lay there together, I could feel his pulse. It was strong, solid... beating for me. I knew that in that moment I belonged with Gabriel, Roman, and Nik. They were my home, and I would do anything for them. My thoughts were interrupted by Gabriel's soft and steady breathing. He had drifted off to sleep, and I cuddled closer to him, feeling his chest rise and fall with each breath.

I felt content, safe, and at peace. I drifted off to sleep, still listening to the sound of his heartbeat.

When I woke up hours later, Gabriel was gone. However, Nik was watching me as he sat on a chair next to the bed.

"Good morning," he said, with a warm smile. "How did you sleep?"

I rubbed my eyes, trying to shake off the sleepiness. "Um, hi. Yeah, I slept well. Where's Gabriel?"

"He had some pack business to attend to. He left before sunrise. He told me to tell you that he loves you and he'll see you soon."

I nodded, feeling a twinge of disappointment that Gabriel wasn't there. But then I looked back at Nik and felt a sudden surge of attraction, followed by a feeling of guilt and confusion.

Nik sensed my inner turmoil, and he reached out to stroke my hair. "Avery, you don't have to feel guilty for feeling attracted to me. It's natural, and it's okay."

I blushed, feeling exposed. "I'm sorry. It's just... I don't want to hurt you or Gabriel or Roman."

Nik tilted his head, his eyes curious. "Why do you assume that your feelings would hurt anyone? We've all marked you, you've accepted us, so why the continued hesitation?"

"I don't know, to be honest. I guess my inexperience with men and my only relationship model being that of a couple, this is just foreign. I know we've slept together before, but now that I'm marked, am I allowed to...?" My face burned at my thoughts. Dirty thoughts. Ones that involved taking control and stripping him naked while I rode him on that very chair.

Nik smirked, watching as I turned an impossible shade of red. "Allowed to what, Avery?" He leaned back, his muscles pulling tightly as I allowed my eyes to trail lower... until I caught sight of that sexy V.

"You know..."

"Of course, I do, I rather enjoy the image you're painting, but I want to hear you say it."

I sighed, shaking my head. "Explore... ourselves."

"How do you want to explore, Avery?" he asked, his voice low and husky.

My tongue slipped out to wet my lips and I slowly crawled over the bed before kneeling at the end.

"I want to feel your skin against mine, I want to feel your lips on my body, and I want to know what it feels like to be the one in control."

A slow smile tugged at the corner of Nik's lips. "Then let's explore," he said, reaching out to take my hand and pulling me onto his lap. He leaned in and kissed me, his hands exploring my body as mine moved to explore his. We kept exploring until I finally felt confident enough in myself and my desires to fully take control. Before I even had a chance to release my primal urges, a knock at the door interrupted us.

"Uh, guys, hate to interrupt, but Jasmine is here."

# Twenty-Five: Roman

As much as I was thrilled that Avery was opening herself to us, that she let us mark her and pleasure her last night, hearing Nik in the room with her filled me with jealousy. *How come he's had a chance to be intimate with her three times and I haven't even had one chance alone? I know it sounds like I'm whining, and really, I'm not... Okay, maybe a bit, but still! It's not fair.*

"Hello! I'm here!" Jasmine's voice floated up the stairs, interrupting my pity party for one.

"Up here!" I called before going to let Avery know that her doctor had arrived.

A few minutes later, everyone—bar Gabe— crowded in the office while Avery and Jasmine discussed her pregnancy.

Avery shifted in her chair, visibly uncomfortable. "So, uh, just about thirteen weeks now?"

Jasmine nodded with a polite smile. "Yes, you're nearly at the end of the second trimester. Remember that pregnancies are faster with wolf pups. How have you been feeling?"

"Pretty good," Avery said softly. "Aside from a few bouts of morning sickness, I've been doing alright."

Jasmine smiled. "That's normal for this stage in pregnancy, especially with wolf pups.They tend to cause more nausea and dizziness due to their quicker growth pattern." She glanced down at her clipboard and made a few more notes before taking Avery's blood pressure, temperature and measuring around her stomach.

She frowned. "You're measuring smaller than I would like to see."

Avery's face paled as she looked up at Jasmine. "What does that mean?"

"It could be a number of things," Jasmine said, her face serious as she wrote down some notes on her clipboard. "It could just be that you're carrying the baby toward your back, or it could be a sign of fetal growth restriction."

Avery's eyes widened in fear. "What does that mean?"

"It means that your baby might not be growing at the rate that it should be," Jasmine explained. "But we won't know anything for certain until we take some measurements and run some tests. I'm going to schedule an ultrasound for you and request some bloodwork to be done to check for any potential issues."

Avery's eyes filled with tears as she looked at Jasmine. "Is my baby going to be okay?"

Jasmine gave her a reassuring smile. "Let's not jump to conclusions yet. We need to get more information before we can determine what's going on. Just know that we're going to do everything we can to make sure you and your baby are healthy."

Avery nodded slowly, still looking shaken by the news. "Thank you, Jasmine."

After Jasmine left, the room fell silent. I could feel everyone's concern for Avery, the tension thick in the air. Nik got up and went to the kitchen, rummaging around in the cupboards.

"Avery," I said, moving towards her, not missing the blank look in her eyes. "I know this must feel terrifying—"

"Terrifying? Terrifying is knowing a monster ejected itself out of your ex-mate's body. Terrifying is not knowing what is going on in the world. Terrifying is not understanding why you are some... weird angel thing. No, Roman. I'm not terrified," she ranted at me, a sharpness falling over her face.

"Then what are you feeling? I can feel you blocked me out, Avery, you have to use your words."

"Numb. Roman. Okay? I feel numb." She stood and folded her arms over her chest.

"Don't shut me out. I want to help you. I want to comfort you. We don't know that anything is wrong, Jasmine said—"

"Don't you think I don't know what she said? I was right here! That doesn't mean I don't worry!"

I took a step closer to her, trying to read her emotions through her body language. "I understand that, Avery. We all care about you and the baby. But you don't have to go through this alone."

Avery let out a deep sigh before looking at me. "I know, Roman. I just... I feel so helpless. What if something is wrong with the baby? What if I can't do anything to help it? I don't want to lose it."

Tears welled up in her eyes, and I pulled her into a tight embrace, wanting nothing more than to comfort her. "Shh, it's okay. We'll get through this together. It's normal to have worries, but we need to stay optimistic and hope for the best. And no matter what happens, we'll be there for you every step of the way. You're not alone, Avery."

She melted into my embrace, her tears soaking into my shirt. I held her tightly, feeling her body shake with sobs as she let out all her fears and emotions.

As I held Avery, I couldn't help but feel my own worry creep in. I didn't want to lose this baby either. Even though it technically wasn't mine, it was mine in every other sense. She sobbed until she could sob no more and suddenly, she lifted the block on our connection and her grief flowed into me. I could feel the weight of her worries and the pain of her grief flooding into me. I knew that I needed to be strong for her, to give her the support she needed to get through this.

"I'm here, Avery. I'm not going anywhere," I whispered, holding her closer as she leaned into me.

For a long moment, we just stood there, wrapped up in each other's arms. I could feel the warmth of her tears on my skin, and the slow rise and fall of her chest as she took deep, shuddering breaths.

Eventually, she pulled away from me, wiping her eyes with the back of her hand.

"I made tea," Nikolai announced at the doorway, watching our interaction.

"You... *you* made tea?" I asked incredulously. The man who would rather eat out than try taming the beast inside enough to cook, made tea. "This is a day for the history books."

Nikolai chuckled. "What can I say? I'm a true renaissance man." He walked over to us and handed Avery a mug of steaming tea. "Here you go, Avery."

"Thank you," she replied, taking the mug from him and heading into the kitchen with us trailing behind her like lost puppies.

As we sat down at the table, sipping our tea, the silence was heavy again. I could see Avery's mind racing, as she thought about the possibilities of what could be wrong with her baby.

"Listen," Nikolai said, breaking the silence. "I may not know how to cook, but I do know how to do research. Let me investigate what could be going on with the baby. Maybe we can get a better understanding of what we're dealing with."

Avery's face brightened at the suggestion, and she nodded eagerly. "Yes, please."

Nikolai pulled out his laptop and began typing away, his eyes scanning the screen as he searched for any information he could find.

As we sat and waited, I couldn't help but feel a sense of unease settle over me. This situation could go in any direction, and there was no telling what the outcome would be.

"Ah ha!" he exclaimed. "See?" he said as he turned the laptop towards Avery, he had pulled up the Supernatural Association Library Archive. "Seraphim babies are naturally smaller. That could be why you're measuring so small!"

Avery's eyes lit up with hope as she read over the article on Nikolai's laptop. "That makes sense. So, I'm not necessarily at risk, then?"

"It doesn't seem like it. Of course, we should still follow up with the doctor and make sure everything is okay, but this is a positive sign."

Avery let out a breath she didn't even know she was holding, and I could see some of the tension released in her shoulders. "Thank you, Nikolai. I don't know what I'd do without you two."

Nikolai waved her off. "Don't sweat it. It's what I do."

"Can we go out?" Avery said suddenly. "I'm feeling a bit trapped here, can we go somewhere?"

Nik's eyes glazed over. "Last time—"

"Okay, but we don't have to go into town, we can explore the forest!" she exclaimed excitedly. Nikolai hesitated for a moment, but then nodded. "Sure, why not? It might be good to get some fresh air and take our minds off things for a bit."

I couldn't help but smile at Avery's enthusiasm. It was the first time in a while that I'd seen her excited about something, and it was contagious.

We quickly prepared ourselves for the outing, putting on warmer clothes since it was getting colder outside. As we headed out into the forest, I could feel the crunch of leaves beneath my feet and the crisp bite of the autumn air on my cheeks.

Avery led the way, her energy infectious as she darted from tree to tree. "You can't find me!" She'd say and then collapse in a fit of giggles.

"Why is she suddenly so... cheery?" I asked suspiciously.

"I may have made her chamomile, which has a mild mood enhancing effect on Seraphim."

"Oh? And when did you learn that?" My eyebrows raised in curiosity.

"While you were comforting her. I wanted to do what I do best and that's solve the problem." he said, pride filling his voice. I couldn't help but chuckle at his confidence, but it seemed to have had a positive effect on Avery. She was no longer weighed down by the uncertainty of her situation. Instead, she was running around like a child, laughing, and playing.

As we reached a clearing in the forest, Avery stopped suddenly, her eyes widening with wonder. "Look at that," she breathed, pointing to a small stream that ran through the clearing. "It's beautiful."

Nikolai and I joined her, and together we stood there, watching as the water flowed lazily over the rocks. It was a peaceful moment, one that felt like it could last forever.

But suddenly, the tranquility was shattered by a loud crack of thunder. Dark clouds rolled in quickly, and soon we were enveloped in a torrential downpour.

"We have to find shelter!" Nikolai shouted, taking Avery's hand, and pulling her towards the nearest tree. I followed closely behind, my heart racing with adrenaline.

We huddled together under the tree, the rain pelting down on us in sheets, but we were safe from the worst of it as the willow's branches stretched far and wide over top of us.

Avery's teeth were chattering, and Nikolai quickly removed his jacket and draped it over her shoulders.

"Thanks," she said, looking up at him gratefully.

A bolt of lightning flickered in the sky, and I watched as her eyes shone brilliantly in that moment.

"I love storms," she said, content to sit in between us and watch as it rolled through. As the storm raged on, a sense of closeness settled between the three of us. We were all huddled together, pressed close against each other, it felt like the storm had brought us closer together.

As the rain lessened to a light patter, Nikolai suddenly stood up. "Come on," he said, holding out his hand to Avery and then to me. "Let's make a run for it."

We darted through the forest, our laughter ringing out against the sound of the rain. It was a moment of pure joy, one that Avery desperately needed.

# Twenty-Six: Gabriel

I f it's not one thing, it's another. After the fires that ravaged the pack village, I was needed to task the crews to deconstruct, clean and reconstruct the buildings. Only this time, I was taking extra careful precautions when it came to our packhouse.

Underground bunker- check.

Safe room adjoining our rooms and Avery's- check.

Prison in the bunker with all the bells and whistles- check.

Avery would never have to live through the anguish of losing her home again. The memories of the fire still haunted me. It was a miracle no one died and that the rescue had somehow not been targeted. But we couldn't afford to let our guard down. There were still too many dangers out there. Amrin was apparently some kind of crazed beast and who knew what he was planning. My heart broke for my love, knowing that she was so young and still had to endure such a big trial, especially while pregnant.

As I finished up the last of the preparations for the new packhouse, I couldn't shake the feeling that something was off. Everyone had been avoiding making eye contact with me, and it just felt... eerie.

"Would someone like to inform me as to why I'm the elephant in the room?" I said as politely as I could while maintaining my Alpha aura. Several wolves bowed and bared their necks, though two were able to resist. Peculiar.

"What's going on?" I demanded, staring hard at the two defiant wolves. Their eyes flicked nervously to each other before one of them stepped forward, his fur ruffled in discomfort.

"Alpha, we have a problem," he said, his voice low. "There's been a sighting—"

"A sighting?" I repeated sharply, my heart rate quickening. "Of what?"

"Two lone male wolves, patrolling the outside of the border. We couldn't detain them both. One scared pretty easy and fled, but we have the other in the cells out back."

Ah yes, the old prison. The inferior one which was constructed in ancient times and hardly ever used because... well, this type of thing hadn't happened in centuries.

"Take me to him," I snarled.

The wolf nodded and came with me to the back of the pile of rubble and down a small hill to where the cells were. I could feel my anger rising as I approached the lone male wolf who was sitting in the corner of the cell, his eyes fixed on the ground.

"What are you doing here?" I growled, my aura making him flinch.

"I meant no harm," he said, his voice hoarse. "I was just passing through."

"You were trespassing," I reminded him. "And why were you patrolling our borders?"

The wolf remained silent, his shoulders hunched in defeat.

I let out a low growl, my anger simmering just beneath the surface. Fortunately for him, he began to sob before I shifted and ripped him to shreds. My control was lacking these days, particularly when it comes to protecting Avery.

"My name is Maddox. Please. Let me stay here. I don't want to go back to him." The young man pleaded on his knees.

"Look at me."

As he raised his head, I saw the long wound trailing down his face. "Who did this to you? Was it one of my men?"

He shook his head, eyes wild with fear. "No, sir. It was... *him*."

I narrowed my eyes at Maddox, my nostrils flaring as I picked up the scent of his fear. "Who is he?"

Maddox looked away, his voice barely above a whisper, "my Alpha. Well, he was my Alpha. I was his Gamma."

I felt a pang of sympathy for the young wolf before me. I knew all too well the horrors of a cruel Alpha having seen their victims filtering into our rescue. "What happened?"

Maddox hesitated, his eyes darting around the cell as if searching for an escape. But there was nowhere for him to run, not in my territory.

"He... died..."

Sighing, I looked at him. "Okay, if he's dead, what is the issue?"

"It's... the thing that came out of him." Tears streamed down his face.

Suddenly, I understood. "Was Braden your Alpha?"

He nodded slowly.

"And something else tore out of him, didn't it?"

Again, he nodded.

"You were wise to flee, but don't expect sympathy from me, much less my counterparts. They will destroy you once they find out who you belonged to." My eyes narrowed. "You held Avery against her will."

Maddox started to sob uncontrollably, and I couldn't help but feel a twinge of sadness for him. He was probably just a victim of Braden's cruelty, after all. Who would have the power to go against a monster, especially if everyone else was just playing along?

But despite this, I couldn't just let him stay in my territory. There were rules to be followed, and justice had to be served.

"I'll make you a deal," I said, crossing my arms. "You tell us everything you know about Braden's death and the thing that came out of him, and in exchange, I will give you safe passage out of here."

He looked up at me, his eyes shining with hope. "You would do that?"

My lips curled into a grin. "Sure. As soon as Nikolai and Roman get here and make their decision, we will release you. So long as the three of us are in unanimous agreement." I winked.

"It shouldn't be too bad though right? You were just an inno-cent bystander when Avery was kidnapped, weren't you?"

Maddox nodded vigorously, his tears finally drying up. "Yes, yes! I was just following orders. I didn't know what he was going to do with her."

I raised my eyebrows. "And what exactly was he going to do with her?"

"I don't know," he admitted, shrinking back slightly. "They didn't tell me much. Just to keep an eye on her and make sure she didn't escape."

I pursed my lips, considering this information. I wasn't sure whether I believed him or not, but it didn't matter. We three made decisions together. If a decision could not be reached, we waited until one could. There was only one time where we accepted a split vote, and it didn't turn out the way it should have. Selene demands the three of us to bring harmony, and act harmoniously.

"I'll be back later. I'm going to go see my *mate* and my brothers and we will come to visit you. In the meantime, get comfortable, enjoy the meal you are served and try to sleep. You're in for a long night if Nikolai has anything to say about it." I chuckled and motioned for the guards to flank the prison.

My thoughts turned to Avery, just as thunder cracked over-head and rain quenched the earth. I didn't mind the rain, in fact, we needed it to help germinate the seeds we replanted. Walking slow, I took in the state of the burnt buildings, and the people who were breaking their backs to rebuild their homes. The smell of charred wood and ash still hung heavily in the air, a reminder of the chaos and destruction that had recently swept through the town. Despite everything, the people here were resilient. They refused to let the tragedy define them and were working tirelessly to restore their community to its former glory.

As I made my way through the streets, I caught glimpses of familiar faces. Some of them nodded in my direction, acknowledging my presence, while others avoided eye contact entirely. I didn't blame them. I was an Alpha that was responsible for maintaining law and order in the town, but that didn't make me popular. Sometimes, rough decisions had to be made and wolves had to be banished. Sometimes, their families stayed and chose to hate me for it despite their ties to the town being too strong to leave for.

Finally, I reached the makeshift packhouse and pushed open the doors. Inside, small groups of wolves gathered and talked in hushed tones. At first, they seemed startled by my presence, but as I made my way around the room to greet people, murmurs of respect followed me from corner to corner. It made me proud to see my wolves still clinging to their morals, even in times of darkness.

"Alpha." One of the men turned to me with a nod. "We were just here to ask what you were going to do to increase security measures around the border? We have a lot of land and not enough men in the guard. What is your solution?"

I sighed. This was really Nikolai's department. However, Nikolai was nowhere to be seen, so I had to step in. "We're working on that. We'll be increasing patrols and bringing in more guards. We have to make sure we're protecting our people."

The man seemed satisfied with my answer and turned to head out of the packhouse. Just as he opened the door, I heard a commotion outside. It sounded like a group of wolves were causing trouble.

Without hesitation, I followed the man outside and found a group of wolves standing around a beaten and bloodied young woman. They were laughing and jeering, taking pleasure in the Omega's pain.

"That's enough," I growled. "What is the meaning of this?"

They all straightened up, eyes focused on the ground, but no one spoke. "What is the meaning of this?" I boomed again, forcing them to their knees.

"Sir, we found her at the gates. She said a demon was ripping at her while a sorcerer conjured spells. We brought her in, but she was hysterical, so we just thought—"

"You thought what?" I growled, dangerously close to snapping his neck. "LOOK AT ME!"

He feebly attempted to make eye contact, "We thought that she was crazy, and we could have a little fun."

Before I could take his head clean off, Nikolai appeared out of nowhere, grabbing my hand. "Guards, take these fine specimens to the prison. Before I kill each of you myself." His eyes flickered before settling on a deep black.

The guards grabbed the men and hauled them off without a fuss. Turning towards the young Omega, I scooped her in my arms and ran straight to Jasmine.

I burst into her room, not bothering to knock. "Jasmine, I need your help!"

She looked up from her work, her eyes widening at the sight of the battered Omega in my arms. "What happened?"

"These bastards found her outside the gates, bleeding and bruised and thought to make it worse for her." I gritted my teeth with rage at the thought of it.

Jasmine didn't waste any time. She moved quickly, grabbing her medical supplies, and commanding me to lay the tiny woman down on the bed. She assessed the wounds and got to work, muttering to herself about the severity of the injuries.

I stood back, watching her work with care and precision. Her skills were unmatched, and I trusted her fully with the Omega's life.

After what felt like hours, Jasmine finished tending to the Omega's wounds. She looked up at me with a small smile. "She'll be okay. She's lucky you found her when you did."

I nodded in agreement, feeling a weight lifted off my shoulder. "Thank you, Jasmine. I owe you one."

She waved off my thanks. "No need. I'm just glad I could help. She needs to rest. I've given her a mild sedative and she should be awake in the morning."

"Thank you."

"Go see your mate, Gabe, I am watching your little fidget dance and know you need to be close to her. I've got this." She shooed me out the door.

I all but ran back to the packhouse, which thankfully, had finally cleared of wolves. It was just Nikolai, pouring himself a scotch. I found myself wondering where Avery was.

"Did you lose her again, Nik? Because I swear to Selene—"

"No."

"Then where is she?"

Nik looked at me before slurping down the drink. That's when I heard the labored breathing and faint sounds of a headboard slapping against a wall.

"She's with Roman, isn't she?"

"Yuuuuuuuup."

I could tell Nik was struggling with jealousy, but I was glad. Roman had spent the least amount of time with her, and after Cassandra, he needed all the good feelings and closeness from Avery he could get.

"Good. Let's go outside and watch the moon."

# Twenty-Seven: Roman

She was the most beautiful thing I'd ever laid eyes on. The way the moonlight bounced off her ivory skin and the glint of our marks shined an even more pale white. As I gazed into her eyes, I felt my heart skip a beat. I had never felt this way before, not even with Cassandra— may her soul rest with Selene— it was like my entire being was consumed by her presence. Time had stopped and we were the only two people on earth.

I reached out to touch her hand, and as our fingers entwined, I knew that I never wanted to let go. She smiled at me, and I felt my heart swell with love. I wanted to stay trapped in her gaze forever as insecurity pooled in my stomach. She was my first. Yes, we'd already done the thing, but I had help. Now that I was face to face with her, I had no idea what to do... Where to touch...

"Roman?" she said as she gazed at me. "Where are you?"

"I'm right here." I tried to smile at her before my anxiety crept in and swallowed me whole.

"No, where are you here?" She tapped my forehead.

I knew what she meant, but I couldn't bring myself to say it. As much as I loved her, there were some things that I couldn't share. The truth was that I was here, but I wasn't here. My mind was consumed by doubts, and fears, and the constant feeling that I wasn't good enough for her. No woman wants to hear the insecurities of an Alpha.

"I'm sorry," I said finally. "I just... I don't know what I'm doing."

"It's okay," she said softly, bringing her other hand up to cup my cheek. "We'll figure it out together."

Her touch was like a balm to my soul, but even as she pulled me in to graze my lips with hers, my stomach clenched. *What if I do this wrong?*

"Roman... relax. I'd only ever had Braden before you guys. I don't know what I'm doing either. What would help you relax? A massage? Maybe some music?" She was so sweet, I felt like I was going to shatter under the love in her eyes.

I took a deep breath, trying to center myself. "Yeah, that sounds nice."

She stood up and walked over to her phone, pressing a few buttons before the music started softly playing. Then she came back over to me, standing behind me as she began to rub my shoulders.

I let out a low groan of pleasure, feeling the knots in my back slowly begin to loosen under her skilled touch. I closed my eyes, letting myself drift away on the waves of relaxation.

"That feels amazing," I breathed out, my head lolling forward.

"I'm glad," she whispered, leaning in to place a gentle kiss on the back of my neck. The sensation sent shivers down my spine, and for a moment I forgot all my worries. But then she started to inch her hands lower, towards the waistband of my jeans, and the knot in my stomach came back.

I tensed up, pulling away slightly. "Wait, what are you doing?"

"Relax," she said, her voice low and sultry. "I'm just trying to help you feel better."

"But... ugh. I just."

"Is it Cassandra?" she said quietly.

"No. No, it's not her. I just don't want our first time to be bad. I want to make this good for you, and I just... don't know what to do." *I am pathetic. What kind of man admits that to the most beautiful woman on earth?* Her beautiful baby bump brushed against my back as she walked around the bed and trailed her fingertip down my face.

"No one is perfect, Roman, and I don't expect you to be. Hell, I didn't know what I was doing with the three of you and we figured it out, okay? You were so confident!"

"Yeah, because Gabriel and Nik were there to help me, and the... *hole* was just there. Easy shot."

She snorted. "Did you just call my pussy a HOLE?"

"Well... it is." Her snort made me chuckle, which lead to full on belly laughing. Poof, just like that anxiety disappeared. "Okay, let's do this," I said, rubbing my hands together.

She grinned, planting another kiss on my neck. "That's what I like to hear."

I rolled over to face her, taking in the sight of her swollen belly and sparkling eyes. She was beautiful, and I couldn't believe she wanted me. I leaned in to kiss her, feeling her lips parting eagerly against mine.

Our hands roamed over each other's bodies, exploring new territory as we shed our clothes. We were both slightly nervous, but the chemistry between us was undeniable. I lost myself in that moment, in the feel of her skin on mine was electrifying.

Spreading her legs, I dipped my head down, trailing hot kisses over her belly and inside her thighs. "You let me know what you need from me," I whispered as I began to circle her clit with my tongue.

Her hips bucked up as she let out a shaky gasp. "Deeper, Roman. Oh god... Deeper." Her fingers ran through my hair before yanking so hard I saw stars.

My tongue dove firmly inside her, and her thighs clamped down on my face. "Fuck Roman, yes!" Her body quivered in delight, my hands steadying her trembling form. I reached up to squeeze her nipples, smiling as she writhed under my touch.

I moved up to kiss her swollen lips, my hands roaming down to grasp her ass. When we broke the kiss, she was breathless with anticipation. Her hips swayed left and right, her body begging me to take her.

I guided my thick cock into her, groaning as I slid inside. The sensation of her inner muscles squeezing me, pulling me in deeper nearly drove me insane.

"Roman!" she cried out as I began to thrust harder and deeper. "You feel so good."

I fucked her hard, before slowing my pace, enjoying the sensation of sliding in and out of her sopping wet pussy.

"Am I good for you, baby?" I whispered in her ear as she wrapped her arms around my neck.

"Yes... oh yes. I love the way you fill me up..." She lamented out, pushing her hips into me again and again.

"I'm ready to come," she moaned out, grinding herself against me as I reached down to push on her clit.

"Come for me, Avery. I want to feel it. I want to feel everything." I plunged faster, watching her face contort as she started to orgasm. Her nails dug into my shoulders as she screamed out.

"Ah! Oh God... Oh, mmm—," she moaned before she slowly pushed me away and got up on wobbling legs. A quick shiver ran through my body as she gently rolled my balls with her soft fingers.

"Yes, touch me, please," I whispered, feeling her lips slide down my body. She grasped my cock tightly, stroking slowly before taking my head into her mouth, groaning as she tasted herself.

"Fuck... that feels good," I growled, watching as she took more of my cock into her mouth. She wrapped her tongue around the shaft, slowly sucking as she pumped me faster. Each stroke was bringing me higher.

I pushed myself toward her mouth as I felt my balls tense up. I was close to coming and didn't want to finish after only a few strokes. I quickly turned her over and laid her down on the bed, moving between her legs. Nipping at her chin and her neck, my hand slid over the curve of her hips and back, caressing her soft skin before one fingertip slipped between her cheeks and tiptoed around her tight asshole. She moaned in pleasure and held my head as I slowly thrust my fingers into her apex which she was already grinding against me.

"What a needy one, aren't you baby girl?" A satisfied moan was my response.

Pushing into her, I found her clit with my thumb and began to stroke it in long soft circles, which made her whole body shudder, the small of her back arching off the bed. Pushing my thumb deeper, I watched as I finger fucked Avery with light strokes, pulling back on each stroke.

"Mmmmm!" She moaned louder, grinding her hips against mine. "Do that again!"

"Like this?" I asked, slowly thrusting my thumb in and out again as I pinched her clit lightly between my finger and thumb.

"More..." She ground her hips up harder against me, me following her perfect rhythm.

Pumping her faster and a little bit rougher with my fingers, I flicked my thumb across her clit a few more times, watching as Avery's hips bucked harder against me, her body trembling as she came apart.

I could feel my cock throbbing against her legs which was pressed tight against me.

"I wanted to suck you dry," she whispered. "It's my first time with you and I wanted it to be special, did I do something wrong?"

"No, you're perfect, baby girl. I'd rather fill you up though." I grinned down at her as her mouth parted before it released a big breath as I pushed inside her.

She was so tight, warm, wet and welcoming as I thrust into her, my fingers threading through her hair, wrapping it tightly around my hand until I pulled her head back. She cried out in pleasure as I released my load, her body shuddering around me, her cries muffled as she bit into her hand. She turned her head away as I eased out of her, but I tugged her head back towards me again and pressed my lips against hers as she sat sideways on my lap, easing my access to her mouth and neck. She was eager, and I kissed her deeply, pushing my tongue into her mouth and letting her taste herself on me.

Pulling back, I took a good look at the goddess before me. Eyelids hooded, hardly open, pink flushed skin starting from her chest and fanning out towards her cheeks, her legs open and limp... and a big wet spot.

"Come here," she said, tiredly pulling me down beside her. "You were... incredible. How is it I'm your first?"

"I guess I'm just that amazing," I said, earning myself a chuckle. "Go to sleep, baby girl. You've been fucked six ways from Sunday."

I got up and fetched a warm washcloth, gently cleaning her before tucking her into my bed and kissing her. Gentle snores filled the room, leaving a satisfied feeling spreading through me. *I did that. I satisfied her. So much, in fact, that she needs to sleep. Never mind that it's well past midnight, I still did that.*

Tip toeing to the bag of clothes on the floor, I threw on the first pair of shorts I could find and made my way downstairs.

# Twenty-Eight: Amrin

T hose pricks. I could hear her screams fill the air as I paced outside of their unguarded packhouse. I could rip them all to shreds right now and get my little prize back, but no. Sion says I must wait, something about gathering a shard to complete my pairing with Belial. So, I wait and wait, and wait some more. Meanwhile MY mate is being dicked down by some insecure little bitch boy while two other full-grown men sit outside like they don't know what's happening.

Disgrace. Since when do we SHARE what's ours? They should have fought for her to the death. Well, I won't be making the same mistake. I WILL fight for her, I will destroy everything and everyone to make her mine and we will rule in darkness, together.

I had to get away from the packhouse before I was found out, not that they could do a damn thing about it. I was faster and stronger than I'd ever been before. I backed away slowly and didn't look back, before running into the woods. The night was chilly, and my breath fogged in front of me as I made my way through the trees, enveloped by darkness. I passed an old oak whose branches hung low like a canopy, and I remembered playing hide-and-seek here when I was younger. Before Braden's father started abusing his mother. And him. Weakling. If he'd have let me out, I would have killed him so much sooner, but he didn't and now I'm... here. At the place where the grim reaper himself would run in terror from me.

My steps grew heavier as I reached my destination— the entrance to the cave that would be my new home for the foreseeable future. Close enough to the pack that I could dip in and out to watch Avery, but far enough away that they'd never suspect I was right here. There were two long spiraling staircases carved right into the wall that led winding down to a small pool where an underground river cut through the cave. I shed my clothes and made my way into the pool until the water hit my shoulders. I stared at the dark moss and lichen that crawled across the rock face until they all turned black and died.

When I heard the sound of footsteps, I knew Sion was at the entrance. No one but him did that particular croak. Something about the way he stepped, he was always on his toes, never fully on his feet. Not because he was weak, far from it. He had devoured enough souls that he was the most powerful sorcerer, Braden had just been too stupid to see it. But I wasn't.

"Report," I barked at him, not moving from my spot.

"That's how you talk to the one that freed you?" He tsked at me. "You'd think you'd have better manners than that."

"I don't care for pleasantries, Sion. We are not friends. We are mutual companions with a mutual goal. Now, report."

"We can't find the shard to complete the transition. And the girl ran away. Somehow made it to the Trio and is now in their care. That complicates things a fair bit."

"Get another girl," I growled.

"It's not that simple. She needed to be from a dormant witch line, 25 years old AND a virgin. Do you know how fucking hard that is to find? It's literally a needle in a haystack," Sion yelled.

"I don't care, get another girl. Whatever you have to do just do it." I commanded him.

"There is no other girl. That brings me to the other problem."

"What now?"

"I think your mate IS the shard."

"Say what now?" I stopped breathing, waiting for his next words.

"Um, so yeah, I've heard through the grapevine that she's a Seraphina. You know what that means?" Sion whispered.

My heart stopped beating as all the pieces suddenly came together. Avery was the missing shard. No wonder she could withstand the mark of the last Lycan. Oh yes, I knew about him too. Legend had it that no one could bare the mark, lest they die. Something to do with balance of light and dark. Who gives a shit? I should have seen the signs. She could turn me into a creature of darkness if I allowed it to happen, something bigger than all of this. Something... unstoppable. And for a moment, I wanted it, but the piece of Belial that was missing allowed the love I have for her to shine through.

"No," I said firmly. "Avery WILL NOT be part of what we are attempting to do here."

"You don't have a choice. She is a Seraphina. Therefore, she is the only one that can restore balance," Sion stated, his gaze never leaving mine. "If we let her go unchecked, she will fucking destroy you. Once she knows what she is capable of, don't for one goddamn second think she won't destroy you, me and everyone in on this."

"Get the virgin and ready the spell. We don't need Avery. We can force the hands of the witches if we must," I said, waving my hand to dismiss him.

"Amrin, you cannot be serious. You knew the deal when we made it. There is no one else to take down Selene. You offered yourself as the vessel because she loves you most. You were the first. The only to be passed down. You can't bail now. Belial..."

Turning, I snarled, "Belial... what? What Sion? What's he going to do? Until the virgin and Avery, apparently, he can't do shit."

It was then that I felt it. A shift, an aching in my bones as they turned into Jello before rearranging. Long spikes forced themselves through my skin.

*Belial...*

*It's time...*

"Fuck...," I groaned. Arching my back, I could feel the bones push up through my skin, moving to put themselves in place. Looking down, I watched it happen, and looked toward Sion as I did so. "Oh shit!"

*What? What is it?*

Tearing out my shirt, I saw that the scars on my chest were rapidly filling in with black. At first a small, hardly noticeable circle. It quickly expanded and pushed outward until it had formed a ball of inky darkness in the shape of a pentagram.

Where the fuck am I? What is going on?

"Hello, you insolent little wolf. I heard you think you can fight against me. Against my will," a dark voice rumbled around me. Swiveling my head, I tried to pinpoint where it was coming from, but the darkness attacked my sight, blinding me. My head was aching, and my memory was hazing in and out. *What the hell?*

"I know you can hear me, Amrin. I'll give you one more chance to complete what we attempted. Before I make you destroy everything."

I ignored the voice. I somehow knew it was Belial and he wasn't exactly speaking with me, but rather through me. His voice seemed to echo without a source. Feeling the violent pain of bones protruding from my skin, I remembered where I had been then.

*Where am I? What did he do to me?*

And then it hit me. Avery. That was why I was in this place. Trying to salvage some semblance of the love I had for her and refusing to hurt her. I growled, voicing my anger at Belial. If I was honest, I was fucking pissed that this was happening. I thought about her, and how he would use her against me. Of course, this wouldn't be happening if not for my rage decision to band with Satan and Satan Jr, but still I couldn't let that happen. Reaching out, I hoped to feel some semblance of life, something to show me that I wasn't fully dead yet. For me to reach out and hold dear to my heart, the one last piece of the happy ending I wished for with her. Without thinking, I curled my claw into a fist, and I punched the darkness.

Which was really fucking dumb, trying to hit a void of darkness.

The black spread and hurt as it met my skin. It brought with it a sleepy tingling feeling, releasing the pent-up agonizing pain of my bones pushing through flesh. Plunging my claws into the black I struggled against it, ripping the massive churning darkness with my nails, but nothing happened. The black appeared unphased by my clawing and kept ripping into me. In a fit of anger and agony, I started to tear at it with my teeth. This was fucking working to some degree as bits started to flake off and away from me, leaving long cuts on my skin that eventually healed. But just as my body began to repair itself, the impossible happened. The blackness pushed back, reeling me in like a fish caught on a hook. I was being swallowed, consumed by the darkness.

In that moment, I screamed out Avery's name. I didn't want her to see me like this, consumed by evil and trapped in a void of darkness. But even as I screamed, my voice was drowned out by the darkness, until there was nothing but silence.

I don't know how long I was trapped in that darkness, but when I finally emerged, I was somewhere else entirely. The air around me was thick with the scent of burning sulfur, and the sky was red with fire. I looked down at my body and saw that I was no longer... me. My skin was black, charred, and ripped away at the places, showing the red flesh and muscle underneath. I had a disgusting set of black horns that I only saw in depictions of demons. When I reached up to feel them, they were cold and hard. Standing up on two legs I surveyed my surroundings and saw that I was in some twisted vision of Hell.

The landscape around me was made up of blood-red dirt and burning lava pits. Beyond all of this was a massive structure that rose from the earth, as high as the sky. It looked more like it was constructed from the very bones of all living things than anything else. Forcing my heavy body up I walked toward the structure, the ground shaking beneath my feet with each step. As I got closer, I could hear screams and cries of agony emanating from within its walls. The closer I got, the more my body began to tremble.

But I couldn't stop now. Something was drawing me closer.

As I approached the entrance, two massive doors made of bones swung open, revealing a dimly lit hallway. The smell of death and decay filled my nostrils as I took my first steps inside. The walls were lined with skulls and bones of every size and shape imaginable, and the floor was slick with blood.

"What am I doing here?" I screamed, falling to my knees.

A chuckle burst forth as a searing pain ripped my heart from my chest. "You are here to rot, you cannot be trusted to carry out the will of the gods, and you will take my place in the Underworld until our job is done. If you don't perish first."

"You can't just leave me here," I said as I watched my own body, the body of a horrific and mangled, half wolf, half demon walked away from me. "What am I supposed to do?"

Belial turned and stared at me. "If you want your precious Avery to live, I suggest you try finding your way out." He gestured to the landscape around me. "Though, that will be hard given you have no body to affix your soul to, and well... you're in your own version of Hell. Welcome to my world."

Helpless, I watched him stalk away, desperately trying to find an entry point back into my body but being forced backwards with each attempt. Despair filled me. As much as I hated Braden, I loved Avery. *Giving up isn't an option. I have to warn her... before it's too late.*

# Twenty-Nine: Avery

I awoke with a start. In the middle of the garden with an ethereal light surrounding me.

"Hello, child."

That voice was familiar, but I couldn't quite place it.

"Yes, it's me. I am here to help you. I see that Selene left you defenseless." Now it was coming back to me. A voice I had heard so long ago for such a brief time.

"Aunt Sapphire?"

"Ahhh," she chuckled. "You remember me."

"Where... how?"

"This is the dream world. Neat, isn't it? I can create anything here. This is my world to play with. Most witches derive their strength from nature or well... the dark, but not me. Mine come from dreams, both manifesting and watching. Please, relax. Or I cannot enter with you."

I closed my eyes, taking a deep breath. As I did, the garden around me began to shift and morph. The flowers grew in size and shape until they became otherworldly creatures with vibrant colors that glowed in the ethereal light. The trees twisted and turned, their branches reaching out to me like beckoning fingers.

When I opened my eyes, Aunt Sapphire stood before me, her arms stretched out in invitation.

"Come, child," she said. "Let me show you the power of the dream world."

I took her hand, and she led me through the garden, which had now transformed into a magical landscape. We walked past waterfalls that flowed upwards, a sky that shimmered with stars in the middle of the day, and trees that whispered secrets as we passed. As we continued our journey, I felt myself becoming lighter, almost weightless, as though I were no longer confined by the rules of the real world.

Finally, we came to a clearing. Aunt Sapphire stopped and turned to me with a smile.

"Are you ready, child?"

I nodded eagerly.

"Then close your eyes," she instructed. "And imagine the most magical place you can think of."

I did as she said, and as I closed my eyes, I felt myself falling into a holding state. Images flashed before my eyes, but the image I settled on wasn't one of my beautiful mates, nor my ex-mate, my family or even her... it was Selene handing me the Spirit Stone.

"Good choice." Aunt Sapphire chuckled. "You want to know more, don't you?"

"I do," I breathed. I couldn't take my eyes off the stone. It was as if I'd never become one with it, dangling there, in all its splendor as Selene stood in the background.

She sighed. "It's a tough road, you've chosen. By molding with the spirit stone, you've set everything in motion."

My heart raced with excitement and trepidation. "What do you mean? What have I set in motion?"

Aunt Sapphire took my hand and pulled me towards a shimmering portal that had appeared out of nowhere. "Come with me," she said. "I'll show you."

I stepped through the portal and was immediately transported to a dark, foreboding forest. The trees were twisted and gnarled, and the ground beneath our feet was covered in blackened, dead leaves.

"What is this place?" I asked, feeling a sense of dread wash over me.

"This is the Shadow Realm," she responded. "It's a dangerous place..." she trailed off.

"What aren't you telling me?"

She sighed again. "This is where the Seraphina come to train. It is meant to be harsh, rugged, so that you learn how to hone your skills and survive. Something like those holos you watch in your movies. Where they train and can't die? Like that."

"Okay... so all of us trained under dream state?"

"No," she snapped, irritably. "You're the only one who gets to do this under dream state and that's because we are literally under duress right now."

"But you just said—"

"Child, listen to me." She grabbed my shoulders with painful strength. "It is here. It is sweeping the earth for you. He has destroyed your ancestors, but I won't let him destroy you, do you understand me?"

Her plea was desperate, wild. Her eyes blown open as her nails raked along my arm as I tried to squirm away. "Yes, okay, yes, I get it, how do I train my skills." I whined until she finally released me.

Aunt Sapphire took a deep breath and composed herself. "First, you need to know what you're up against."

She led me deeper into the forest, pointing out strange creatures lurking in the shadows. There were creatures with multiple eyes, large fangs, and tentacles that writhed in the darkness. They all seemed to be watching us, waiting for a moment of weakness to strike.

"What are those?" I asked, my voice barely above a whisper.

"They are the shadows that haunt the realm. They are the remnants of beings who have perished here but remain, trapped in the darkness. They are restless, hungry, and will attack anything that crosses their path."

She handed me a small knife. It was sharp and glinted menacingly in the moonlight.

"This will be your weapon. It's not much, but it will do. You need to learn how to use it well."

She showed me how to grip it, how to move it swiftly, and how to strike. I practiced with her under her watchful eye until my muscles ached. But she was patient and kind, never once losing her temper.

In the days that followed, my daily duties would be fulfilled, but at night, I ventured further into the Shadow Realm with Aunt Sapphire. She taught me how to track prey, how to stay hidden, and how to strike without being seen. We hunted strange creatures together, taking down grotesque beasts with our bare hands. We moved silently, gliding through the darkness with ease.

As we walked deeper into the forest, I felt something stir within me. It was as if a dormant power had awakened, and I could feel it coursing through my veins. Aunt Sapphire noticed the change in me, and a smile flickered across her face.

"Good," she said. "You're starting to feel it. Your power is growing, and soon you will be able to harness it."

"What kind of power?" I asked, intrigued.

"A power that only the Seraphina possess."

"How do I harness it?" I asked eagerly.

"It comes with time and practice," she replied. "But for now, focus on using your senses to navigate through the shadows. Listen to the sounds around you, feel the vibrations in the earth, and smell the scents in the air. Let them guide you."

I closed my eyes and took a deep breath. I focused all my senses, trying to home in on the sounds.

Suddenly, I heard a soft whistling wind, and a gentle warmth spread across my body. I felt the air around me shift, and just like that, I was in control of the wind. It was a strange sensation but exhilarating at the same time.

As we walked further into the darkness, a bright light lit up my surroundings suddenly. Flames danced from my fingertips like clockwork spinning erratically before engulfing everything in sight with an inferno's grace. I moved my arms ever so slightly to control the fire, manipulating it as if it were an extension of myself.

The different elements of air and fire had become part of my being, and I couldn't wait to see what other powers awaited me as a Seraphina.

Aunt Sapphire nodded approvingly. "Impressive," she said. "But remember, with great power comes great responsibility. You must use your gifts wisely, and never let them consume you."

I nodded, understanding the gravity of her words. We continued our hunt, moving deeper into the forest. As we walked, I felt a wave of gratitude for her coming to visit me in my dreams. She had taken me under her wing when no one else would, and now I was unlocking powers I never knew existed.

Suddenly, we heard a bloodcurdling scream in the distance. It was a sound that chilled me to my very core.

Without hesitation, we took off running towards the direction of the scream. As we got closer, we saw a figure lying on the ground, writhing in agony. I quickly realized it was a man, dressed in tattered clothes and covered in dirt. His skin was ripped, and he was moaning in desperation.

As we approached him, he cried out for help. "Please, someone help me!" he gasped.

Aunt Sapphire knelt beside him, looking deeply into his soul.

"Avery, you need to go back now."

"No, Aunt—"

"Avery. You need to go back now."

"How? I don't control my dreams."

"Yes, you do. Think of your mates, your home, go, leave. NOW."

I closed my eyes, trying to focus on home. I could feel a pull like a tugging sensation deep inside of me. With one final glance at the injured man, I allowed myself to be pulled back into my body.

As soon as I opened my eyes, I knew something was wrong. I wasn't in my bedroom anymore. Panic and confusion set in as I realized I was lying on the cold ground. Looking around frantically, I searched for any sign of my bed or my mates. Nothing was familiar. It was then that I noticed the thick fog surrounding me and the eerie silence that permeated the air. Fear started to take over, paralyzing my movements.

Suddenly, I heard a rustling sound coming from behind me. I turned around and saw a pair of glowing red eyes staring at me. My heart raced as I tried to look for a way out. But I was surrounded by a dense forest, and the only path available was a narrow one leading deeper into the woods.

The eyes seemed to be getting closer, and I realized that whatever creature they belonged to was now standing right in front of me. It was a massive wolf. Its teeth bared at me, I could hardly contain my terror as it stalked closer, until it slumped down and lay beside me panting. I hesitated for a moment, wondering if the wolf was friendly or not. I knew my mates shifted, obviously, but...why wasn't this one shifting back? When it didn't make a move to attack me, I cautiously reached out my hand to stroke its fur. Surprisingly, it leaned into my touch and closed its eyes in contentment.

As I sat there petting it, I began to wonder where I was and how I got here. Was this still a dream? Or had something gone terribly wrong with Aunt Sapphire's spell? I tried to focus on going back home once again, but nothing happened. The fog around me remained thick, and the wolf seemed to be my only company.

Hours passed, or maybe it was days, but suddenly, I found myself back in bed.

"Avery?"

# Thirty: Nikolai

I found her lying there. Stupid brothers still fast asleep. The minute she left, I felt it, but damn, something blocked her movement until the moment she touched down. 6 hours later. Night after night, I'd been tracking her through her dreams and bringing her back home. Why was I the only one able to sense what was happening and where she was?

Exhaustion crept over me as I tucked her into bed. Not in mine. Not tonight. I was pissed. Sure, we SUPPOSEDLY can't control our dreams... except she could... and I could. I watched her for a moment, her chest rising and falling gently as she slept. She looked so peaceful, so vulnerable, that for a moment, I forgot my anger. But then I remembered the frustration of watching her slip away night after night, leaving me to track her once again.

I shook my head, trying to clear my mind. It wasn't just her dreams that were the problem. It was the fact that I couldn't stop thinking about her, even when she was awake. She had this hold over me, this pull that I couldn't escape. And it was driving me insane.

I turned to leave the room, but she called out in her sleep. Rushing to her side, I tuned in to listen.

"Belial, Amrin, coming for the shard. No, no drop that, there is no time to waste. Yes, sir, I'd also like a cheesecake to go, oh my god, you have blackberries. Yes, they're my favorite. Thank you," she murmured in her sleep.

Her lips ended their rant on a beautifully parted note. Her skin looked soft and supple in the moonlight. Ugh... she was... everything.

I tried to shake her awake. "Avery, hey baby can you wake up for me?"

She groaned in response, but her eyes stayed shut. I sighed, wondering what she could be dreaming about. It seemed like every time she fell asleep, something pulled her away from me. It was like she was being called to some other world. And for some reason, I couldn't shake the feeling that I was supposed to follow her there.

I started to leave the room again, but then she called out my name. "Nikolai," she murmured, her voice husky and full of need.

My heart skipped a beat. Was she dreaming of me? I turned back to her, watching as she shifted in her sleep. "Nikolai, please, where are you?"

My heart swelled with the desire to hold her in my arms, but I knew that wasn't possible. Not while she was in this state of mind. I couldn't risk hurting her in her sleep.

I sat by her bedside, watching her toss and turn. Her breaths came out shallow, and her skin was slicked with sweat. I knew I had to do something to bring her back to me.

Without thinking, I leaned forward and brushed a gentle hand down her cheek. The contact seemed to soothe her, and she let out a sigh of contentment. I felt my own heart race at the sight of her melting under my touch. But I needed to focus on her dreams. I had to find a way to enter them and bring her back to me. I closed my eyes, taking deep breaths and focusing all my energy on her sleeping form.

Suddenly, I felt a jolt of electricity pass through me. My eyes snapped open, and I found myself standing in a strange world. The sky was a deep shade of purple, and strange plants with glowing flowers surrounded me.

I looked around, trying to find any trace of Avery. And then I saw her, standing in the distance. She looked lost and scared, and I knew I had to get to her.

I ran towards her, my heart pounding in my chest. The closer I got, the clearer her form became. She was wearing a long flowing dress that looked like it was made of pure moonlight. Her hair was unbound and fell in wild tendrils around her face.

As I reached her side, she turned to me with a look of relief. "Nikolai," she whispered, her voice filled with longing.

I pulled her into my arms, feeling the warmth of her body against mine. "I came for you, Avery," I said, breathless. "I followed you here."

She looked up at me with eyes filled with wonder and love. "You shouldn't have come here."

"Why not?" I asked, feeling a twinge of fear at the uncertainty in her voice.

"This place is dangerous. It's full of traps and illusions," she said, her grip on me tightening. "We need to leave before it's too late."

I nodded, taking her hand in mine. "Let's go then. Together."

We ran through the strange world, dodging obstacles and fighting off creatures that seemed to come out of nowhere. But the more we advanced, the clearer it became that this place was designed to keep Avery trapped.

The air grew thick with a strange energy, and I felt my own strength waning. Avery stumbled, and I caught her before she fell. "We need to find a way out of here," I said, struggling to keep my own fear at bay.

Avery's eyes widened in realization as she looked around. "There," she said, pointing to a faint glimmer in the distance. "That's the way out."

We sprinted towards the glimmer, our hearts racing with hope. As we got closer, the glimmer became a bright light that seemed to be coming from a portal.

Without hesitation, we jumped through the portal and found ourselves back in our world. We collapsed on the ground, gasping for breath, grateful to be alive. When I looked down, she was wrapped in my arms, sweat slick upon her face. Her whimpers drove me to madness.

"Avery? Sweetheart, wake up."

Her eyes flickered open, and she looked up at me with a dazed expression. "Nikolai?" she murmured.

I pulled her closer to me, feeling the warmth of her body against mine. "Thank God you're okay," I breathed, relief washing over me in waves.

She nodded weakly, her eyes still unfocused. "What happened?" she asked, her voice trembling.

"We made it out," I said, stroking her hair gently. "We're back in our world now."

Avery's eyes cleared, and she looked up at me with a mix of emotions— relief, love and hunger.

"Thank you," she whispered, her glistening forehead marking my own as she pressed her lips to mine. I don't know that I'd have made it out without you... it just kept..."

She trailed off, looking at me expectantly.

"What do you need?" My voice was gravelly.

She hesitated for a moment before answering. "I need you, Nikolai," she whispered, her breath hot against my ear. "I need you to make me feel alive again. Control me, control my body, help me remember, but most of all, help me forget."

I leaned down and kissed her hungrily, feeling her response as she opened her mouth to mine. I could feel the intensity of her desire as she wound her fingers through my hair, pulling me closer as our tongues tangled.

Avery moaned softly as I trailed kisses down her neck and over her collarbone. I could taste the salt of her sweat, mingled with the sweet perfume of her skin. I could feel the heat rising between us, the need building with each passing moment.

I pushed her gently back onto the ground, my lips never leaving hers as my hands roamed over her body, exploring every inch of her. I could sense her giving herself over to me completely, trusting me with her body and soul.

As I trailed my fingers down her stomach, Avery let out a soft moan of pleasure. She was so responsive to my touch, so alive in my arms. With each stroke of my hand, I could feel her surrendering to me completely, giving herself over to the intense pleasure that I was providing.

I looked up at her, seeing the desire in her eyes. She wanted this just as much as I did, and nothing would stop me from giving her what she craved. I leaned in and whispered in her ear, "I'm going to make you forget everything except this moment, Avery. You're mine now."

She whimpered in response, her body trembling with anticipation. I took my time exploring every inch of her body, mapping out her every curve and contour with my hands and lips. I wanted to make this moment last forever, to savor every second of her sweet surrender.

"Okay, princess, I'm going to cuff you now, and then I'll take your sight, you ready?"

Her moans were enough for me to start the process. I reached for the handcuffs by the bedside table, my fingers grazing over the cool metal. Avery's eyes widened with excitement as I secured each cuff tightly around her wrists. She was completely at my mercy now, and I could feel the power coursing through my veins.

Next, I reached for the blindfold, carefully tying it over her eyes. I trailed my fingers over her naked body, feeling her shiver with pleasure as I grazed her nipples and traced the curve of her hips.

I lapped at her engorged clitoris, wanting more, more pleasure, more stimulation, but how? How could I send her over the edge with nothing to hold onto except me? I teased her nipples, seeing them harden and jump at my touch. Oh, I was going to love owning this body.

I covered her clit with my mouth and lapped at her pussy, feeling the warmth of her skin on my face, the sweet sticky juice flowing from within. Finally, I felt her tense up and I slowed the pace, but not the intensity. I felt her desperate need for release and her inability to hold on any longer. Avery was a delicate flower in my hands. She needed to be nurtured and cared for. She needed my guidance and protection. There was no questioning how much I wanted her to cum all over me.

"Come for me, princess."

I felt the warm flood of her orgasm around my fingers as she finally let go. I couldn't wait any longer. It was time she could now feel the real me. I pulled up the blindfold and picked up a condom from the drawer by the side of the bed.

I quickly slipped it over my engorged cock before plunging into her, only stopping in surprise when she whispered in a tiny voice, "take the condom off, I want to feel you."

Pulling the barrier off, I sighed in relief as I buried myself inside her. Slick with need she tried wiggling her hips against me, until I flipped her and pressed her head into the mattress. "Oh no princess, you don't dominate me, I dominate you."

My hand wrapped around her hair, pulling her body taut against mine, I watched as the scream she was about to release died on her lips as I captured it on mine.

"Say my name," I growled.

"Nikolai," she whispered, her pussy quivering around me.

"Louder."

"Nikolai, oh god..."

"As loud as you can, I want the windows to rattle with the sound of your cunt dripping for me," I snarled against her neck.

I felt her whole body stiffen as she cried out my name. I released her lips and watched as her back arched up and her whole body froze in pleasure. Her pussy convulsed and grasped my cock in its vice-like grip as she came hard. I quickened my pace and felt my own orgasm rise.

Finally, I could see the tension building within her, a tension of another kind, the kind that was greedy, needy, the need for release almost overwhelming. I leaned down and kissed her deeply, plunging my tongue into her mouth as I felt her body climbing towards the skies.

It was then that I came. I spilled my seed so deeply within her... and it was then that she rose like a phoenix rising against a darkened sky.

# Thirty-One: Gabriel

"Nik, why did you put on a condom last night? You've never worn one before..." I heard Avery's whisper as they sat on the porch together enjoying a coffee.

"I... I don't know, Avery. I was really tired, and it was late... I wore them with all my other partners, and I guess it was just second nature..." He tried to reach for her, but she pulled her hand away. "I'm sorry. I wasn't thinking."

"I don't care about the condom, Nik, it just kind of hurt my feelings the way you flippantly describe how many other partners you've had."

He chuckled, "Avery... I was no saint before we met, hell, I'm not even a saint now that we HAVE met. I didn't mean to be callous with your feelings, but it's the truth."

I could see her intake a big breath. "I know," she said quietly. "I just feel jealous, that's all."

"Why, baby girl? You have me. I'm right here. No one will ever take you from me. You're it."

She let out a breath with a small huff and leaned into him. They were so perfect together, but a small roll of irritation spread through me. I desperately wanted to be so flippant with my time, I wanted to hog her to myself and have my own way with her, but for some reason, I just couldn't let go. It wasn't that I didn't want to be with Avery, I did. But there was just something holding me back, a deep-seated fear that ached within me. It was as if I was always waiting for the other shoe to drop, a fear that one day, she would be gone, and I would be left alone. That fear caused me to withdraw more and more into myself.

Avery was my everything, the reason I woke up in the morning and the last thought before I went to sleep. But that feeling was tearing me apart. It was like a monster lying in wait to devour whatever precious time I did get with her, always ready to pounce and consume me whole.

I should just talk to her, to tell her that I was built differently to Nik and Roman. They were both able to express themselves outwardly with such ease. Even with Roman's insecurities and abandonment issues, he was still so jovial. But me... I struggled to connect. Not just with her, but with everyone. These guys were my brothers, but I still kept so much of myself bottled inside. Most times, the words to explain myself escaped me and I was left stumbling over how I felt. It was frustrating to say the least.

The irritation flared again when I saw that the coffee pot was empty. Refilling and resetting the pot with new grounds, I leaned against the counter to watch them enjoying each other's company. Nik's shoulder was moving ever so slightly, and her small sighs of pleasure told me all I needed to know. *Maybe I should just go to work. There's so much to be done in town. Stuff that both Roman and Nik should really be helping me with, but instead they're spending their days busting out their peashooters while mine turns a crazy shade of blue.* Flicking the pot on to start, I gasped as the glass shattered, embedding in my stomach.

In a flash, Avery was standing beside me while Nik led me to the table. "I'm fine guys, really. No need to stop your shenanigans on my account."

Avery levelled me with a glare. "Shut up Gabe, what climbed in your ass?"

I winced at her choice of words, knowing she was just trying to get a reaction out of me. But with the pain still radiating from my stomach, I couldn't bring myself to play along.

"Sorry, just feeling a little off today," I muttered, trying to pull away from Nik's grasp. "I can handle it."

But as I stood up, my vision suddenly went black, and I stumbled forward, blindly groping for something to hold onto. Nik's arms caught me before I hit the ground, and I was vaguely aware of Roman and Avery rushing over to us.

"What happened? Is he okay?" Roman's panicked voice hit me.

"He's fine, he needs to rest. The coffee pot shattered, he's got some glass embedded in his stomach and his dumbass didn't want our help to remove it. Let's get him to his room and we can pull them out before his body tries to heal over it. Roman, you're gonna need to go do some work and take over for Gabe, he's been spending too many nights working on everything alone." Nik barked orders.

"Why," Roman whined. "Why don't you go, and I'll stay here?"

"Because, I said so," Nik jeered, roughly carrying me to my room and unceremoniously dumping me on the bed.

"Here, let me do it," Avery said. "My touch is clearly gentler then yours."

I groaned, feeling embarrassed. I'd always prided myself on my toughness and independence, but now I was lying helpless on my own bed with glass in my stomach.

Avery's hands were gentle as she lifted my shirt up and inspected the wound. I could feel her breath on my skin as she murmured to herself, examining the area closely. Her fingers were nimble as she carefully probed the broken glass.

"Okay, I think I can get it out in one piece," she said finally. "But this is going to hurt, Gabe. A lot. Nik grab me a small knife, I've gotta cut a bit, it's already trying to heal."

I gritted my teeth, bracing myself for the pain. Avery's fingers were cool against my skin as she made a tiny incision where the largest piece of glass was embedded and then slowly began to extract the shard. The pain brought tears to my eyes, but I didn't make a sound, partly out of stubbornness and partly because I didn't want to scare Avery.

She worked quietly and efficiently. I watched her focused expression, admiring how beautiful she looked in the soft light filtering through my blinds. She had always been the nurturing type, the one who made sure everyone was taken care of, and I had always admired her for it.

Finally, the glass was out, and she kissed my forehead and tucked me in.

"Nik, you AND Roman go to work today. I'll heal in a few minutes, and I'll spend the day with Avery," I said firmly, not leaving room for argument.

Nik and Roman grumbled, but eventually left the room, leaving Avery and I alone. I could feel her eyes on me, concern etched into every line of her expression.

"Are you okay? Do you need anything else?" she asked softly.

I shook my head, wincing as the movement pulled on the wound. "I'll be okay. Thank you. I appreciate that you're caring for me."

She smiled, her eyes shining with emotion. "That's what mates are for Gabe. I couldn't bear to see you hurt."

We sat in silence for a few moments, the air heavy with unspoken words. Suddenly, Avery leaned forward and pressed her lips gently to mine. The kiss was soft and slow, and I felt myself melting into her touch.

As we pulled away, I looked at her, my heart racing. "Avery, I always have these really strong feelings for you. I just never knew how to express them."

Her eyes widened, and for a moment, she looked surprised. Then, a slow smile spread across her face.

"Well, maybe now is the perfect time to explore those feelings," she said, leaning in for another kiss.

"Avery... wait..."

She pulled back and held my hand. "Talk to me Gabe. I've noticed you're always the quiet one just watching me with the other guys. Why don't you ever make a move on me? Are you regretting this? Are you regretting me?"

"No, of course not!" I gingerly put my arms around her. "It's just... I'm just struggling right now. Watching you with them, you're so relaxed and at ease, and I just get in my own head a lot and it's..."

"It's what?"

"It's embarrassing."

Avery looked at me with a mixture of confusion and sympathy, giving my hand a gentle squeeze. "Why is it embarrassing, Gabe? You don't have to hide anything from me."

"I know," I said, looking away from her. "It's just that I don't want you to think less of me, or to think that I'm weak."

She leaned in closer, touching her forehead to mine. "You're not weak, Gabe. You're strong, and you're brave for telling me your feelings. I'm here for you, no matter what you have to say."

I let out a deep breath. "I... can't get it up lately..."

Avery pulled back from our embrace and looked at me with a hint of surprise. "What do you mean?"

I felt my face flush with embarrassment, but I knew I couldn't keep this bottled up any longer. "I mean, when we're... together, or whenever, I think about trying to be intimate with you... Or even by myself in the shower, I just haven't been able to... you *know*."

Avery's expression softened and she cupped my face in her hands. "Gabe, that doesn't make you any less of a man. Sometimes things like that happen, and it's completely normal. We can work through this together."

"I just can't make you feel good." I ducked my head so she couldn't see the shame burning in my eyes.

Her fingers cupped my chin and forced me to look at her. "Gabriel, yes you can, there's more to intimacy than fucking, you know?"

I nodded, but I couldn't help feeling like I was letting her down. "I know, but it still feels like I'm not enough, you know? Like I'm not giving you everything you need."

Avery leaned in and kissed me gently, her lips soft against mine. "Listen to me, Gabe. You are enough. More than enough. You make me feel loved, and cherished, and desired. And that's all that matters."

I felt a lump form in my throat as I looked into her eyes. "I love you, Avery."

"I love you too, Gabe." Her voice was soft, but steady. "And don't feel ashamed. We can go at your pace, whenever you're ready to explore, we can try other things. Maybe it's due to the stress, you know? There's a lot of stuff going on right now and Nik and Roman haven't really been pulling their weight. I know they haven't and it's mainly my fault." Her face looked crushed.

"No, it's not your fault, it's theirs. They've always slacked a bit and I've always naturally taken the lead with things, but I can't do everything for everyone anymore. Maybe you're right. Maybe once some of this stress is lifted, he will rise once again."

She chuckled at my poor sense of humor, leaning in to give me a soft kiss. I felt a sense of relief wash over me at Avery's words. She always knew how to make me feel better, how to ease my worries and doubts.

As we continued to kiss, our hands started exploring each other's bodies, I knew that Avery was right. There was more to intimacy than just sex. We could explore each other in other ways, take our time, and discover new things together.

I pulled away from the kiss, looking into her eyes. "Thank you," I whispered. "You always know how to make me feel better."

She smiled. "That's my job, now be quiet and let me enjoy you."

I leaned back, covered in dried blood, but fully healed, watching as this glorious angel worked her way down my body, peppering me with kisses. I stopped her before she reached my waistband. "Avery..."

"Shhh, I know." She respected my wish and instead, knelt, one knee on each side of me and pulled off her shirt slowly, dropping her hands to caress her breasts. Then she stood and pushed her pants over her hips before standing over top of my face, giving me the best view a man could ask for. I couldn't resist. I grabbed her hips and pulled her down to meet my waiting mouth. She moaned, and I felt the vibrations run through me. The taste of her hit me like a drug and I couldn't get enough.

Avery's hands were tangled in my hair as I worked her over with my tongue. The soft whimpers that were escaping from her lips were my undoing and I wanted so much more.

But Avery was in control, teasing me with her body. She moved away from me for a moment before leaning backwards and rubbing her pussy over my stubble and moaning while she did so.

She whispered, her voice lusty and full, "I want to fuck your face until I cum all over it."

I grinned. "That so?"

"Mmhm." She licked her lips. "You have a problem with that?"

She groaned and worked on grinding against my chin as I pulled her down, my tongue going to work on her clit. I didn't stop until I had licked her to the point of madness and by then, she was so wet, it was dripping down my face.

"Enough," she moaned as she pushed up from my face. She got up, pulling off my pants as I gasped, my exposed cock was semi.

"What are you doing?" I said, fear creeping into my voice.

"I'm going to blow you while you eat me out, if you get hard, you get hard, if not that's fine because this is for me. I want to do this for you. For us. Are you willing to be vulnerable enough to let me try?"

I swallowed hard. "Okay... Bring that sexy ass over here." As long as I was distracted by bringing her pleasure, my embarrassment would abate. Hopefully.

She smiled, a satisfied gleam in her eye and moved herself over top of me. I began to kiss her thighs as she suckled my cock, taking it into her mouth with abandon. I could feel the pleasure start to build up inside me and I closed my eyes, diving into this beautiful moment of being taken care of for once. Her moans sent me through the roof as I felt myself harden inside her mouth. We continued like that for what seemed like an eternity, our bodies rocking in unison as we each brought the other over the edge until finally, we both came down from our high and settled against each other in blissful exhaustion.

It seemed that Avery was right, doing away with the stress might be the catalyst to keeping my dick hard.

"See? I knew you just needed to get out of your head. There's nothing wrong with you Gabe, and even if you didn't get hard, there STILL wouldn't be anything wrong with you. You're incredible, gorgeous, brilliant, and MINE."

The cute way she half-snarled the last word made me chuckle. "Yes ma'am."

"Should we sleep or go get something to eat?" she said, yawning into my chest.

"Definitely take a nap," I whispered as her snores carried me into my own peaceful dreams.

# Thirty-Two: Avery

Selene met me in my dream. This one was different to all the others. In this one she looked... tired, worn down. She wasn't glowing anymore, and her hair looked dull and lifeless. Her eyes, though, held a ferocity they hadn't before.

"Avery, you need to hurry. Please. You need to go a bit faster with your learning. I know you're enjoying your mates, and that's lovely. That's why I gave them to you. But he's here and he's growing more powerful with each passing day. The dream realm was supposed to be for you to learn, but there's more evil lurking in the shadows than in the light. I am going to block your access to it. You need to find other ways to continue your training. He's coming for you, Avery. I don't know when, but it will be soon."

Her words sent a shiver down my spine. Who was she talking about, and why did I need to hurry my training? Was it Belial? Amrin? Something else entirely? So many questions and she was just cryptic as fuck. I had only just discovered my powers, and I was still struggling to control them. The more time I spent in the dream realm, the better I got, but I still hadn't practiced outside of that space.

"Selene, please, who do I go to for help? I'm all alone. I don't know what to do, or where to go." I looked at her and watched as her eyes welled with tears. "Go and find Osric. He will help you. He's always been loyal to me, and he will be loyal to you too. He will guide you, but you must be careful. The darkness is coming, and it will consume anyone who isn't strong enough to resist it."

"Who is Osric? How do I find him?"

"He is an ancient being, one that has not been awoken for many centuries. He lies in the depths of the forest, hidden away from prying eyes. You must seek him out and awaken him from his slumber. But be warned, Avery. He is not to be trifled with. He will test you, push you to your limits to ensure that you are worthy. But if you pass his test, he will become a powerful ally in the fight against darkness."

I nodded solemnly, taking in her words. It was clear that I had no choice but to heed her advice. I needed to find Osric and wake him from his slumber. But how? I had never heard of this ancient being before, and I had no clue where to even start looking.

"Use your Spirit, Avery. You have it in you to seek anyone, heal anyone... destroy anyone. You just need to use the Spirit."

Before I could ask any more questions, her eyes darted around. "He's here. You must go. *Now.*" With a quick shove, I fell back into my body, drenched in sweat and shivering. Gabriel was sitting at the edge of the bed, his mouth gaping wide.

"Avery... you're..."

Glowing. I was glowing. In fact, with each passing second, the light got brighter. So bright that Gabe had to shield his face.

"Gabe... I think you should leave. I don't know what's happening to me." Gabe nodded and backed away, still shielding his face from the bright light emanating from me. I closed my eyes and focused on my Spirit, feeling its power course through my veins. I could sense the darkness all around me, pulsing as if the earth was allowing me to feel the root of evil, while it was lurking just below the surface, waiting to pounce.

But I wouldn't let it consume me. With a deep breath, I stepped forward, my entire body now engulfed in a brilliant white light. I could feel the power within me surging, pulsing with an intensity I had never felt before. My skin tingled, it felt indestructible as my eyes adjusted to the brightness emanating from within me. As I stood there, basking in the glory of my light, I smiled. This was what true power felt like and I wanted more. I wanted to be able to control it, mold it, use it to protect the ones I love. Osric was out there, waiting for me to find him, and with my Spirit residing inside of me, I was confident that nothing could stand in my way.

I raised my hands, and from within the light, a beam shot out, piercing through the ceiling of the room. The beam continued upward, reaching high into the sky until it disappeared. I had no control over what was happening, but it felt like my Spirit was leading the way, guiding me towards my destiny.

I closed my eyes and focused on quelling the light. There was no way I could face my mates shining like a lighthouse on crack. Within a second, it had disappeared, and I was normal again.

"Gabe?" I called out, just as he barreled into the room.

"Oh, my Goddess, Avery, what the hell was that! You were all glowing and then I heard something... I guess the roof," he said, looking up at the giant hole, "break and I couldn't get in because the doorknob was basically on fire. What the hell?"

"I don't know. I went to the dream realm and saw Selene and then came back and I was glowing. I think this is one of my powers."

Gabe's eyes widened. "You can basically harness the power of the sun?" he asked incredulously. "That's amazing! I don't even know what to say..."

I nodded slowly, still in shock myself. "I think so. I don't know where they came from or how to control them, but I can feel them inside me."

Gabe stepped closer and reached out a hand to touch my arm tentatively. "Do you feel different?" he asked softly.

I closed my eyes and focused on the sensation. "Yes," I whispered. "It's like there's something inside me, something powerful and ancient. It's like a second heartbeat, pulsing and surging with energy."

Gabe's expression shifted from awe to concern. "Are you okay?" he asked, his voice laced with worry.

"I'm okay, Gabe," I assured him. "I just need to figure out how to control this power. I... I can also control fire and air... but I don't know how to control it."

"Damn, Avery... You're something else."

"You're right, I am. And now I've been tasked with finding something named Osric."

"Osric? Are you sure? How do you know that name?"

"Selene told me to find him, and he will help me channel my powers. Why what do you know?"

He hesitated. "I think we should chat about this with Roman and Nik. Nik especially, he will want to hear this."

Before I could agree or disagree, they both crashed through the front door like a couple of drunk frat boys. We quickly ushered them to the table.

"What's up, guys?" Roman slurred, throwing his arm around Gabe's shoulders. "Did we miss anything exciting?"

Nik, who was a little more sober than Roman, eyed us all curiously. "What's going on?"

A moment of hesitation swept over me before I decided to tell them everything. I explained about Selene, the dream realm, and my powers. Their reactions ranged from disbelief to surprise to awestruck wonder.

"And then Selene told me to find someone named Osric who can help me control my powers," I finished.

"Osric," Nik repeated thoughtfully. "I've heard that name before..."

"Yes. You have." Gabe cut in smoothly. "He is the ancient Lycan. The first. Built in the image of the titans. Large, imposing, terrifying in every aspect." My pulse quickened at the thought of meeting an ancient being like Osric. It was hard to imagine what kind of power he could possess.

"I think we should find Osric," Roman said, his eyes glittering with excitement. "It'll be an adventure."

"An adventure?" I repeated, incredulous. "This isn't a game, Roman. This is dangerous."

"I'm not saying it's a game," he replied, his tone serious now. "But it's obvious that you can't control your powers by yourself. We need someone who can help you. And if Osric really is as powerful as Selene says he is, then he might be our best bet."

I frowned, unsure. It did make sense, but the idea of seeking out an ancient Lycan filled me with unease. "But how do we even find him? Selene didn't give me any clues other than that he's in the forest and I should use my Spirit to find him."

Nik spoke up, a sly grin on his face. "I have a contact who might be able to help us. He's well-connected in the supernatural world, and he owes me a favor. I can give him a call and see what he knows about Osric."

I nodded slowly, feeling a sense of relief wash over me. At least we had a plan now.

"Nik..." Gabe said.

"Yes?"

"Osric is your ancestor. He's where you came from."

"How did you know I was a Lycan? I only just found out like... recently-ish," Nik said inquisitively.

"I've sensed for a while, that you're not like us. I didn't want to push you, but you must know that Osric was put into a slumber by his own people?"

Nik's expression darkened, his eyes narrowing in suspicion. "Why would they do that? And why haven't you told me about this before?"

"It's complicated," Gabe replied, his voice low. "Osric was a powerful Lycan who believed in using our abilities to enslave humans. He was so powerful, he could have done it, and many of our kind rebelled against him. In the end, it was the Lycans who were able to put him into a deep sleep, but it came at a great cost. Many Lycans were killed, and those who survived went into hiding. Like your family, Nik. They created ties with the werewolves and our pack was created."

"So why would we want to wake him up?" I asked, now terrified of waking this blood thirsty super-being.

"In order to beat evil, you either become it... or release it." Gabe said, carefully guarding his next words. "Selene believes he can help you, Avery. Likely because you are a Seraphina, another of a long-lost line of ancients, he will help you hone your skills. He has his own set of skills that he had to learn how to control on his own. He was created by Selene for balance. When she realized that he felt superior to the humans, she created the Seraphina to balance him. You and Osric are complete opposites, but you create. You are balance."

"So, what do we do now?" Avery asked.

"We go to the place where they put Osric to sleep," Gabe replied.

"Where is that?" Nik asked.

"It's a place that only a few of us know about," Gabe said. "We have to travel to the other side of the world to get there."

"Wait a minute," Roman interjected. "How do you know so much about all of this? And Nik, what the hell man?"

"Sorry dude, I wasn't ready." Nik shrugged, stuffing his mouth full of chips before turning back to Gabe. "Yeah, how do you know all of this Gabe?"

"My father was meticulous about passing history down to me. You know, while you were out shagging girls and Roman was busy playing sports. I was learning for my role."

"Right. Stupid question." Roman grinned.

"So how do we wake him up?" I asked tentatively.

Gabe sighed. "There is a ritual that must be performed. It involves a great deal of power and must be done correctly. Selene will be there to guide us, but we must first retrieve Osric."

"Right, so where is his body?"

"In the rainforest of the Amazon. Strap in guys, we're going on a plane."

"Okay... but not right now, right?" Roman said.

Gabe chuckled. "No, I need to contact a friend to arrange a private flight, it'll take a few days."

"Great, can we order some pizza? I'm starving." Roman said as he patted his belly.

"Yes, drunk too by the looks of it. How did you get any work done today?" I asked, throwing him an apple.

"By the grace of the Goddess and the sweat on my brow." He frowned, putting the apple down and moved away to call in for a pizza delivery.

Nik took the moment to move closer to me. "How are you feeling about all this Avery? It's a lot to take in."

I took a deep breath, trying to keep my emotions in check. "I'm terrified, but also excited. I never thought I'd be a part of something like this, you know?"

"I know what you mean," Nik said with a smile. "It's like we're living in a fantasy or something."

Gabe nodded in agreement. "The journey we're about to undertake is not for the faint of heart. But I believe in all of us. We can do this."

I smiled at my three men, knowing that Selene had picked the best of the best, just for me. Watching as they bantered back and forth to release some of the tension, brought me a sense of peace. There was nothing these guys wouldn't do for me, and somehow, knowing that made me want to protect them even more.

# Thirty-Three: Amrin

I'd found a body to inhabit. It was old. Weathered. It was hot as hell down here too, so half the time I roamed naked. It stunk to high heaven and quite frankly, I missed the cold darkness of living inside the cage Braden loved to keep me in. Searching for a way out of the Underworld was no easy task. Pretty much everyone I came across refused to help, or tried to and was subsequently eaten by these massive flying creatures that circled over top of me all hours of the day.

Fortunately, after a particularly grueling day, I stumbled upon a small village that looked like it had been untouched for centuries. The buildings were made of stone and vines crawled up the walls. I cautiously approached a group of unfortunate looking people who were huddled together, whispering frantically to each other. They stopped talking as soon as they saw me, their eyes widening in fear.

"Who are you?" one of them asked, trembling.

"I'm looking for a way out of this place," I replied, trying to sound as friendly as possible.

They whispered amongst themselves before one of them spoke up.

"There is a way out, but it's dangerous," she said, her voice quivering. "You—" Her eyes widened. "Oh no, no, I can't be talking to you. Everyone is under strict orders not to engage with you unless they want—"

A loud screech sounded in the sky as one of those things swooped in furiously. I instinctively ducked, but the creature didn't seem to be interested in me. Instead, it grabbed one of the villagers and flew away with them in its sharp talons.

"The Harpies," the woman whispered, her face pale. "They're your curse. You won't be able to go or do anything without them finding you."

I looked up at the sky, watching as the other creatures circled around us, screeching and cackling. It was then that I noticed something strange happening to my body. My skin began to shimmer and glow, and as I looked down, I saw that it was covered in intricate, glowing symbols.

"What's happening to me? What is this place?"

The woman gasped as she looked at me. "You have been marked by the goddess," she whispered, her eyes wide with wonder and fear.

I suddenly felt a chill run down my spine. "What do you mean?"

"The markings are a sign that you have been chosen by the goddess to perform a great task," she explained. "It is said that those who bear these symbols will be able to pass through the Underworld."

I looked at the symbols on my skin in amazement. It was like nothing I had ever seen before, yet somehow, it felt familiar. "What task?" I asked her.

"I don't know, I don't know. I just know that you can pass back, IF you can find a way out, but I cannot speak with you anymore." She turned in a huff and went inside just as another Harpy slammed on the door, rattling its hinges.

*Well then. If I'm somehow marked by Selene, I need to find a stronger body to carry what's left of my soul because this one was old, and it is starting to stink.* I shuddered at the thought of my decaying, frail body, but there was no time to dwell on it. The Harpies were getting closer to breaking down the door, and I needed to find a way out of this cursed village.

As I ran through the narrow streets, I caught sight of a group of warriors gathered in the town square. They were armed with swords and shields, ready to defend their homes against the Harpies.

I approached them cautiously, my glowing symbols drawing their attention. They eyed me warily, unsure what to make of me.

"Hello." I said, smiling. "Mind if I ask for a favor?"

"Wh... what is it?" one of them said, eyeing me up and down, puffing out his chest.

"I need to... borrow your body."

The warriors looked at me in shock, unsure what to make of my strange request. I could see their hands twitching on the hilts of their swords as they evaluated me.

"Why do you need one of our bodies?" one asked, suspicion in his voice.

"I assure you, it's for a good cause," I said, trying to sound as sincere as possible. "This old body is frail and weak. But with your help, I can continue on my way."

They exchanged a glance before squaring up. "No. I know what you are. You're a soul jumped. I do not consent to giving you my body to house your filth."

I laughed so hard I started sputtering, "I don't need your consent. What do you think this is the 5th grade and I'm asking to share your candy bar? No. I have someone very important to me that I need to get back to. You can either choose who I will inhabit, or I will choose for you."

At the mention of choosing for them, the warriors bristled, their hands tightening around their weapons. But as they looked at me, with my glowing symbols and ragged appearance, they hesitated.

"We cannot simply offer our bodies to a stranger," the tall one said, his voice low and concerned. "What would happen to us?"

"I'd return it to you as soon as I am done with it." I wouldn't, buddy was going to die the minute I entered him, but he didn't need to know that. Quite frankly, I was surprised he was even considering it. He seemed kind of like a simpleton. *Perhaps I should go for the quiet, broody one standing off to the corner, cleaning his teeth with a rusty knife.*

"I don't know..." the simpleton continued.

"Enough. I have chosen," I bellowed as they all stared at me. As fast as lightning, I lifted my soul out of this bag of bones and went straight for the quiet one, entering him without resistance and feeling the strength of his body humming under the weight of my soul.

"Ahhhh, much better." Cracking my neck, I watched the men scatter, terrified. As if I was going to devour them. *Silly guys, I just needed a stronger host until I could claim my own body back from that wretched demon I made a pact with.*

Turning back the way I came, I trudged straight past the house where I gained the glowing tattoos. It was rubble now, flesh and bone everywhere. The Harpies had moved on, but I could feel their eyes on me. It was time to find the door that would lead me out of this hellhole.

I walked for hours, navigating through the barren wasteland that used to be a lush forest by the looks of these giant tree stumps. It was a strange place. The Underworld. It was almost as if it used to be a beautiful place. You could still see the remnants of beauty every now and then, but it was mostly the further out from the main hub you got. It felt like a petulant child set fire to everything during a tantrum and ignored the fact that he was destroying the very thing he created. The quiet one's body was strong and agile, and I felt invigorated with every step I took. The tattoos on my arms glowed brighter with each passing moment, signaling that I was getting closer to my goal.

Finally, as the moon was high in the sky, I reached an ancient oak tree that was unlike anything I had ever seen before. Its trunk was massive, easily big enough for ten men to circle it and still not touch hands. The branches stretched up into the sky, disappearing into the darkness overhead. It was strange. The only tree for miles and miles and it was untouched by the death around it.

Without hesitation, I placed my hand on the rough bark of the tree trunk, and a shock ran through my body. I knew this was it— the door to the other side.

I pushed against the tree, and it gradually began to open like a portal. As the gap widened, I could see a faint light shining from the other side. I stepped through, and the world around me changed instantly.

I was standing in a grand hall, with columns of marble stretching up into the darkness above. The air was thick with a nauseating scent of decay and sulfur, and I could hear the groans of lost souls echoing through the hall.

At the end of the room, on a raised platform, sat a hooded figure, staring at me with soulless eyes. A beautiful woman stood to his right, watching me curiously.

"Amrin, you've finally made it."

"Is this?"

"Yes, child, you've been here before. Many lifetimes ago. Much has changed since your last visit." Her voice was weak, tired.

"Selene." Falling to my knees, I began to sob. "I... I..."

"Yes, I know. You are sorry for the hell you've unleashed. It is too late to take it back. In fact, you now stand on the graveyard of the other council members. Him and I are all that remain." She cracked as she stepped closer to me.

I looked up at her, tears streaming down my face. "Selene, please tell me there's something I can do. Anything to make this right."

She laughed bitterly. "Make it right? You can't make it right, Amrin. You've doomed us all. Your lust for power has cost us our world."

I hung my head in shame, the weight of my actions crushing me. "I... I didn't know it would come to this. I only wanted my mate back."

"She was never yours, child. She always belonged to them. What happened to you was unfortunate, but it was written in the threads of time to begin and end the way it did. She needed to experience heartache, to accept her love, her powers, her destiny."

"But what about me? I loved her!" I wailed.

"Oh Amrin. I had someone for you. She was beautiful. She would have brought you peace and joy. Braden would have destroyed that too and then I would have given you the choice to leave him and find a suitable counterpart. But your foolishness got in the way. And now look." She waved her arms around the hall.

"They're all dead," I said, numbness finally settling over me. "Because of me."

"Lost souls, doomed to wander these halls. Unless Avery can make it right."

"Avery?" I looked up at Selene, a glimmer of hope in my eyes.

"Yes, Avery. The only one who can save us now." She looked at me with sadness in her eyes. "But you know what it will cost you, don't you?"

I nodded, understanding dawning on me. "My life. It's the only way."

Selene nodded solemnly. "It is. But it's not just your life. Avery will need to take a part of you with her, a part of your soul. It will be painful, but it's the only way to reverse what you've done."

I took a deep breath. "And if I don't?" I wasn't ready to die. I didn't deserve this. All of this was because my stupid human rejected the most divine being. Everything I've done was so I could get back to her. She was the light in the darkness, and she was the only thing I wanted.

Her eyes flashed. "Then you will have made the decision to be the beginning of the end."

# Thirty-Four: Roman

"Yo guys, this plane is siiiiiick," I said, dumping my bags on the floor and lounging on the bed in the back. "Hey babe, wanna come take this puppy for a spin?"

Avery's laughter was music to my ears. "No," she said before winking. "At least not right now. The flight is long with several stops so... let's just enjoy, yeah? See where the mood takes us."

Nik shot me a disgusted look. "Yeah, Roman, she doesn't wanna play with your wang, she wants to play with mine," he said jutting his hips out and made a slow grinding motion.

"Dear Goddess, you are both like horny dogs. Sit in your seats," Gabe said, but not without a small smirk. "The hostess will be on board shortly and we need to TRY and behave so we don't terrify her. She doesn't know about us." His tone was low, warning.

*Ahh, so he booked us with some human friends of his. It's so weird to think that he even has any of those, what with his powerful aura he almost never controls. Most of our pack has gotten used to the way it feels, but he has one of the strongest presences I know of. Dude is an absolute beast and I'd never want to be on his wrong side. Thank the heavens he got his anger issues under control when he did, or this pack would have been burnt to the ground long before someone else did it.*

"Gabe, we will behave," Nik and I said simultaneously.

"So, tell me, is the plane ours for the journey or are there other passengers?" Avery said as she busied herself putting her bags away. She was an organized lady. Truly a woman after my own heart.

"Nope," Gabe said. "All ours." I didn't miss the way he said it, that seductive, sultry tone turning my girl's ears pink. *Oh boy, is she in for the time of her life.*

"Time to join the mile high club," Nik and I high fived before scrambling to our seats under Avery's death glare. Gabe shook his head in amusement, a small chuckle escaping his lips before he settled into his seat. The hum of the engines surrounded us as we lifted off the ground and into the air.

Avery's eyes widened as we ascended through the clouds, her grip on the armrests tightening slightly. I reached out and placed my hand on top of hers, giving it a reassuring squeeze. She turned to look at me and flashed a small smile, grateful for the comforting touch.

The flight attendant soon made her way down the aisle, her eyes flickering over our group with a mixture of curiosity and apprehension. Gabe stiffened beside me, his gaze never leaving the attendant's face. It was as if he was sizing her up, testing her. I knew that he could easily detect any lies or hidden intentions, so it made sense that he was wary. Always the cautious one, Gabe was.

"Can I get you all something to drink?" the attendant asked, breaking the tense silence that had settled over our group.

"Whiskey, neat," Gabe said, his voice firm.

"A Bloody Mary for me," Nik said, winking at the attendant.

"A glass of water, please," Avery said politely.

"I'll take a gin and tonic," I added, grinning at Nik's playful antics. "And the lady will also have a ginger ale and some crackers. Motion sickness." I gestured to her rather large bump.

The flight attendant nodded, scribbling our orders down in her notebook before making her way to the front of the plane. I could see Avery relaxing a little, her shoulders dropping as the attendant disappeared.

"So, the Amazon, eh?" *This is going to be interesting.* I'd never been to the Amazon, let alone on a hunt for some old petrified Lycan, but hey, adventures were always fun.

"Yeeeeeep," Gabe said, closing his eyes.

I watched as Avery unbuckled her seatbelt and made her way out of her seat before laying down on the bed. "Ah, so much better. That seat is so cramped."

I didn't have the heart to tell her that it's because over the last few weeks her ass had grown a few inches in width, along with her feet. But to be fair, every time I saw the sway of her hips, my dick wouldn't stay down. I was insanely attracted to her in her non-pregnant body, but with child? This woman would straight up rival Selene for the title of Goddess.

"Lemme just scooch on by here," I said, ignoring the glare Nik was shooting my way.

"Don't even think about it, Romeo. She is all of ours and if she's joining the mile high club today, so am I."

"And me," Gabe said lazily.

"I just want to go snuggle," I whined.

"Sure, you do. Come on, let's all go snuggle her then."

"Fine," I huffed before rushing to the bed and hopping in beside her. I slung an arm around her torso and pulled her close, ignoring the small elbow jabbing in my side and the loud laughter from Nik as he made his way to the bed.

The waitress handed us our drinks before scurrying back to the cabin at the front.

"Phew, this is strong," I said, sputtering as I took a sip.

"Lightweight," Nik said before he downed his drink.

"Can you be the designated drink mule the rest of the trip?" I asked Avery.

"What the hell is a drink mule?" she said, eyeing me in suspicion.

"You know, the person who carries the load for the drunk ones. AKA, me and Nik. I don't think Gabe has ever been sloshed out of his tree, because that would mean giving up some control for like the hour it takes for our systems to be rid of the poison."

"I resent that comment," Gabe said as he pushed me away from Avery and settled in front of her. "However," he said, extending his arms and putting them behind his head. "I don't have anything to gain from being drunk, so I'll take the drink mule duty if you must get hammered. Avery can take sexy duty and strip for us."

I frowned, but he winked at me, and I couldn't help but snort. The guy knew how to work it. Not that Avery had any complaints, as she was currently munching on crackers and drinking her ginger ale while her features flushed a deep red.

Gabe started off by unbuttoning her blouse and then removed his own, tossing it on the floor. He moved down and kissed her neck as he slowly undid the buttons of her jeans. His strong hands worked around her body as if he was making love to her with just those tiny actions, and I could see Avery visibly trembling from anticipation.

His lips met hers in a hot passionate kiss that I felt through my entire body. Nik pushed me aside gently so he could suckle on Avery's breasts, while Gabriel's hands moved up and down her body exploring every inch of skin that was visible to him. They both knew how to make a woman feel like she was the most beautiful creature on the planet, and I watched as Avery closed her eyes and moaned softly. I almost got up to go and "brush my teeth" from watching her half naked body respond to the touch of her men, but I was transfixed. This little minx had such a hold over us, I don't even think she understood it. Pulling my pants off, I lounged on the side of the bed, letting Nik and Gabe pleasure her to within an inch of her life as I slowly stroked my dick.

She had tiny pearl-like beads of sweat on her forehead and cheeks and was breathing slowly through her parted lips. She was completely exhausted and completely pleased by the looks of things. Nik and Gabe were coming up for air as she came down from a strong orgasm. My heart pounded as I considered taking her then, but I couldn't move as I watched the rise and fall of her chest.

It wasn't until she looked at me and licked her lips that my control broke like a flood. Rushing over to her, I kissed her with such force, I bruised her lips instantly. The groan in my mouth was all the encouragement that I needed.

"I want you all to come on me... at the same time." She panted. "I want to feel every single way that you want me."

"Jesus Christ." I wasn't sure who said it, but even my cock jumped a little at those words. Clearly this woman was magic.

"You really want us to... *together*... with you?" My voice sounded hoarse, but she nodded, and I looked back at Nik and Gabriel for confirmation.

"Please," she begged between desperate breaths.

"I want everyone to see me, to get on me and around me," she said with a little rational thought in her voice. "I want my pussy to be drenched with all your babies."

Nik burst out laughing, but Gabriel and I chuckled.

"Your wish is our command." I smiled and kissed her head.

Gabe and I moved in at the same time and before she knew it, we were both taking turns kissing her. It was the first time we got to kiss her at the same time and something about it was... I don't know... right. The four of us together were perfection at its finest.

Gabe pulled her hair back as I licked the delicate skin between her breasts, and she moaned.

I couldn't hold on any longer. This woman was the devil with the body of an angel. Within seconds, I'd unleashed my load all over her inner thighs, painting her the prettiest picture. Next came Gabe, followed quickly by Roman. She squealed as I pressed my thumb into her clit, pulling out one last orgasm before collapsing beside her.

"Wow," she said.

"Wow is right," Nik chuckled, playing with her hair. "I didn't know sex could be so intimate without like... actually fucking, you know?"

Gabe slapped him upside the head. "You're such a moron, shut the fuck up."

"Go to sleep Avery," I whispered, watching as Nik went to grab a cloth and gently wiped her clean. "We still have many... many hours of flight time left."

"You're a dog, you know that?" Gabe said, getting up and pulling on his clothes.

"And you're so perfect, Mr. White Knight. God, let go once in a while. Don't you wanna be down and dirty sometimes? Doesn't it get exhausting being in control all the time?" I said, genuinely curious.

He turned to look at me. "Yes, actually, it does. But if I don't keep things running, who will? The goofball or the reformed man-slut?"

His words were like a slap to the face. "Woah man, easy. That was a bit harsh."

He sighed. "I'm sorry, that was uncalled for." Running his hands through his hair, he looked at Avery before going and sitting down, Nik and I following.

"What's going on man? You're wound tighter than a virgin."

"I dunno. I've been so stressed, my dick stopped working for weeks. I can't handle everything on my own anymore, you know? I really need you guys to step up and help. That means actually getting stuff done without me asking, and not getting drunk while you're doing it." Gabe sighed and I could see the exhaustion now that I was really looking.

"Man... I'm so sorry," Nik said, putting a hand on his shoulder. "I had no idea you felt this way."

"Why didn't you tell us sooner?"

"I don't know. I guess I thought that if I shouldered the load, you two could keep Avery safe, but now I kind of understand that we all need to rotate," he said with a sigh.

"We fucked up, dude. When we get back, things will change. We will do better. Promise," Nik said, downing another drink.

"And we promise not to get drunk on work hours," I added before taking a sip of my own.

"Well... drunk no, but drinks... yes?" Nik said, his eyes pleading. "Please Gabe, this shit is so boring, I can't tolerate it without a small buzz."

"Fine," Gabe said with a small smile. "But no excessive drinking, we have images to uphold."

Before I could say another word, the speaker boomed. *"Please buckle yourselves, we will be landing for a refuel in 25 minutes."*

# Thirty-Five: Avery

I t was weird dreaming but not being in the dream realm. I'd gotten so used to finding my way there and exploring that I'd forgotten what dreams without purpose were. Somehow it brought me a sense of comfort, but also a mild feeling of terror. Selene said I'd never be able to go back there, but I wanted to. I was finally getting the hang of creating my own environments and she pulled my entry ticket. Instead, I started practicing how to lucid dream. I'd alternate between dreaming of being boned by my sexy mates and saving the world like some kind of superwoman. Sometimes, both.

I'll say, I wasn't expecting to be thrown into a dream where I was giving birth, but here I was, laying on a table in a white room with my legs up in stirrups. Honestly, it was uncomfortable. How ridiculous that I have to birth on my back, rather than on all fours like intended. Listening to my body seemed much more intuitive than to well-meaning nurses who had no idea the physiology of birth. As the sharp pain of a contraction hit me, I let out a deep groan and closed my eyes. This wasn't the first time I'd had a dream like this, but it always felt so real. I looked around the room and saw Amrin standing at my side,

nervously wringing his hands. Somehow, he felt out of place...
like he didn't belong, but I couldn't place the source of feeling.
He was watching me with a burning intensity as he tried to
speak but no sound came out.

I took a deep breath and focused on the sensation of the
contraction. My body was working hard to bring new life into
the world, and I was determined to let it do its job. As I pushed,
I felt the baby's head crowning and a wave of relief wash over
me. Suddenly, the room began to spin, and I was suspended in
mid-air. When I opened my eyes, I saw that I was no longer in
the white room, but in a dark forest, with Amrin nowhere in
sight.

Panic set in as I realized that I had no idea what had happened. Had the birth been successful? Was my baby safe? I
struggled to stand up, but a sharp pain in my abdomen made
me double over. Looking down, I saw blood pooling at my feet
and my heart raced with fear. What was happening to me?

Suddenly, I heard a rustling in the bushes behind me. I turned
around frantically, trying to see what was coming. Was it a
predator? Was it a rescuer? But as the bushes parted, a figure
emerged that made my heart skip a beat.

It was the big black wolf with the red eyes. He was large and
imposing as he stalked towards me, watching me with curiosity
before eyeing my life spill down my legs into a dark puddle. Who
was this wolf? What did he want? It paced back and forth before
I understood that I was to follow it. I stumbled behind the wolf
as we navigated our way through the dark forest. My breaths

came out in short gasps as I clutched my stomach in agony. As we walked, I couldn't help but feel as though I was being led towards something... or someone.

Eventually, we reached a clearing and I saw him. A figure, petrified with time, laying like a massive boulder. Beautiful wildflowers grew in a circle around him, not too close to where he lay in his slumber. As I turned to look at the wolf, he had disappeared, leaving me with the being before me. My inquisitive nature just couldn't leave well enough alone, so I walked closer. As I walked, the blood stopped flowing and life returned, my legs grew stronger and my stomach stopped aching.

That was when I saw it. My baby was laying at its feet, while color began to swirl around the figure, leeching life from my own child. I felt a surge of anger and fear rushing through me as I watched this ominous figure draining my baby's life away. Without hesitation, I lunged forward to grab my baby from the grasp of this monster. As I picked up my infant, the figure slowly got up. My hands started glowing as the wind picked up, swirling ominously around us, creating a shield. Lightning crackled in the distance, striking closer and closer the more anger spread through me.

His eyes met mine and I could see the agelessness reflecting back at me. He was old, yet there was a strange light that shone from within him, almost like he was imbued with otherworldly powers. I held my baby close, ready to defend her with everything I had.

The figure spoke in a voice that seemed to resonate within me, "You should not have come here."

Just as I was about to open my mouth and speak, a rumbling outside of my control startled me. I was being shaken, faster and faster while indiscernible yelling filtered through the sky.

"Avery! Avery!" Nik was screaming at me while he shook me violently.

"Wake up, Avery!" Gabe sounded panicked.

I didn't want to wake up, I wanted to stay in this dream. It felt important that I be here, but the longer I stayed, the more I was being yelled at.

Waking with a start, I saw the sky around the plane descending into darkness as the windows rattled. Nik was still shaking me, trying to get my attention, trying to snap me out of it. "What's going on?" I asked groggily.

"We're in some kind of storm," Gabe shouted over the sound of the wind and rain battering against the plane's metal exterior.

I looked out the window and my heart sank as I saw lightning illuminating the thick clouds that surrounded us. This wasn't just any storm; it was a full-blown tempest.

My mind raced as I tried to figure out what to do. We were way too high up to try to land the plane, and the turbulence was only getting worse. We were at the mercy of the weather.

Roman figured it out first. "Avery, take deep breaths."

Fixing my eyes on him, he helped me count. "1...2...3... that's it, good girl."

As my panic subsided, the rain dissipated, the storm clouds disappeared, and the turbulence ended.

"Avery..." Gabe looked at me incredulously. "Did you know you could do that?"

Not fully understanding what was happening, I looked at him. "Do what?"

"You realize you changed the weather, right?"

I stared at him, unable to comprehend what he was saying. It was crazy. Mystic powers of the likes of which I couldn't even imagine, that I hadn't even understood as something that could even be controlled.

But then I remembered the dream I had been having, and the anger I had felt. Maybe that was the key to controlling all of this... my emotions. I had been in the middle of something powerful, something that felt like it had the ability to change the world. This being was real and I could feel we were getting closer to him.

Maybe, just maybe, there was something to what Gabe was saying. I clutched my stomach protectively as I stared at my mates, and they stared right back, no one able to process what had happened at a speed faster than that of a turtle.

"I need a drink," Roman sighed and walked to the front of the plane.

Nik just sat beside me, frozen, clutching my hand as if it were a lifeline. I'd never seen him so... still. Even Gabe had no idea what to say, confusion etched on his features.

"Avery... We are landing in a few minutes. We... we can try to piece all this together then, okay?" he whispered hoarsely. I nodded, grateful that he was trying to help me make sense of everything. The plane landing was a blur, and before I knew it, I was standing in a new place. The sun was shining down on us, and I felt the heat permeate through my clothes.

As we walked down the steps of the plane, I noticed that there was something different about the air. It was thick, charged with something that I couldn't quite put my finger on. As if on cue, the sky darkened, the wind picked up and a sound like thunder erupted in the distance.

My heart pounded in my chest as I looked around for any indication of what was happening, but all I felt was an unsaid warning. One that was clear as day: leave and don't come back.

"Where are we?" I asked, trying to shove the lump that had grown inside my stomach away.

"Somewhere between home and the Amazon, we were supposed to have more stops, but the pilot couldn't land with the um... storm."

"So how far until we start looking for Osric?"

"4 or 5 hours, give or take. I don't quite know. Not much longer though."

I looked around. "How long are we stopped here?"

"They said we have a day. The pilot is tired, he was getting off a 36 hour run when he was asked to step in for my friend. He obliged, apparently owing him one, but really, he shouldn't have been flying," Gabe said, squeezing my shoulder as we hurried into the small terminal.

"Right. Okay."

Roman came up beside me. "Let's go find some real food, okay? Peanuts and crackers suck and I'm starving."

As we stepped out of the airport after grabbing our carry on, the thick, humid air hit me like a wall. It was almost suffocating. The sky was still dark, but flashes of lightning lit up the horizon in the distance.

"This doesn't feel safe," I muttered, feeling a shiver run down my spine.

"We'll be fine," Gabe said with a reassuring smile. "We'll find Osric within the next day and get out of here as soon as possible."

We headed towards a small town not far from the airport, and as we walked, I couldn't shake off the feeling of being watched. The streets were empty, and the only sounds were our footsteps and the distant rumble of thunder. Eventually, we stumbled upon a small diner with an open sign still lit, and we made our way inside.

The diner was empty except for one other patron, a man sitting at the counter with his back turned towards us. The sound of his spoon scraping against his plate echoed in the empty space.

"Hey, do you guys have any food left?" Roman called out to the man behind the counter.

The man didn't turn around but nodded his head slightly.

"Yeah, sure. Grab a booth and I'll bring you guys some menus."

We sat down and waited for the man to come over.

"Where is everyone?" I whispered.

"I have no idea, but I agree, this place is hella creepy. Do we even trust the food?" Nik said.

"I don't care man, if its poisoned, our healing will fix us, so just eat and we can go back to the airport and sleep there," Roman said, motioning for the waiter to come quickly. The waiter approached our table without so much as a smile, placing the menus down.

"What can I get for y'all?" he asked.

"Some real food, okay? Snack foods suck and I'm starving," Roman said.

The waiter chuckled. "I hear ya. How about some burgers and fries? Goes great with this weather."

We all agreed, and the waiter jotted down our orders before heading back to the kitchen.

As we waited for our food, the man sitting at the counter suddenly turned around to face us. He was old, his face lined with wrinkles and his eyes a piercing green. He stared at us for a moment, making us all uncomfortable, before he finally opened his mouth.

"You kids shouldn't be here," he said in a raspy voice.

"What do you mean?" I asked, my curiosity piqued.

"This ain't a safe place to be, especially at night. You should leave while you still can," he replied, glancing at the window.

"We have no choice. Our pilot needs to rest. Trust me, we don't want to be here either," Nik said, his tone bitter.

The man chuckled, but there was no humor in his laughter. "There are things in this town that shouldn't be messed with. I've seen things that would make your skin crawl," he said, his eyes widening in fear.

"What kind of things?" I asked, my curiosity getting the better of me.

"The kind of things that go bump in the night. The kind of things that lurk in the shadows. You kids should leave while you still can, before it's too late," the man said, his voice shaking.

I glanced at Nik and Roman, who looked just as uncomfortable as I felt. But before any of us could say anything, the waiter returned with our burgers and fries, placing them in front of us.

"Enjoy your meal," he said with a smile before turning to leave.

As we started on our food, the old man's words lingered in my mind. I couldn't shake the feeling that there was something off about this town. Something dangerous that we had stumbled upon. But I pushed those thoughts aside and focused on my meal, knowing that we needed to keep our strength up for whatever lay ahead.

After we finished eating, we paid the bill and headed outside. The air was chilly and the sky was dark, but there was a strange energy in the air. I could feel it buzzing around us, like the town was alive with some kind of hidden power.

Suddenly, we heard a sound and before we could make a break for it, a giant flying monster came barreling towards us.

# Thirty-Six: Nikolai

These things were huge, barreling straight towards Avery. No time to think, we all shifted, forming a circle around the love of our lives.

"Protect Avery at all costs," River snarled, snapping at the wing of one of one of the creatures.

"No shit, Sherlock," Enzo said as he took a chunk from its soft underbelly.

Silver moved in to take it down, not noticing another one behind him. Avery, who had been standing petrified, flew into action. She closed her eyes, focusing all her energy on the magical powers that had been dormant within her for years. Suddenly, the air around her began to vibrate with an otherworldly energy. I couldn't help but stare at her. She was magnificent.

As she opened her eyes, Avery saw the second creature closing in on Silver. Without hesitation, she raised her hand and a beam of brilliant light shot forth, piercing the darkness like a beacon.

The creature let out an ear-splitting screech as it was engulfed by the light, dissolving into a cloud of ash. The first creature, sensing the power of Avery's magic, fled into the night, screeching loudly.

Collapsing to the ground, her body trembled. We shifted back, closing in around her, lifting her and running back into the airport terminal. Laying her gently on one of the old, worn seats, we caressed her forehead.

"Avery," Gabe started, "are you alright?"

"Damn dude, she was amazing!" Roman said a mixture of pride and concern showing on his face. "Did you see how she shot that beam at that thing? How did you even do that Avery?"

She groaned and held her head. "Roman, I love that you're so excited, but honestly, I have a massive headache, so maybe tone it down a bit?"

Avery's words were barely a whisper, but we all heard them. We took a step back, giving her some space. She sat up slowly, rubbing her temples with one hand, and with the other, reached for my hand.

"That was really... strange," she said slowly. "What were those things?"

"They're harpies," a strange voice said from behind us. He was large and imposing as he leaned against a pillar.

Growling, we flanked Avery once more. "Who are you?"

He sighed, making a move towards us, but thought better of it and stayed where he was. "Avery, you know who I am."

She studied him, jealousy coursing through me. "No, I'm sorry, I don't recognize you."

"Right, of course. This isn't how you'd remember me. Last time... I was rather... different." He sounded sad as he said it, casting his eyes to the floor. "I'm Amrin."

She gasped. "Like Braden's wolf? Or demon? Whatever you are..."

He had the decency to look sheepish. "I'm sorry about that... I... made a deal with the devil, literally, to—"

"What do you want?" I snarled, staring daggers at him.

Averys palm was warm as she held my arm tightly. "Let him finish, please, I want to know."

"I wanted to get you back. Belial said he could make that happen. Turns out I made a gross error in judgement and have basically unleashed the Underworld."

"You... you opened the gates of evil for me?"

I couldn't tell if she was flattered or disgusted. Or both.

"Basically. I'd been fighting against Braden for two years to accept and love you. I wanted you, but he kept locking me away. When he rejected you... I... lost it. Sion said he had another way to get you back and like a love-sick puppy, I agreed." A single tear trailed down his face.

"But why do you look like that now? Last time I saw you..."

"Yeah, basically, I refused to obey Belial and he split us in two. Sent me to the Underworld, where I've been fighting those things to get back here. In coming back, I opened the door."

Avery got up. "I need coffee, and a pain killer. This headache is getting worse. When's our flight?"

"Four hours give or take," Gabe responded while checking his watch before quietly eyeing the intruder. "I will go get you a coffee. Roman... Nik..."

"Don't worry, we got her," Roman said, moving to sit beside Avery. She looked so tiny squished in between us.

"Try anything, Amrin, and they will tear you apart."

"I won't," he simply replied before taking a seat opposite us. "I'm just here to talk."

"What do you want to talk about?" she asked, her voice laced with annoyance as she rubbed her temples.

"I wanted to apologize for what I've done," Amrin replied, his voice low and solemn. "I know that opening the gates of the Underworld was a mistake. I never should have made a deal with Belial."

"You think?" Avery muttered, rolling her eyes.

"I'm serious, Avery. I never wanted to hurt you or anyone else. I was just desperate and thought I had no other choice."

Avery sighed. "Okay, I hear you. But what now? You can't just undo what you've done. People have been hurt, killed even. How do we fix this?"

"I don't know," Amrin admitted. "But I want to try. I'm willing to do whatever it takes to make things right. Even if it means letting you go."

Avery looked at him skeptically. "And why should I believe you?"

"You don't have to," he said. "But if you're willing to give me a chance, I can prove to you that I'm on your side."

Avery hesitated, considering his offer. She knew that they were running out of options and time. Maybe giving Amrin a chance was their last hope.

"Fine," she finally said. "But know this, Amrin. If you betray us, I will make sure that there are consequences."

"I understand," he replied, his eyes serious and determined.

Gabe returned with a cup of coffee for Avery and sat down next to her.

"What's going on?" he asked, noticing the tension in the room.

"We're giving Amrin a chance to make things right," Avery replied, taking a sip of her coffee.

Gabe raised an eyebrow. "And how do we know he won't betray us and take you?"

"We don't," Avery admitted. "But we're running out of options and time. We need all the help we can get."

"Well, I don't trust him," Gabe said firmly. "But I'll go along with it for now. If he does anything suspicious, I won't hesitate to dispatch him."

"Understood," Amrin said, nodding his head in agreement.

For the next few hours, he sat silently, watching Avery while she leaned on me, trying to catch a snooze.

"Nik, can you come with me please? Roman, watch over Avery. And you"— Gabe pointed at Amrin— "don't try anything stupid."

"Sure thing, boss," I said with extra attitude. I wanted to stay with Avery, but there were some things I excelled at that Roman didn't and I had a feeling this was one of those things. Probably something bloody. My favorite.

"So, what's the plan?" I asked Gabe, knowing that he wouldn't have asked me to come along just for a casual chat.

"We need to get some information out of this guy," Gabe replied, his tone serious. "He claims to be on our side, but we need to verify it."

"Want me to get rough with him?" I offered, cracking my knuckles. "I can make him talk."

Gabe shook his head. "Not yet. Let's try the good cop, bad cop method. If things turn ugly, Roman can always take Avery on the plane and get out of here."

I nodded. "Sure, but I get to be the bad cop, right? I haven't gotten my hands dirty in a long while."

Gabe smirked. "Of course. I wouldn't have it any other way, Nik."

We walked back to find them all in the exact same position they were in when we left. "Amrin, can we go for a chat?"

He chuckled. "Let me guess, the big scary one is going to rough me up, and the one who looks like a CEO is going to try pretending he wasn't the one to plan this whole ordeal? Sure, sounds fun, let's do it. But just know... I bite."

Excitement curled in my stomach. Oh, he was going to be fun to break. Very fun. Not counting the fact that he scared the living hell out of my love, his arrogant attitude was enough to infuriate me.

"Right, then let's go for a walk. Roman?"

"On it," he said as he shifted Avery so she was curled into his lap, fast asleep.

Gabe and I took on either side of Amrin, leading him down the long dark corridor of the airport. We had noticed that no one was around so it was the perfect place to interrogate someone. Nobody would hear us, nobody would see us.

We stopped in front of a door marked 'Exit'. Gabe banged on the rusty hinges, pushing it open to reveal dead silence and darkness within. I grabbed Amrin's wrist tightly in my hand as we entered the small, abandoned room with only a few chairs and a broken light bulb hanging from the ceiling casting eerie shadows on the wall. The textbook creepy torture room.

"So... You were mates with MY mate and now you're not. You became increasingly salty about that and decided to make horrible life decisions, essentially making the Prophesy come true and now, MY mate will have to fight for her life—technically everyone's lives— to save us all. Did I miss anything, Gabe?"

"Sounds about right, anything to add, Amrin?"

Amrin grinned, a wicked glint in his eye as he leaned back in the rusty chair. "Seems like you have it all figured out. What are you waiting for... Nik? You don't seem the type to have much self-control, so what's stopping you from ending me right now? Unless..."

My hackles were up. This motherfucker thinks he can insult me. "Unless what?"

*Don't say it... don't say it...*

"Unless you're afraid of me. Afraid that Avery will see you for the darkness you really are and will come crawling into my—"

The first fist landed with a heavy thud, snapping his head backward. I saw red as my knuckles connected with Amrin's jaw. I couldn't help but revel in the satisfaction of seeing him wince, blood trickling down his chin. It was exhilarating, and for a moment, I forgot about everything else.

"You're going to pay for what you've done," I growled, the room spinning before fading away and he was all I saw. Gabe grabbed my arm, pulling me back before I could land another blow.

"Nik, stop! This isn't the answer," he said firmly.

I shook my head, trying to clear it. He was right. Violence wasn't going to solve anything. But it sure felt good.

"Get off me, Gabriel. I will only warn you once."

"Or what, Nik? You'll hit me?"

"If I have to, yes. Now move." River was shining through, and Gabe sensed that I was no longer in control. With a heavy sigh, he moved to stand on the opposite wall, giving Amrin a nonchalant shrug.

"I'd suggest just taking it, Amrin, he will keep going until you're nothing but a fleshy pulp if you try to fight back." He gave him a friendly smile. "Not that I really blame him, you know? I have my own dark urges, but I have better control over them than he does."

"Can you shut up please?" River said before landing another punch straight into Amrin's nose. "You're fucking with my flow."

Amrin stumbled back, clutching his face. Blood streamed down his chin, staining the front of his shirt. I grabbed his shirt, pulling him forward until we were nose to nose.

"Don't you ever talk about her again," I growled my voice barely above a whisper. "I know what you want and as long as I breathe, you will NEVER have it."

"You're about to find out what I am," he countered. "And I'll tell Avery everything. I'll tell her what a degenerate person you really are. I'm not afraid of you, Nik."

I punched him again and again until I couldn't feel my hand anymore. "You think she doesn't know about this side of me? She craves this side of me, you mutt. Besides, why would she listen to you anyway? You broke her and I put the pieces back together."

He was struggling to heal as my hands slowed and I wiped the blood off on his shirt. "Because, Nik. I have something you will never have."

"Yeah? And what's that?"

"The child growing in her belly."

# Thirty-Seven: Nikolai

"That's it. Gabe, can I kill him now?"

I looked at him and saw him struggling not to shift. I guess Amrin laying claim to OUR baby, did his head in too. Man, I didn't want to have to stop him from shifting, but I had to become the reasonable one.

Part of why Gabe was so in control all the time was because when he had first shifted, he went on a rampage. He couldn't control Silver and was basically feral. Roman and I had to lock them in the dungeons for a good few months while we taught him how to work with Silver and not give him control. Since then, Gabe had been a beacon of self-control. So much so, that he became incredibly boring. I don't even know how he fucks Avery being so boring, but whatever. Not my can of worms.

"Gabe... Gabe... look at me." I tried to keep my voice calm and steady, but I could feel the anger and frustration bubbling up inside of me. "We can't kill him. As much as I want to rip his throat out, we can't forget that we have a baby on the way and that baby only needs one psycho dad and unfortunately for you, that's me. You of all people should understand the importance of self-control."

Gabe's eyes met mine and I could see the agony in his gaze. He was torn between the animalistic desire to kill and the human understanding that his actions would have consequences.

"You're right," he said softly, his voice barely above a whisper. "I just... I can't stand the thought of him laying claim to MY child."

"Actually, it's mine. You three just decided you'd take in a bastard because you love Avery, but for all your 'it's mine', 'it's ours', it's actually my seed that created it." Amrin smirked, the dried blood cracking on his skin.

"If I were you, I'd shut the fuck up because if Gabe loses control..."

"Oooooh, I'm so scared of buddy in the suit."

He was taunting us now. I'd half the mind to just rip his throat out and be done with it, but we'd wasted enough time with this fool, getting no answers and only receiving frustration in response.

"Gabe, go back to Avery. I'll deal with this."

I could see the tension in his eyes as he fought the warring sides of himself. Finally, his shoulders sagged, and he left without a word.

"Good job, buddy. You got rid of the mentally unstable one. He should really see a shrink for that." Amrin snorted. He wasn't the least bit worried about me.

Ignoring the insult, I leaned in, my fangs sliding into place. There was absolutely nothing I wanted to do more than tear through him, dick and balls first.

"Now, be a good boy and stand up... real slow," I said softly.

"I don't think so."

Opening my eyes, a long string of profanity left me in a fit of incoherent rage. How dare he!

I violently kicked him off the chair, wood splintered as metal cracked, but did nothing but make the chair even more unstable. This time I picked him up by the throat and slammed him against the wall.

"Fucking freak!"

Underneath my hold his face contorted, and a fresh flow of blood whipped through the air as he spat at me.

"Kill me if you want, but then you won't figure out what's coming."

"You sure about that?"

I sank my fangs in deep, the blood pooling out slowly, but he was hesitant now and still very much full of life. He struggled to pull away, but stopped when he felt the rip of his skin. Letting go of him slowly, I grinned.

"Now, tell me about Belial and Sion, and what exactly you did."

Before he could answer, an earth-shattered scream erupted from the terminal.

Amrin's eyes flew wide open as the stench of sulfur floated through the air.

"Belial," he whispered at the same time as I screamed.

"Avery!"

I dropped him like a sack of potatoes and tore out of the room, in time to see the large demon towering over Avery.

"No!"

I watched in horror as the demon locked eyes with me before it grinned and picked her up in his hand. Roman and Gabe were lifeless, smashed against the wall in unnatural angles. I didn't have time to worry about them as I let River take control and rush towards the demon. Before I reached Avery, she looked at me, lifting her arms, she created a shield around them, blocking me from getting to her.

"Avery, don't do this!" I screamed, my voice hoarse as I battered against the shield.

"*I love you*," she said through the mind link before staring directly into the eyes of hell incarnate and disappearing in a brilliant flash of light.

"Oh, my Goddess." Crumpling to the floor, grief consumed me. I could hardly understand what Amrin was saying. I watched, half-dazed, as he went to check on Roman and Gabe.

"They're okay. They're breathing, but they're badly battered," he said, sighing.

"This is all your fault!" I shouted at him, trying to make a move towards him, but my body was frozen.

"Just sit there, I will help Roman and Gabriel. You can kill me after, okay?" he said quietly. "For what it's worth, I didn't know he was going to come here. Nothing would have stopped this."

I couldn't breathe, couldn't think. My mind replayed the image of Avery in Belial's clutches, over and over, as if it was a tape stuck on repeat. Watching as Amrin cracked Roman's broken bones back in place before working on Gabe, I turned off every emotion I had. The grief was all-consuming.

Amrin finally returned to me, helping me sit in a chair before speaking, "he's taken her to the Underworld. She is the only one who is able to stop him, so he will keep her bound tightly."

Roman's eyes were red, as if he had been crying, but his voice was steady. Strong. "How do we get to her?"

"I don't know. I got out through a portal, but I don't know if it's still open, or even how to find it if I did."

Gabe hesitated. "We were on our way to find Osric before"— he choked back a sob— "Maybe he will know? Maybe he will have some answers."

"Osric? The Lycan God?" Amrin pursed his lips. "Perhaps he will."

The sound of the terminal speaker sounded overhead, "*Boarding for the Amazon, starting now. Will all passengers please head to terminal 5, all passengers to terminal 5.*"

We stood, staring at each other, until I finally found my voice, "Let's go get that Lycan and get our baby girl back."

Broken and battered, we stood before the air hostess as she tsked at us. "You boys look awful. Is this all? Where's your luggage?"

"Just let us on the plane, ma'am. It's been a long day," Gabriel said with as much politeness as he could muster.

"Well," she huffed. "Fine."

The plane felt different. I looked at the bed where just hours ago, Avery had been delighting in the pleasure we brought her. Now the cabin felt empty. Hollow. Just like my heart. We sat in silence, the only motion was us shifting uncomfortably in our seats. It was Roman that broke the silence first.

"I thought we needed Avery to wake him?"

Amrin looked at Roman like he had two heads. "You don't know how to wake him?"

"Well, we thought we needed Avery. She's the light to his dark, right, so she is theoretically the only one who can wake him from his slumber." He looked at Gabe. "Right, Gabe?"

"I dunno man. I don't want to think about anything right now. None of this even matters. What is Belial doing to her? Is he hurting her? Is the baby safe?" I wasn't sure if he realized he was speaking these questions out loud, but we sat and listened to his despair before he burst into tears.

I moved to sit beside him, putting my arm around him. "It's going to be okay, man. We will get her back." I don't know who I was trying to convince, but it came out as empty as I felt. "She knows we will come for her. I know she does. We just need to get Osric. He will know what to do."

"Yeah? And what if he kills us instead? What then? Then Avery is stuck with that demon and the world will die," he spat bitterly.

"Do you guys really not know what's involved in waking Osric?" Amrin was still looking at us like we were stupid. "If you did, you'd be glad she is with Belial, because at least Belial can't hurt her. If he does, he will only hurt himself."

"What are you talking about man? Enough with the riddles," Roman snapped.

"To wake Osric, there needs to be a sacrifice."

# Thirty-Eight: Avery

One minute Roman's hands were down my pants and the next, Gabe and Roman had shifted, trying to protect me from a giant black demon. He was terrifying. I screamed as the demon descended upon us, his body creating a gust of wind that nearly knocked me off my feet. Gabe and Roman both stood and waited, to protect me. In a flash, both of them were sent flying into a wall, their bodies making a sickening crunch as their bones broke.

When I saw Nik's face, I knew. I knew exactly what I had to do. I couldn't let them die because of me. The shield I summoned was impenetrable. I'd finally mastered my use of emotions in conjunction with my power. The fear I felt crawling up my spine was enough to ensure there would be nothing going in... or out. In a flash, Belial had sent us into another realm.

The Underworld.

It was dark, oppressive and eerie. Everywhere I looked, there were all sorts of creatures just waiting to snag a soul. There were fire demons with beady eyes and sharp teeth, ghouls that weaved in and out of shadows on silent wings, and huge spiders lurking behind every corner. Then there was Belial himself, looming over us like a giant beast. He seemed to fill the whole area with an overwhelming darkness, almost as if he had the ability to suck away hope from everyone around him.

I felt a chill run down my spine as I took it all in. I knew, without a doubt, that if I even caused the slightest disturbance, the creatures would swarm me, absolutely devouring me in darkness. Having them this close was almost as bad as having them visit me in my dreams, but not quite. Their presence gave me comfort. It meant I was there.

In this other realm.

I could feel them all. I could hear them whispering, breathing, moving about. I even smelled the thick, humid air as it expelled from their lungs, steaming out of their nostrils.

"Let's go," Belial said, his voice scratchy and rough. Gripping me tightly in his hand, he lumbered forward. Toward the fire that spewed from within the bowel of the Underworld.

"What do you want with me?" I asked, trying to will my voice to be strong. To be brave.

"Ah, little Seraphina. While I cannot kill you, I can put you away. No one will find you. No one can cross the Eternal Soul Realm to retrieve you. The only way is through sacrifice, which was intentional. Any sacrifice ends in death of the sacrificee, ergo, you will never get out. I'm brilliant, really." At this point he was only talking to hear his own voice than to tell me anything.

"When I get out, I will kill you. I'm going to hunt you down," I replied, my voice steady, I wasn't going to let this demon keep me there any longer than it took me to figure out how to escape.

"Of course, I know that," he began. I wasn't sure where he was headed with this, but I didn't like the sound of it. "After a few thousand years you'll find me, and I'll still be on the other side. Havoc and chaos are in my blood. I was built for destruction. Even if you manage to get out, it won't matter. Nothing in your world will exist as it is. It will become"— he motioned around at the barren landscape— "like this."

A screech made me shudder. The swarming wings fluttered around me, as if a skeletal bird was suddenly caught in the heart of hurricane. These birds were different. They were somehow darker. More sinister. Harpies swept before me, hovering in the air while they screamed their own song.

"And that's where you'll be. Trapped." More demons broke off from the sea of the viscous river and began to circle me as they drew closer. I felt Belial lift me as he swatted them away. "These creations of mine, they never listen."

"Okay, great, so the plan is to destroy Earth? That's very... unoriginal of you," I said.

"Unoriginal?"

"Well, yeah. You already have an Underworld. Here. Why would you want to turn the beauty above into this?" Honestly, talking to him kept my panic at bay. I couldn't even describe how weird it was to be having a conversation with a demon the size of a mountain while he dangled me above shooting bolts of molten lava.

Belial chuckled, the sound echoing throughout the barren landscape. "Unoriginal, you say? I have never been one for originality, my dear. Destruction is my passion, it's what I was created for. What better way to showcase my mastery than to destroy all that is good and pure in your world?"

"But why?" I asked, struggling to make sense of his madness. "What did we ever do to deserve this?"

Belial's grip on me tightened, and I winced in pain. "Deserve it? That's the thing, my dear. None of you deserve anything. You are mere pawns in the grand plan. Your kind, the Seraphim, were made to tip the scales in favor of the light. As a result, creatures like me were created to ensure that would never happen. It took centuries of battle before we killed every one of you. We were told to wait, to bide our time. When the truth is, we should have destroyed Earth when we had the chance. You and your supernatural *mates* are the abominations. Not us."

I sighed; this was pointless. "How are we the abominations? We just want to live and let live."

"Because you were all born with darkness that you hide. Darkness that you ignore. Instead of embracing what you truly are, you pretend to be what you're not. Pure. I have no such compulsion. I am darkness."

"That's the point though. To be balanced." Though, the more he spoke, the more I could see his super twisted point. *We do whatever we can to hide the darkness we have inside. Nik is the closest to balanced out of us that I can see. The rest of us hide that darkness.*

Belial threw his head back and roared with laughter. The ground began to shake, and the sky rumbled and crackled around us. "Balance? You believe in balance? That is like a condemned man telling himself he will walk away from the gallows because he still has faith in life! Such naivety." He threw me high up into the air, and I screamed as I watched him grow smaller below me, before I plummeted down, down, down into the pit of flames far below.

The pit was lined with walls of jagged rocks that stretched out for miles, blocking out any light that could have possibly reached me. Demons lined the walls of the pit, armed with swords and axes, circling and twirling on the ground as they waited for me to fall. Even Lilith flew far out and laughed as I fell, waiting for the fall to end. The last thing I remembered seeing was Belial walking up to my broken body near the top of the pit with malevolence in his eyes.

My heart raced as I waited, unable to move my arms or legs. The pit gained a life of its own and swallowed me up, placing me inside a cage made of bone and crude steel.

"Now, Seraphina. This will become your home. I trust you will appreciate that I've made it especially homey for you." He laughed as he watched her struggle to move. "Don't worry, you will heal soon enough. If you can figure out how, that is. Now. I have business on the upside to attend. You will be alright, yeah?"

He laughed as helplessness settled in the core of my stomach. As if on cue, my baby kicked out at my rib, causing me to gasp.

*How am I going to get out of here? I cannot have this baby in the pits of hell.* I tried to mind-link Nik, but it was closed. *Ugh. What luck. Think, Avery, think.*

A lightbulb went off. *Selene. If I can somehow call her, maybe she will come down here and save me.* It was worth a shot. Looking around the pit, it was devoid of life, both demonic and otherwise. Lifting my eyes to the black above, I called on her. Willing her to appear.

Crickets. If crickets could exist down here, that's what I'd hear. I was well and truly alone.

"*Ahhh, but are you child?*"

I tried to look around as my bones shifted painfully, beginning to rearrange and heal. "Aunt Sapphire?"

"*Indeed. Of course, I'm not actually here, here, but good enough. Now what is this conundrum you've gotten yourself into? You couldn't have used any of your other powers to fight him? You just gave yourself to him like a willing slave? What on earth possessed you to do that?*" She chided me, gently pushing and pulling on my body as my bones snapped back into place. "*That'll be sore for a while, but it's healed.*"

"How are you here right now?"

"*I guess Selene lifted your ban on the dream realm. Welcome back.*"

As I looked around, I could see small streams of color coming through as my aunt came into view. "What do I do? I don't know how to get out of this?"

"*Ah, child.*" Aunt Sapphire sighed. "*You have always lacked sense when it comes to thinking things through.*"

"I know," I said, my voice barely above a whisper. "I just wanted to save my mates. Now I'm stuck here, and I willingly chose to put my baby at risk. What kind of mother will I be if I can't even make the right decisions?"

Aunt Sapphire's expression softened, and she took me in her arms, her golden skin glowing in the dim light. "Oh, I know, child, I know your fear. But you must keep your head. Think of your training. Remember, your powers are not just for show. Use them."

I took a deep breath, feeling the strength from my aunt's embrace. She was right. I had to think and act quickly if I wanted to save us. Closing my eyes, I focused on my powers, calling upon the elements of fire, water, earth, and air. As Aunt Sapphire disappeared into the background, the cell I was caged in came into view.

My powers began to build, the electricity in the air coming alive as I chanted ancient words of power. Words I'd never heard before but were as clear as day. The cell doors soon began to disintegrate around me, replaced by images of fire and ice that danced before my eyes. Before long, the flames evaporated, and I was standing outside of what was once my prison.

With a sigh of relief, I stepped out into the darkness where a demon stood guard at the entrance. His face filled with hatred as he recognized me. I saw his hands start to shake and without hesitating, I brought forth a shield of fire that encircled him completely, burning away any possibility of escape.

"Leave us alone," I commanded, my voice filled with fierce determination.

The demon's eyes widened in shock as he tried to break free, but it was no use. My powers were too strong. I was unstoppable. The knowledge inside me had finally broken free and I felt... incredible. He fell to his knees, defeated, as I walked away from him, my heart pounding with the triumph of my victory.

As I made my way through the maze of the dungeons, my eyes took in the horror that surrounded me. The stench of death and decay was overwhelming, and I knew that I had to hurry if I wanted to save my mates.

But then I saw him. The large black wolf with red eyes, pacing impatiently inside a cell similar to mine.

"Osric?"

# Thirty-Nine: Avery

T he wolf looked at me, flames burning in its gaze.

"I can't understand you; can you shift? Into something... else?" I finished lamely.

Within seconds a large, imposing man with red eyes sat naked in front of me.

"You are the Seraphina?" He scoffed.

I felt a shiver run down my spine as I nodded in response to his question. He looked at me with a mixture of annoyance and amusement.

"What do you want from me?" he asked, his voice deep and gravelly.

"I need your help," I replied, trying to keep my voice steady. "There's something happening on Earth. Belial is out for blood. He's going to destroy everything. I was hoping that you could help me figure out how to stop it."

The man's expression darkened, and he leaned in close to me. "You humans always come to us when you need something," he growled. "Why should I help you?"

I squared up to him. "Because Selene said you would."

His gaze faltered. "Selene?"

I nodded, seeing the flash of recognition in his eyes.

"You know her?" I asked, hoping that he did.

The man stood up, towering over me. "I do. She is a wise one. If she sent you to me, then she must be desperate. Belial is not one to be trifled with."

"I know," I told him. "But I can't do this alone. I need your help, please."

He considered my words for a moment before nodding. "Very well. I will help you stop Belial. But it won't be easy."

"I know," I said, relieved that he had agreed to help. "But... how do we get you out of there?"

"You don't," he said.

"Then how are you going to help me?"

"I mean YOU don't. Not that I don't get out," he said cryptically.

"That makes no sense."

Suddenly, a movie-like vision appeared on the ground in his cell.

"These are your mates, yes? And ex-mate?" he said, motioning to a grainy image of Roman, Gabe and Nik walking towards Osric's still form in front of them. Amrin trailed behind, guarded and watchful.

"What's going on? Why are they headed towards you?" It dawned on me. They were going to wake him up... without me. Panic rose in my chest. "If they go try wake you... without me... what happens?"

"A sacrifice must be made."

I held my belly, cradling the child that— in my dream—was being sacrificed to wake him and terror turned my blood into ice. "No... no, no this cannot be happening."

"Unfortunately, this is the part of the Prophesy where you can make a decision. I have enough power left in me to send you to them, stop them from waking me and you can all try to fight Belial on your own. Or you can let what happens, happens and I will be released. You have my word that I will stop him with you. I am your counterpart, for lack of a better term. Together we would become an unstoppable force. Destined to set balance back in the world."

*I don't know what to choose. This is the darkness that Belial was talking about.* I so badly wanted—no, needed—to save my mates, but my driving need to be good was overwhelming.

"Tick tock little girl."

I watched in horror as they stood around his petrified body, talking and arguing as to how to wake him when suddenly their life forces started draining out of them. "Stop, okay, stop." Osric began to glow the longer he sucked their lives from their bones.

"I SAID STOP." Unleashing a force field, I knocked him back in his cell.

He chuckled, his skin a sickly dark glow. His veins stood black against his forearms as he tilted his head and looked at me. "Ah, I see you've chosen to embrace the darkness within you. Good choice. You're going to need it if you plan to try stopping Belial without me. Very well." He yawned, snapping his fingers as the projection cut off. "I will send you back now. They've given me what I need. For now."

I stood waiting, but he continued speaking, much to my chagrin.

"You will be back here, little girl. Once Belial realizes that you've left, he will come for you. He has every intention of making you his bride. What did he call you? Ah, yes, Belial's Bitch. I thought it was kind of sweet, but then he ate some other poor wench and that was disgusting. I'm more of a quiet violent type. Superiority complex and all."

"Listen, not to be rude, but can you shut up and send me back?" I said through gritted teeth.

"Impatient, are we? Sure. See you soon." His laughter echoed around me as I fell upwards, back through the dark tunnel that landed me here, through the fields filled with demonic creatures, back through the portal. Landing on my ass with a thud, I came face to face with 3 pairs of very relieved eyes.

"Avery? Is that really you?" Gabriel said as he rushed forward, grabbing my shoulders and examining me as if I were a dream come true.

"My Goddess, you're really here." Roman stared at me.

I could see the relief in his eyes, and the fear that seemed to be simmering beneath the surface. I couldn't blame him, not after everything that had happened.

"Yes, it's me," I said, pushing myself up from the ground. "We need to get out of here, now. Belial is coming for me."

Gabriel's eyes widened, and he quickly moved to the side, allowing me to see what was going on behind him. Dozens of demons were making their way towards us, their eyes glowing an eerie red in the darkness.

"We have to go," Roman said, grabbing my hand and pulling me towards him. "Nik, Amrin, hold the line."

"No. This time, I fight too," I said, standing my ground. "I can control it now."

Nik side-eyed me. "Fine. But stick with us and don't go off alone."

Without wasting another moment, the five of us stood shoulder to shoulder, ready to fight the demons coming through the portal. I could feel my power beginning to bubble inside me, almost begging me to release it. Roman and Gabriel had already shifted into their wolves. Amrin and Nik were holding off, choosing instead to flank beside me, ready to defend me with their lives.

The demons finally reached us, barely five yards away now. The air around us began to buzz with energy as we all tapped into our abilities and prepared for battle. I braced myself for what was sure to be a harrowing fight as I widened my stance and intertwined my fingers in front of me, focusing on channeling my energy. The air seemed to crackle with energy as my power surged outward, a thunderous roar emanating from my palms and filling the night sky.

The demons charged at us, their claws and fangs glinting in the dim light. I raised my hands towards them, as beams of light flew out of me, hitting the demons head-on.

They flew backward, slamming into the ground with a sickening thud. But they didn't stay down for long. More of them were already climbing over the bodies of their fallen comrades, their eyes fixed on us with soulless stares.

The taste of power was like an electric current on my tongue, emanating from the tips of my fingers and rushing up my arms. The stench of sulfur filled the air as the demons disintegrated into ash, mixed with the faint smell of burning wood and incense.

But there were too many of them. More kept coming through the portal, and we were quickly becoming overwhelmed. Even with the combined strength of all of us working together, it seemed like we were fighting a losing battle.

"We have to close the portal," Roman shouted over the chaos.

"But how?" I yelled back.

Roman looked at Gabe and Nik and nodded as he rushed towards the portal. The sound of my scream stilled the chaos around us as I watched in horror as one of the men I loved was willing to lay down his life to seal the entrance. Before he hit the murky shimmer, Amrin came out of nowhere and pushed Roman just before his body made contact, veering him to the left into a crowd of adversaries. Amrin's bones instantly shattered as he hit the portal, sending pieces of flesh flying over the battlefield. The portal whirred and stilled as it began to contort before shining brightly and disappearing.

The demons followed soon after, vanishing with a thunderous crash that echoed throughout the night.

Roman lay on the ground unmoving, his eyes closed and his chest barely rising and falling. I rushed towards him, tears streaming down my face as I tried desperately to get him to wake up. "Please," I whispered through my sobs. "Don't leave me." He was covered in bites and scratches. One wound was deep enough that I could see his heart beating.

Nik was by my side in an instant, pulling me into a tight hug as he whispered words of comfort in my ear. "Let me go, I can heal him."

Concentrating with every fiber of my being, I began to chant. Words rising and falling with the intensity of my breath, my hands resting on his chest. A single, small beam of light emanated from my fingertip as it travelled over Roman's body, gently pulling and pushing at the wound until it sealed, leaving a slightly raised scar where it was once gaping.

"Avery?" he said, his eyes finding mine.

"Yes, yes, oh my Goddess, Roman," I sobbed into his chest.

"Hey now, I only want to hear those words when you're coming around my cock, not when you've just healed me from impending doom." He smiled weakly.

I couldn't help but laugh as I cried, relief flooding my entire body. "Oh, thank the Goddess, thank you, thank you, thank you," I said, kissing his neck and continuing down to his chest.

He collapsed back onto the ground and closed his eyes, his entire face a mask of pain. I rubbed my hand across his chest trying to sooth the aches and pains. "Did we get them all?" he asked.

"Yeah, I think so," I said, taking in my surroundings. Slowly the bloodlust that was within us was abating and the adrenaline was wearing off. My ears were ringing as I heard Nik clear his throat behind us.

"Listen, as much as I'm always down for some exhibitionism, Amrin just exploded all over the battlefield, Osric is still asleep, there was literally just a pile of demons here that just disappeared, and well, Avery? You're peeing yourself. So I think it's time we get home."

Looking down, I saw a small trickle down my legs.

*Oh shit.*

# Forty: Avery

"Guys... I don't think that's pee," Gabe said, his mouth falling open.

"What do we do? We're in the middle of nowhere, guys, what do we do?" Out of all my men, Nik was the last one I thought would panic about labor and birth. It was so comical, I snorted.

"First, you calm down a bit Nik. I don't even feel contractions yet, we likely have a lot of hours to go. First time moms can take hours to enter active labor, so maybe we can just hurriedly walk back the way you came? Yeah? Okay, here we go," I said, earning myself a handsome Alpha on each side of my arm, trying to fight each other about who is going to carry me.

"How about none of you," I snapped, irritation creeping in at being grabbed incessantly. "Walk nicely beside me like good boys."

Roman and Nik shut up, straightened out and walked silently next to me, while Gabe tried to get some reception on the cellphone, he miraculously had the foresight to stash in the trunk of a tree.

"Nope, no reception. We gotta keep going. How are you doing, Avery?" he asked, his eyes trailing down to where the steady stream of fluid leaked down my legs.

"I'm doing fine, Gabe," I said, trying to sound confident. However, the truth was that I was scared. This wasn't just any fluid leaking, and I knew that it wouldn't be long before the pain set in.

"Guys, stop," I said, holding up my hand. "I can feel it now. The contractions are starting." I closed my eyes and took a deep breath, trying to ignore the discomfort. "Honestly, that wasn't so bad. Just some twinges, like if I had gas."

"Maybe we should hurry—" Nik started and stopped as he saw my glare.

"I'm going as fast as I can, okay?" Truth was, it hurt like hell, but given his earlier reaction, I figured it might do more harm than good to let on exactly how much it hurt.

"Maybe someone can keep track of the time... How far apart they are? I read something about that somewhere," Roman said hesitantly.

"Finally, someone with a brain," I muttered.

"Gabe, keep an eye on your timer for when the next one starts."

The sky was starting to brighten, as the sun was peeking out between the trees, piles of smoke were rising in small puffs. I hoped that it meant we were getting close to civilization. My contractions were getting closer, but I tried to remain calm. The last thing we needed was for me to panic.

As we walked, Gabe kept track of the time between each one. They were coming faster and harder, making it difficult to keep up. I was sweating and panting by the time we finally stumbled upon a small cabin on the outskirts of the woods.

"Thank god," I gasped as Gabe grabbed the doorknob and forced it open. The cabin was empty, but it had a small bed and some basic supplies. A small towel lay draped over the bedside table. *Gross, but it'll do.* I collapsed onto the bed and tried to breathe through the pain as the others frantically worked to make me comfortable.

"What do we do? Guys, anyone? Did anyone read the parenting books? How do we deliver a baby?" Nik was whispering loudly to Roman and Gabe as they stood there, watching me writhe.

"You guys are idiots, someone come hold my hand, and one of you can— I dunno? Take off my pants? I can't push a baby out through jeans, alright?" This was ridiculous. You'd think not one, not two, but THREE Alpha's could figure some basic biology shit out. Finally, Roman stepped in, freeing my legs from the pants and sliding my underwear down as his eyes grew wide.

"Avery, uh…" He looked like he was about to faint.

But as the contractions grew stronger, I realized I didn't have time to wait for them to figure it out. They tried to help, grabbing at my hands, but now I was in pain and I was pissed off. I shoved Gabe and Roman aside and grabbed the towel, gritting my teeth in pain as I spread my legs wide.

"Alright," I said, my voice trembling. "One of you needs to catch the baby, and the other needs to make sure nothing else goes wrong. Leave Roman in the corner. He will just faint, or puke on my vagina. Got it?"

Nik and Roman exchanged a horrified glance as Gabe looked like he was about to turn green.

"I'll do it," Nik said, taking a deep breath. "I mean, I helped deliver a calf once. How much different can it be?"

"That's the spirit." I groaned out, involuntarily pushing. "Motherfucker!"

The pain was unbearable, and I could feel sweat running down my forehead. I let out a primal scream as another contraction hit me, and Nik quickly moved closer to be in position to catch the baby.

The room was filled with tension as everyone held their breaths. I pushed again, harder this time, and felt a sense of relief as the baby's head emerged. The fire inside my body calmed as I rested for a moment.

"Almost there, Avery, you've got this. You're the strongest person I know," Nik encouraged me as he carefully cradled the baby's head in his hands.

I pushed once more, unleashing the powerful roar only a woman in labor could muster, and the baby slipped out. Nik grabbed it, staring down at my vagina as I collapsed back onto the bed.

"Uh... Gabe, can you take this one?" Nik asked.

"This... *one*?" I squeaked, just as another contraction hit and that ring of fire started up again. Gabe hesitated for a second but then nodded, cradling the newborn in his arms. As he moved to the side, Roman rushed in to take his place.

"Okay, Avery, I need you to keep going," Nik said, his voice soothing and calm. A massive difference from the panicked man from just an hour ago. He continued, "you're doing amazing."

I nodded, gritting my teeth and pushing with all my might. A moment later, the slippery feeling of the second baby's emergence filled me with relief. Nik caught the baby with ease and held it tightly, gazing at it in awe.

"Can you guys stop staring and give them to me, please?" I said in a huff. "Check my lady bits and make sure the placenta detaches and that everything looks... normal."

"No offense, but it kinda looks like ground—"

"Do not finish that sentence if you wish to live much past the end of it," I said.

The sound of crying babies filled the room as Nik handed them to me, one after the other. They looked so small and fragile in my arms, yet I felt a surge of love for them that went beyond words. Looking down at them, I saw a little girl, with hair as white as snow, and a little boy with jet black hair. Both perfect, both beautiful.

"How did Jasmine miss this?" Roman finally spoke the question out loud.

"I don't know... And I was measuring small, but that was weeks ago..."

"A mystery for another day. Just relax Avery, you did so well," Gabe said, kissing my sweaty forehead, before giving each baby a kiss too. "We will have to think of names."

"Yes, but for now, I think I'm just going to relax and enjoy their new baby smell," I said, snuggling both little ones into my neck as they nestled in.

"Technically, that's the smell of your vag—"

"Seriously, Nik? What the fuck is wrong with you?" Gabe clapped him upside the head, as we all burst into laughter.

"Hey, I'm supposed to be the funny one," Roman said with a grumpy look on his face.

"And you are, but I needed to release some tension, I literally just had my hands elbow deep in my mate. I deserve to crack some jokes. Now, does this Goddess forsaken cabin have any drinks? I could use something to wash my pallet," Nik said as he bent down to kiss us, before turning to rummage around the small kitchen.

As Nik searched for drinks, I couldn't help but feel overwhelmed with emotion. I had just brought two beautiful children into the world with the loves of my life by my side. It was a moment I never thought I would experience, yet here I was, holding my little ones close. After all the chaos, the death, the darkness, this was the light I desperately needed to help me hold on.

Suddenly, a piercing pain shot through my stomach, and I gasped for breath. Gabe and Roman were at my side in an instant, their concern etched on their faces.

"Avery, what's wrong?" Gabe asked, placing a hand on my forehead.

"I... I don't know. It just hurts so much," I managed to say before the pain intensified, making it impossible for me to speak.

Nik came rushing back into the room, a worried expression on his face as he saw me writhing in pain. "What the hell is happening?" he exclaimed.

"Take them," I moaned. "Take the babies. Please." I doubled over in agony as Roman rushed forward, taking my beautiful babies before I dropped them.

"Guys, something is happening to her, look at her arms." Gabe said, grabbing my arm and turning it over. "Oh, my Goddess, it's spreading. Someone do something."

He was right, a blackness was settling through my veins, spreading up my arm and across my chest. The pain was unbearable, like nothing I had ever felt before. I could feel my body convulsing, my breathing becoming more ragged with each passing moment.

Gabe and Roman quickly sprang into action, trying to look for the source of whatever was causing this. Nik rummaged around the cabin, looking for any medical supplies that could help. But it was no use. Whatever was happening to me was beyond their abilities.

As the blackness continued to spread, I started to lose consciousness. I could hear their panicked voices, but it was like they were coming from far away. All I could focus on was the voice coming from inside of me.

   "*There is no escaping me, little girl.*"

# Forty-One: Gabriel

Watching Avery give birth was the most terrifying and amazing thing I'd ever been fortunate enough to see. She was so powerful, her body working perfectly to bring two beautiful babies into the world. I was looking forward to being able to maybe relax a bit, get to know these two little ones, and help her recover— until her veins started turning black. The further it spread, the more pain she seemed to be in.

"Guys... What do we do?" Roman asked, panic edging into his voice as he tried to hold a wet washcloth to her sweaty forehead.

"I don't know man... I don't know what's happening, or where it's coming from..." Nik replied. "Hey baby girl, you're going to be alright, everything is going to be okay. Do you think you can heal yourself?"

"No," she panted, leaning forward to clutch at her stomach. "He's here. He's inside of me."

"Who, Avery? Who is inside of you?"

"Belial. Osric said something about him wanting to make me his bride. I think..." She strained. "I think he put something in me when he caged me. I don't know, a piece of him, his soul."

"Okay, so how do we get it out?" I asked, wanting so desperately to help her, but not knowing what to do.

"I need help. Someone, something, greater than me." She sat up, wide eyed. "The dream realm. Selene opened it to me while I was in the Underworld, maybe I can still get in. Maybe I can find my aunt, she will know what to do."

"That's too dangerous Avery, we can't help you there," Roman said, in between cooing at the babies. *He is going to be a fantastic dad.*

"Uh..." Nik started. "That's not entirely true actually."

"What do you mean that's not entirely true?" I demanded.

"I can follow her and have been for weeks. I don't know why I have access to her dreams, but... I can go with her. Protect her." At least he had the decency to look sheepish as he spoke.

Avery's eyes widened as she took in Nik's words. "You've been following me in my dreams?" she asked, her voice trembling.

Nik nodded, his gaze locked onto hers. "I couldn't help it," he said softly. "I didn't mean to invade your privacy, but I couldn't resist. You're so beautiful, Avery. And your dreams ..."

Avery's face flushed with anger and embarrassment. "You had no right to do that," she said, but I could tell the words held no punch. "But... thank you. For keeping me safe."

"I know, I know I shouldn't have, but I didn't really have a choice. It just kind of happened," Nik said, looking contrite. "I'm sorry. But I promise I was only watching to make sure you were alright. Avery, it's not just your aunt that you can access in the dream realm, its Selene too."

"Give me my babies and someone go outside and find some lavender, I could have sworn I saw some growing around out there," She said, reaching for the babies.

"What are you going to name them?" Roman said as he handed them over, sitting beside her in case she needed a hand.

She looked down at the raven-haired boy, his eyes a deep blue with yellow circles becoming brighter the closer to the center they got. "Onyx," she said, beaming at him before inhaling deeply and giving him a kiss. "And you, little girl... you are my beautiful Aurora." Running her lips over Aurora's hair, she sighed.

"I will make sure nothing happens to them, Avery," I said, coming to sit on the other side of her.

"I know, I just... want this to be over. Selene was right, these babies are my weakness. I don't understand why I have two, but I know both of them are mine, and they're both so small, and so fragile and I just..." Her eyes started watering. "I just don't want to live in a world where danger lurks around every corner. How am I supposed to protect them?"

"With us," Nik said, peeking out from a bouquet of lavender. "We will stand by your side until the end. Onyx and Aurora are safe because they have a mother who would rather die than have them see harm, and they have 3 dads who would kill any motherfucker who came too close." Nik paused for a second.

"And they have a dad who already sacrificed himself to save us all."

Avery looked at him, tears streaming down her face. "Thank you," she whispered. "Thank you so much." Her pain was momentarily forgotten as she held the two beauties in her arms, nuzzling them close to her chest. "Okay, I'm ready. Well... ready as I'll ever be. Gabe?" She looked up at me, waiting for me to respond.

My nerves were on alert as I took the tiny babies in my arms. Immediately, they settled, cooing softly, contentment washing over their faces.

"What about food? Don't they need to eat?" Roman said suddenly.

"Shit... Okay, here's what we will do, and don't make this weird. My milk is coming in, so just pop them on when they cry and take them off when they're done. I don't have a better plan and it is the only one we've got so they don't starve."

I nodded as she spoke. Nik handed her the lavender and they both lay on the bed, deeply inhaling the fragrance.

"Can one of you sing to me?" she asked, as exhaustion overtook her. Her body was tired, worn. I could see the light from within her trying to fight back the darkness that was swimming in her veins.

"Sure," said Roman as I settled into a nearby chair. He began to hum a tune, a lullaby from his childhood. The sound filled the room, and I watched as Avery's body relaxed, the tension slowly leaving her.

I looked down at the content babies in my arms, feeling a surge of love and protectiveness. We were all in this together, a family born out of happenstance and love rather than blood. But that didn't make it any less real.

As we waited for her to sleep, thoughts of the future rolled around in my brain. The dangers that threatened us at every turn, the unknown horrors waiting to strike. It felt like one horrific event after another. But then I felt the warmth of the babies in my arms, and heard Roman's cracked yet soothing song, and it reminded me that even though life was unpredictable and sometimes cruel, it also held moments of beauty and joy. That as long as we had each other, we could find a way to carry on, no matter what happened.

I rocked them gently in my arms and whispered promises to them. Promises that I would always be there for them. That I would protect them from anything the world threw at us. Sure enough, within minutes they had fallen into a peaceful sleep, along with their beautiful and courageous mother.

"And now... we wait," Roman said nervously.

"What do you think is happening?" I asked, not wanting the silence to swallow me whole.

Roman let out a sigh, looking over at the sleeping Avery and then at the twins.

"I think we've only seen the first glimpse of what's to come," he said, his voice low. "Whatever Belial is after, it's clear he won't stop until he gets it. And we have to be ready for that."

My heart sank at his words, the weight of the situation heavy on my shoulders. But I knew he was right. We couldn't let our guard down, not for a moment. Not when there were so many dangers lurking in the shadows, waiting for the perfect moment to strike.

"We need to be cautious," I said. "But how do we protect her when he's basically a ghost? We don't know when or where we will challenge us for her. He wants her, for whatever reason, and we all know we won't give her up without a fight. Is that what was meant by the sacrifice? We sacrifice ourselves to save her?"

"I kinda thought we circumvented that when I was going to leap into the portal and Amrin kind of took one for the team..." Roman said.

"Man, I don't think that's how it works. I think we each need to make a sacrifice and I don't think any of us will sacrifice anyone other than ourselves to protect her."

"I dunno, dude, I would have readily sacrificed Amrin, but he took that joy away from me." Roman laughed.

"Ha. Yes, very funny. Except he did redeem himself, and who knows, maybe Selene will have mercy on him and grant him a new body with a counterpart who will love his mate. Lord knows he deserves a damn break."

"Why are you being so nice about it all?"

"Because... I almost lost it back in the airport. I almost killed him, Roman. I almost..."

He grew quiet. "You're not that person anymore, man. You can forgive yourself. You didn't and that's what counts."

I nodded my head slowly, his words hitting me hard. It was true. I wasn't that same person anymore, but the old me still lingered, always just beneath the surface. It was a constant battle, one that I often found myself losing.

"I know," I said softly. "But it's hard, you know? To let go of the past and move on."

"I know," he said. "But we have to keep pushing forward. We can't let Belial win. We have to do whatever it takes to protect her."

I sighed, knowing he was right. "On the bright side, if we all die and manage to save the world, maybe there's like a quadruplet Alpha squad who will mate her next."

"Ew, dude, what the fuck. Don't think like that. She will never let another dick near her if it's not one of ours. She would never cheat on us like that," Roman said, indignantly.

I rolled my eyes at his protective behavior. "I know, I know. I'm just saying, it's not a bad deal for her."

"Yeah, well, let's not talk about dying anymore. We've got this. We're going to protect her and win this war."

We fell silent for a while, and before long, Roman's snores filled the room. Somehow, he didn't wake up the babies with that chainsaw-like racket. My own eyes were growing heavy, but I didn't want to fall asleep in case Avery needed me. Looking over at her, I saw her twitching in her sleep, the darkness slowly moving like sludge, closer and closer to her heart.

"Hurry guys... please. She doesn't have much time," I whispered, willing them to listen.

# Forty-Two: Avery

Nik stood beside me as we surveyed the dream realm. It was dark. Eerie.

"Can't you like... change this? There's so much dust. And the lava is kind of off-putting." He said, taking my hand.

"I'm trying, but nothing is happening. It's like this place is infected too." I sighed, looking down at my hands. At least the black veins were gone.

We moved forward cautiously, Nik gripping my hand tightly, afraid to let me go. As we walked, the terrain changed from an open flat land to tall cliffs and jagged rocks. I could see some of the creatures that lived within it, their sharp eyes sending chills through me.

The atmosphere was uneasy and oppressive. There was a darkness that clung to us like a heavy blanket, making it hard to breathe. Everywhere I looked, there were shadows dancing around without direction or purpose.

It felt like something unseen was watching us from the dark corners, waiting for us to make a mistake so they could snatch us up into their world forever. It was the first time I'd come here and not felt a sense of peace.

"Aunt Sapphire! Auntie!" I yelled as the wind howled around us. "Damnit, where is she?"

In an instant, a blinding light flashed before us. The shadows fled, and the wind died down. In front of us was a figure cloaked in white, holding a staff with a glowing crystal on top.

"Hi, Avery," the figure said in a gentle voice as the light subsided. "I am here in the place of your aunt. She... cannot be here right now."

Nik and I stared at the figure in awe. The magic emanating from her was palpable, and it filled me with a sense of wonder and enchantment.

"Alara? Is that you? You look..." I was shocked.

"Different?" She giggled. "Indeed. This is my Ethereal body. You have one too, though I suspect your mate has seen it."

I looked at Nik quizzically and he simply stared at Alara. "What are you?"

"Silly boy, I am Avery's ancestor. She met with me long ago, though I was quite depleted at the time of our meeting. I am feeling better now, and I'm here to help you."

"How...? How did you regain your Ethereal...ness?" I finished lamely.

Her face downturned. "Avery... your aunt..."

"My aunt WHAT? What Alara? What about my aunt?" Panic was rising in my chest.

"She asked Selene if she gave her soul, if mine would be whole again... if I could come here and help you."

My heart stopped as the words sunk in. My aunt, my kind, generous Aunt Sapphire had given her life for me. Tears streaming down my face, I knelt on the ground and covered my face with my hands.

Nik murmured something comforting before standing and pulling me up into his arms. He held me tight while I sobbed uncontrollably at the overwhelming sense of grief that had descended upon me. The grief was red and raw, cutting like a thousand papercuts, leaving marks all over my soul.

Alara stood silently watching while I mourned the loss of someone who meant so much to me and whose selfless act was so deeply appreciated. When I composed myself again, Alara spoke softly, "She will always be with you, Avery. She is resting peacefully, that I promise you. Selene carved out a special garden for her, so she can practice her magic in peace. You do not have to mourn her, my girl. Celebrate the fierce woman she was and let's honor her legacy by defeating the monsters who caused her to sacrifice on your behalf."

Nik squeezed me tighter and I nodded, taking deep breaths to steady myself. Alara was right. Aunt Sapphire wouldn't have wanted me to fall apart about her death. She would have wanted me to keep fighting and making her proud. I wiped my tears and looked up at Alara.

"What do we do now?"

Alara's expression turned grim. "We must prepare for the final battle. They will be coming for you, Avery. We need to heal you first and foremost. And then we need to find allies."

Nik stepped forward. "Who will help us? We can't do this alone. We cannot ask our pack to put themselves in danger."

Alara turned to him, exasperation on her face. "Young Lycan, did you ever wonder why you were able to wander the dream realm while the two wolves cannot?"

"I mean, sort of, but not really. My concern was to keep Avery safe. Not really on why I could be here," Nik said, shuffling his feet.

"Goddess you three Alpha's are so intelligent, but sometimes you're really dumb, you know that?" Alara sighed. "Because, young man, we need to awaken Osric."

"We tried that on earth... Avery stopped us. Well technically a bunch of demons did, but then Avery didn't want us to die, so..."

"Yeah, I also tried to free him in the Underworld, but I couldn't get him out." I chimed in.

"Right. This is why we are here now. While you were talking to him, he infected you with a piece of his soul, so that you would have to go back and free him," Alara said, matter-of-factly.

"I thought that was Belial? Doesn't he want to make me his queen or something?" I was dumbfounded.

"Yes, he does, but the infection raging through your veins was activated when your children were born. At least he was kind enough not to infect you until after they were out safely. Thank the Goddess for small mercies, I suppose." Alara said, motioning for us to walk and talk.

As we walked, Alara continued to speak, her voice low and serious, "Belial wants you as his queen, but he knows he cannot have you until Osric is out of the way. Osric was the only one standing in his way. Now that he has infected you with a piece of his soul, you are tied to him in a way that even Belial cannot control. You are the only one who can free him, and in doing so, you will be freeing yourself."

I frowned, trying to make sense of it all. "But how do we awaken him? We've tried everything short of sacrificing my mates. And why is Osric the one who is standing in his way? I don't understand."

Alara glanced at Nik, who had fallen silent. "When Selene created Osric, she tied his soul to that of the first Seraphina. It was her way of ensuring balance. Now that all of us except you are... well, dead, and Osric has been in hibernation, he found a way to ensure your souls remained tied. The longer he is chained and you are not, the worse your infection will get, until, unfortunately, the darkness will consume you. Selene's spell was only supposed to be for when both light and dark walked the earth at the same time. Belial is a minor setback, one that alongside Osric, we can conquer. The true darkness comes from your mates Lycan line."

I gasped, my hand flying up to my chest in shock. "What? What do you mean?"

Nik finally spoke up, his voice tight with emotion, "When a Lycan line is corrupted by darkness, it can lead to catastrophic consequences. The power that comes with it is immense, but it's too much for a single person to handle. It's why we always knew we needed to find our Seraphina, our balance. It's why you are my mate. The balance to the darkness I fight daily."

Alara nodded, her expression grim. "Your mate has a long history of darkness within his bloodline. It's something we thought we could keep at bay, but with the rise of Belial and the split in the realms... it's all happening much too soon. We can no longer contain the evil that's spreading through the Above World, because the Underworld has gained the upper hand. If we do not rebalance earth soon, the split will be too catastrophic to close. Demons and the like will walk among us."

"So... Where are we going now?" I asked, watching as the horizon changed from dark and terrifying, to beautiful hues of purple and pink.

"We have to find where Osric's spirit resides in the Dream World. It's the only way we are going to break his chains without killing your mate in the real world."

"Wait, what?" I screamed. "Nik could die?"

Alara gave me a sympathetic look. "It's a possibility, but we won't let that happen if we can help it and we plan correctly. We need to remain focused on the task at hand and use our magic wisely."

Nik, who had remained quiet, spoke up, "I won't let anything happen to me, or to you, Avery. We'll get through this together. But... if it comes down to it, you know I'd stop at nothing to keep you safe. If this is the sacrifice I make, then I am at peace with that."

I nodded, a small blossom of hope blooming in my chest. There was no way I would let Nik die, even if he was ready and willing. I loved him. More than I could ever express. Looking over at the broody, handsome man standing by my side, a rush of emotions heated me.

"Alara, how many days do you think we will be stuck here?" I asked, a sudden rush of need filling me.

She smiled slightly. "It could be a while. I have a general idea where Osric has hidden his soul, but it could be a decoy. Would you like to set up camp somewhere and rest?"

"I would, actually. I am rather... tired." I faked a yawn.

"I see. Well, I do have some things to attend with Selene. Stay here, do not go back to your realm. Your infection is delayed the longer you are here. Have... fun." She winked at me before disappearing in a brilliant display of lights, leaving me and Nik staring in wonder.

"How does she do that?" he whispered.

"I have no idea, but I hope I can do that too. That was awesome!" I said, grabbing his arm and turning him to face me. "You're awesome."

"I'm... awesome?" He chuckled. "Thanks... I guess?"

"You know what I mean." Swatting at his arm, a blush crept up my chest. "Let's go find somewhere to sleep for the night... day? For a few hours. Time is weird in here."

"On it, baby girl."

# Forty-Three: Nikolai

My head was spinning with the reality that in the next few hours, or days or weeks... I might die. Not that I hadn't been preparing for this moment since the witch told us that we would each make a sacrifice to save us all, but now it just felt so real. Looking at the bodacious babe on my arm, my heart ached. I wanted to be here with her, forever. I wanted to raise our twins, fuck her long into the night, make her round with child again and build a home with her. I'm not one for emotions, but frankly, the thought of all of that ending before it even had a chance to bloom was depressing.

Nevertheless, my baby girl asked for shelter, and shelter she shall receive.

"Voila," I said, waving my arms around.

"...this? This is what you chose?" She looked around with dismay.

"What? A dark, dingy cave isn't good enough for the angelic little princess?" I teased.

She smacked my arm. "No, this is actually perfect." Her eyes glinted mischievously.

"In fact, how do you know I didn't want to lure you here to have my way with you?"

"Your what? Your way with me? Baby girl, I could over-power you ten ways from Sunday and there's not a God-dess-damn thing you could do about it." I slapped her ass, satisfied at the yelp she made.

"Oh yeah?" She snickered as she turned to walk away. "Catch me if you can."

Without another thought, I was in hot pursuit. Avery's petite frame ran like the wind and my long strides barely managed to keep up. She gracefully weaved through the tall trees, jumped over fallen logs, and arched around boulders. Meanwhile, I was more of a bull-dozing force, flinging my-self off of ledges just in time to catch her soft hand before she could sprint away again. Her soft giggles caught me off guard as she twisted before kicking me and off she went again.

I was tempted to let River out for some fun, but I wanted this moment to myself. My little bunny, running. She had no idea what she was running from, but the moment I saw those luscious hips swaying, my cock sprang to action like a soldier in salute. No, my baby girl would not get away from me.

"Avery... Where are you baby? I could shift into River and sniff you out. Where'd you go. Hmmm, are you... here?" I said, jumping behind a tree, only to be met with giggles from behind me.

"Tag," she said, "you're it." And she was off again. My heart pounding out of my chest as I watched her strip pieces of her clothing off.

"You little... You wait until I catch you. I will have no mercy." I growled, willing my legs to go faster.

Finally, she was slowing, I could see her ribcage expand and contract with each breathless gasp. I slowed, hiding behind a tree as she frantically looked for me before relaxing and stopping to gather a breath.

I leapt out and wrapped her in my arms. "I win." I said, sniffing her hair before biting her shoulder.

She yelped, but I felt her ass move against my hard cock. "Now I really win." She sighed before collapsing in my arms.

I scooped her up and she wrapped her legs around my waist, sucking and biting at my ear while her hands tugged at my hair. "Fuck me like it's the last time."

"Gladly." I started walking towards our cave, but she stopped me.

"No."

"No?"

"I want you to take me right here, right now. I can't wait anymore. I need you, on me, around me... in me," she whispered breathlessly.

I growled and pulled her up to a sitting position, wrapping her legs around me. With my eyes still locked with hers, we both lifted my shirt in a hurry. I looked down at her pert tits covered by a small bra lace thing, a baby bra? Cloth bra? I don't know but it was hot. *She wasn't wearing this before... Oh maybe she was able to put it on for me.* The purple lace kissed the tops of her breasts delicately, just hidden enough to tease me, while the same purple lace hugged her hips in a thong that disappeared under her short skirt.

"Fuck." I leaned down and bit one piece, ripping it off, revealing her perfect nipple as my teeth grazed it. Her hips rose to meet the bulge in my jeans, rubbing herself on me. I grunted moving back upwards, biting her ear before sucking her earlobe, biting down hard and tugging.

She writhed. "Take off my skirt." Her voice was husky and broken, thick with lusty desire.

I picked her up and placed her on a fallen tree, sitting her on top before roughly shoving her skirt down her legs. "The panties too." I took my time pulling them down, enjoying the familiar scent of her already.

Her eyes rolled back in her head as soon as I had her underwear off. "Fuck me," she groaned, gripping the tree with her fingernails while I snuck a finger into her slick entrance. "Right now."

I looked up at her, she was flushed and ready. "Turn around."

She nodded. I unbuckled my belt, and pulled down my jeans slow enough to tease her, before pulling them back up, the anticipation driving her crazy. She turned around and her legs became weak, so I gripped her waist before she fell. My fingers pushing into her skin so hard it'd leave marks. *Good. I want her to have a piece of me on her, just in case.*

"Push yourself back on me," I ordered her. She nodded, her face in her arms as she backed into me, stopping when she felt my jeans against her sensitive mound.

"Please, Nik... fuck me..."

"No."

I gripped her hips, digging my nails in and grinding my hip bone between her ass cheeks. She moaned my name. I smacked her ass hard, and her body bucked forward.

"Fuck!"

"Get on all fours."

She got on all fours, pushing her ass out wiggling it back and forth. I smacked the other cheek, and she leaned forward, rubbing herself furiously. I unbuttoned my jeans and pulled my cock out, slamming back into her in one swift movement. "Oh, fuck!" I yelled out, squeezing her hips holding her in place as her tight pussy contracted around me, allowing me to fill her until she was stretched.

She started to moan louder and louder as I picked up my pace. "Nik, please... oh God... fucking hell." She was sweating and flushing red, ready to come apart.

"Tell me you want this," I told her, dragging her hair back and pulling her head back. She could barely focus, I smacked her ass again. "Tell me you need this." I grabbed her neck, tightening my grip until she was gasping for air.

She was biting at her lip when the moans turned to grunts and she gripped the tree rebounding her body back onto me, wanting more.

"Oh, dear God!" she managed to choke out, clenching me so fucking tight it lit me up like a firework.

I ground my teeth together, trying to keep myself from blowing my load. I started ramming her harder and just as she was about to cum, I pulled out.

"Run, baby girl."

"Nik, please, I can't..." She was almost a sobbing mess, but I needed this. I needed her to do as I say, just this once.

"Avery, you're going to run as fast as you can, and you're not going to stop. Do you hear me? I want you to run, because I'm going to chase you, and then I'm going to destroy that pussy, maybe your ass too, if you can take it. But right now, I need you to run."

She started to open her mouth to argue.

"Baby girl, you better run. Unless you want me to just fuck your mouth and leave you needy and sopping."

And just like that, she turned around and ran. I watched as she zig zagged around trees and branches, collecting scratches and scrapes, but I didn't care. She was just waiting for me to catch up with her, so I took off behind her, only listening to my pounding chest and straining legs.

What felt like forever, two minutes at most, she took a sharp turn and ran through the opening. It looked like another small cave, and I followed her in. I caught her off guard and pinned her to the wall kicking her legs open and gripping her ass tight, my breath coming out hard and heavy. "Tell me you want this."

She nodded, but no words came out.

"Tell me you need this." I ground my cock against her, not to hard and not slow enough either.

She tried to lick her lips, but instead grinded into me, avoiding eye contact. I held still, but said nothing. She was squirming against me, and I narrowed my eyes to where she held my gaze.

"I do. Nik, please. I can't run anymore. My legs will fall off."

My response was an approving nod, but I needed to hear those words.

"Please... I need you."

With one hand pinning her ass to the wall, I pulled my belt from my jeans, and with a snap, my mother-fucking Levi's dropped around my ankles. I drove into her with nothing but animalistic rage and lust, barely able to control my instincts when all I wanted to do was consume, possess and remind her she's mine. She met my thrust with a bite to my shoulder, drawing blood. It was the hottest thing she's ever done, if I'm being honest.

She wrapped her legs around my waist, digging her nails into me as I fucked her harder and faster. "Faster, Nik! Harder, fuck me!" she begged and so I did.

I hit that spot within her that had her screaming my name and bucking against me, it felt like she was milking every ounce of cum from me, but I kept pounding away until we both came apart. I felt the warmth sink deeper within us both as I drove into the back wall until we were both completely satisfied.

"You..." I said, kissing her fervently. "Are... amazing..."

# Forty-Four: Avery

Nik was the type of guy that made you wet without even trying. His raw, primal energy coursed straight through him and into me. He unlocked aspects of my sexuality that I'd never thought I'd be pleasured by. But being fucked like an animal... BY an animalistic man, was some hidden dream come true. I truly wanted this man to take everything I had, and everything I am, and make it his to own. To keep. To possess.

As we lay in this dank cave, his arm curled around my shoulder and my leg resting atop his semi-hard dick, I just wanted more. I craved more. More of him, more of this lust, more of the primal energy we shared. Of all my amazing mates... he was the one that balanced me, and up until today, I didn't know why. Gabriel and Roman completed our foursome, but Nik was the one who brought me to my knees and then raised me up again. I couldn't lose him without losing myself.

I slowly dipped my hand lower, until I was stroking his half-hard cock, reveling in how I could make him aroused without even trying.

My tongue ran across my lips as I looked at him, his beautiful eyes still closed in blissful sleep. I bit my lip, then moved closer to him. My hand still held his dick as I leaned over and kissed him tenderly on the lips. His eyes opened quickly as he stirred awake, and before he even had a chance to utter a word, I pressed down onto him with all my body's might. His soft moan escaped out of his mouth straight into mine, sending electric sparks throughout my body.

With every movement, there was friction which sent my arousal through the roof.

"Baby girl, what are you doing?"

"I'm fucking you."

"It's like... super late, shouldn't you get some rest? You don't know if tomorrow—"

I cut him off with a kiss. "Please? I just want to be close to you."

"As you wish," he said, before flipping me on my back and kissing a blazing trail down my body and finding my soaking pussy waiting for him.

My legs fell open as he licked up and down my inner thighs, inhaling deeply as his shuddered. "You smell like heaven."

"Since when?" I breathed, my hands automatically snaking into his hair, pulling him in close.

"Always."

And then he started to lick me, teasing me, dipping his tongue in and out of me.

I sighed in relief. "Oh, yes..."

He sucked me before running his tongue in circles around my throbbing clit and swirling it around before moving further down and diving back inside.

"Wait. Wait, no. Don't move away."

He smiled mischievously and circled the tip of his tongue all around the curves of my thighs. I ached, my actual pussy ached, my body crying out for more of his touch.

"Fuuuuuck." He breathed as he continued his torment.

My hips bucked into the air, thrusting my clit into his mouth as he sucked and lightly nibbled, before he bit down harder, drawing out an orgasm that had been hovering on the cusp. Trembling, my thighs closed around his head as he chuckled.

"More?"

I nodded ferociously. "More."

He smiled as he came up for air. "What do you want, baby? I'm yours for the taking."

"Well... in that case..." I pushed him off of me and settled my hips over his upper thighs as I leaned down to lick the precum that had beaded on his tip.

"Ah, shit..." he groaned as I trailed my tongue back up to take him inside of my mouth.

My pussy rubbed back and forth over his thighs, the friction creating lovely bolts of electricity, his cock sliding gently in and out as I played, my hand grabbing and lightly squeezing his balls.

"Tell me what you want," I begged, wanting to feel him, taste him, bathe in his scent, his touch and his sounds.

"I want to fuck you all night," he said and I could only moan in response, jutting my hips against his legs.

One big hand gripped my ass, making me sob around him as I fucked his leg, bringing myself toward another orgasm. His hand curled around my head, pushing me further and further down his hard cock.

"Yes, that's it, baby girl, relax, you can take it all, I know you can."

I writhed as I sucked, whimpering and moaning like a wolf in heat. I wanted him. I needed him. I loved him. I loved him so fucking much... I wouldn't have done anything or said anything differently if I had a thousand chances to do it again.

"Oh, fuck, baby, this is so fucking good... you're so fucking good." He twisted and tugged my nipples, making me quiver with pleasure. I was about to come again, the build to orgasm getting more intense by the second, when he gripped my shoulders and he pulled me up, slamming me back on the rocks.

I moaned in protest, wanting to take him deeper down my throat and feel the milky streams of hot cum spill into my mouth as I sucked him dry, but he had other plans.

"Alright, I've had enough of you taking control. It's my turn."

I pouted and frowned at him. "But I was having so much fun," I whined. But he just laughed, his eyes flashing and cock twitching.

"You'll be having more fun soon enough, baby." He growled, positioned between my legs, draping them over his shoulders as he leaned towards me.

I slowed my breathing and took every detail of his face in. The way his jawline clenched, his lips parting a little as his breath came in short, excited bursts. I stared into his eyes, trying to see how he felt. I wondered if he understood how I felt about him. Could he read between the lines of my confessions, could he feel how much I adored him, loved him, how completely and totally I was in love with him? I searched his face for recognition, for reflected desire.

"Please fuck me," I whispered, waiting for an answer. "Fuck me."

"Is that what you really want, baby girl?" He purred at me.

I nodded, moving my hips slightly, my legs wiggling on his shoulders. I tried to reach down and play with my clit, and he grinned, reaching towards my hand and taking it away.

"No... I think tonight, for the first time in my life, I am going to make love. Relax, princess. I know you're scared, and this is your way of showing me your feelings, but I'm not going anywhere... In fact, I'll be coming right here," he said as he played with my nipples.

I sighed, relieved and aroused at the same time. "I want you to make love to me. Make me yours, in body, mind and soul."

He grinned, then leaned down and gently bit my nipple before moving to my other breast. He didn't bother hiding the tears in this side of his eyes when we kissed. His emotions flooded into me. Desire, lust, love... acceptance.

I cried out and screamed his name as his cock stretched me, slowly pushing its way inside my wet pussy. He groaned, burying himself in me to the hilt, pushing hard against my hips, holding himself still. I looked up into his eyes, knowing that this was how it was meant to be, this was the only way that it could be. I called out his name again as he started to move, slowly thrusting in and out of me, then picking up speed. Pounding into me harder and harder as I dug my nails into his back, letting him know I wanted it hard. He was so deep inside me, there was no room left for anything but love. He was fucking me with his cock, his heart and his soul...

I struggled not to cum as he led me to the edge of the cliff before pushing me off with a gentle kiss.

"You're mine, Avery. No matter what comes to pass. You are my heart, and you always will be."

And then he unleashed his seed, deep within me. And deep within me, I felt a healing energy awaken as it began to spread through our connected bodies, shattering the chains that held us captive.

There was no more pain. Nothing that this world or the next could put between us would tear us apart. The click of our souls felt like the breaking of the wind. It just was.

"I can hear it... your soul. Your soul is so sweet, like warm honey flowing through my heart. I will never let you go, Avery. I'm holding on to the last remnants of this world because of you. Life might forsake me, but you have not," Nik said, as he collapsed beside me.

I cradled him against me as he shuddered, breathing hard, clutching me tighter and tighter, making me realize what a gift it is to have him in my arms.

"I love you," I said, as we held each other, seeking a life raft from a world rife with darkness. There might not be a tomorrow, but at least for today, I felt whole.

# Acknowledgements

This is in no particular order.

Julie, thank you, chaos wrangler, for keeping me in check and taking care of those things that I quite frankly... don't want to do and don't have time to do.

Megan, for talking to me and keeping me sane. Appreciate how real you are and how you're always quick to lend me a hand when I feel like I have too much on my plate. Thank you for proofing this with me and doing so quickly. I owe you a drink, or ten.

Kassia, you are such a beautiful soul. I just appreciate you for being you.

Ashley, my incredible beta reader. You are so amazing at pointing out what needs to be worked on, and you're always so willing to be that shit draft reader, I have no words to express how grateful I am to you.

Cassie & Noel, you both have been such a fixture in my life, through the ups and downs, the highs and lows, you two are forever in my circle. I love you both so much.

Brittany, for always listening, being the first to say you'll help me with someone and being so supportive.

Jamie, for being an ear when I need one & being in my corner.

Beth, for editing this beast and making hilarious comments that had me laughing.

I know I'm forgetting people, and for that I am sorry, but if you're reading this and are miffed I didn't mention you, know that I absolutely do appreciate and love you, I just have the memory of an ant and screaming children who are distracting me.

# About the Author

Always being told she is a daydreamer, Stephanie uses her gifts for escaping into a fantasy world to bring those worlds to life. Unable to write solely in one genre, she has found herself enjoying writing a wide array of books. From historical fiction to fantasy, Stephanie loves it all. Hoping to instill a love of books in her children, Stephanie spends her days reading, writing and going on adventures with her family, allowing imagination to lead the way and creativity to write the stories. Her favorite adventures are the ones where her son leads them through magical portals to new lands in discovery of the mystery that lies there.

# Also By

Historical Fiction:

The Milkmaid: https://books2read.com/u/3yQJOe

The Betrayal: https://books2read.com/u/4NeqNx

Fantasy:

The Forest Keeper's Princess: https://books2read.com/u/meq

aVz

Ream:

https://reamstories.com/stephanieswann

# Contact Stephanie

You can contact Stephanie at: stephanieswann.author@gmail.com if you'd like to know more about her upcoming works!

**Instagram: authorstephanieswann**
https://www.instagram.com/authorstephanieswann/
**Facebook: Stephanie Swann**
https://www.facebook.com/StephanieSwannAuthor/
**Tiktok: stephanieswannauthor**
https://www.tiktok.com/@stephanieswannauthor
**Other Links:**
https://linktr.ee/stephanieswannauthor

Printed in Great Britain
by Amazon

29490077R00209